CHAPTER ONE

They were expecting me, but I didn't think they'd be expecting *this*. I arranged myself in the doorway and waited for them to notice me. I was just wondering if there was a sexy way to clear my throat to get their attention when Owen Palmer looked up from his notebook and said, "I'm sorry, but you're not supposed to be here. I'll call for someone to escort you out."

On the one hand, it was nice to know that my boyfriend's head wasn't easily turned by every curvy blonde who came along. On the other, his lack of reaction made me wonder if I'd missed the mark. Rod Gwaltney's reaction was more like it. When he noticed me, he looked like a cartoon wolf, with his eyes popping out on springs and his tongue unrolling to the ground. Yeah, I'd done it right, I thought, ever so smugly.

I dropped my voice down an octave or so and tried to create a hoarse, breathy tone that fit my bombshell exterior to say, "I thought you were expecting me." I didn't think that sounded like my usual voice, but Owen frowned in suspicion. Rod was still ogling me. I had to bite my lip to keep myself from smiling. This was too much fun. Then it became absolutely impossible for me to keep a straight face one minute longer, and I dissolved into giggles.

"Katie?" Rod blurted.

"I think she gets an 'A' for illusions," Owen said with a smile as I let my va-va-voom illusion drop. "Nice work. You had us fooled. Where did you get the image?"

"From the Victoria's Secret catalog, though I added clothing," I said as I crossed the room and took a seat at the table where the guys were. I conjured myself a cup of coffee, not so much because I needed it but because I could, and that was a trick I never got tired of doing. "And, you know, that illusion stuff is harder than it looks—not so much the magic part as all the stuff that goes with it to make it convincing."

Rod made an "ew, I just mentally undressed my sister" face but said, "Yeah, the trick to making an illusion work is to create the whole character: the voice, the walk, the body language, the attitude. Once you've got all that down, the magic is just the finishing touch." And he should know, since he regularly relied on an illusion to make himself more handsome. Until very recently, it hadn't worked on me, but a freak incident had turned my magical immunity into magical powers, so magic now worked on—and for—me.

Which was why I was there in an improvised classroom in the bowels of the Magic, Spells, and Illusions, Inc., headquarters building. Rod was teaching me to use my newfound powers, while Owen was studying me to see how my magic worked. Apparently, my situation was rather unprecedented.

Rod continued lecturing me. "Most situations require only minor disguises, like a different hair color or clothing, but for more extensive alternative identities, I'd recommend creating a few regular characters. Work on those characters before you even add the magic, practice their voices and body language, and then it'll be easier to pull off the illusions."

"Not that she's likely to need to create any alter egos," Owen said.

"In our line of work?" Rod countered. "You never know when you'll need a good disguise. Just remember, the attitude—the nonmagical part—is what's most important."

"I would think, then, that if you got good at the attitude you might not even need the magical part," I said with a meaningful look at Rod. He was making improvements and had dropped the attraction spell he used to use along with the handsome illusion, but I still hadn't managed to convince him that he could be attractive as himself. Although the illusion was better-looking, I missed seeing his real face.

He ignored me and changed the subject. "We should start working on defensive spells. Without your magical immunity, you're vulnerable to attack spells, so you'll need to be able to defend yourself."

"But only in extreme circumstances," Owen put in.

"That's so annoying," I said with a sigh. "I have magical powers, but can't use them outside this room." But I knew why. The same incident that gave me magic had restored Owen's lost powers. Things in the magical world were still too touchy for that secret to be let out, given that Owen's birth parents had been evil wizards. Our enemies had revealed that fact to discredit him, and now most people in the magical world distrusted him. His life was easier while his restored magic remained a secret, and that meant my newfound powers had to be a secret too.

"I've developed a few shield spells that mimic the effect of magical immunity," Owen went on, passing some handwritten pages to Rod.

"They'd block and dissipate any attack spells. The use of magic would be apparent to anyone who's really paying attention, but in the heat of a fight when there's a lot of magic flying around, no one should notice." He gave me the shy smile that always made my knees go weak and added, "After all, us being affected by magic would also reveal more than we'd like."

Then we settled down to the lessons. Owen was developing spells for me to learn, but Rod handled the teaching. It had turned out that Owen, while being an expert in the science and theory of magic, wasn't a very good teacher. He used magic instinctively, so he was impatient with anyone who didn't automatically grasp it the way he did, and he didn't understand the need to break it down into steps. Instead, he studied the way my magic worked while Rod worked through preschool-level magic lessons with me.

Or maybe elementary-level. I must have worked my way at least to second grade by now, which was pretty good, considering I'd only been working at it for a few weeks. My job for the time being was to learn enough to be useful and play guinea pig for Owen's research while still putting up a front of doing my old marketing job at the company.

Rod jotted a few notes on Owen's spell—probably adding those necessary steps that Owen forgot to mention because they were instinctive to him—then said, "Yeah, I think this'll work. Let's see what you can do. Owen, I'll need you to provide an attack in a second."

I listened as Rod talked me through the combination of words, mental images, and magical control needed to carry out the spell. I had to memorize and then internalize the words so that all I'd need to do was think them to make the spell work. Once I got that down, the rest was easy because the magic just flowed for me. I was having more fun learning magic than anything else I'd ever studied. It was truly *awesome*.

"Okay, I think you're ready to test it," Rod said with a satisfied nod when I'd mastered the magical manipulations. "Owen, something relatively harmless and visible, please."

I maintained the spell while Owen sent a ball of light flying at me. I fought not to duck and to focus on my spell as the ball came toward me and then fizzled harmlessly a fraction of an inch away from me.

The guys turned to each other. "Whattaya think?" Rod asked. "Did it look like a shield to you, or just like magical immunity?"

"It looked like a shield, but only because I know what to look for. In a real-world setting with a fight going on, I think it should be okay. They're not going to just use fireballs, and it'll be less obvious in blocking other spells."

"So while I'm doing this, no one can turn me into a frog?" I asked.

Owen grinned. "No, you should be safe from that."

"Then why don't I just keep this shield up all the time? And why don't you people shield yourselves all the time?"

"People would notice the magic," Owen said. "And it's an energy drain. If I did some tinkering, though, it might be commercially viable as a shield for certain situations, like the magical equivalent of body armor ..." His voice trailed off as he started mentally developing the idea.

"I think we've lost him for the day, and he may have just made his next million," Rod said with fond amusement. "Now, let's see how fast you can put that spell up."

He drilled me in spells for the next hour while Owen scribbled frantically in his notebook, occasionally mumbling things to himself. I knew I should have been exhausted by the time the lesson ended, but I was exhilarated. I felt like I'd finally found something I was really good at. "You're a natural," Rod confirmed with a proud smile.

"Not too natural," I said. "More like a freak of nature."

"That just means you're special," he said, patting me on the shoulder. "Now I'd better get back to work. I've got a ton of paperwork waiting for me that I wish I could magic away. It's strange how many people are just not showing up to work these days. Same time tomorrow?"

"Yeah." I shot him a grin over my shoulder as I headed out of the room. "And you never know who'll show up."

Owen joined me on the way out, and as soon as we were out of earshot of the schoolroom, he said, "Although that illusion was nice work, I like what's behind it a lot better."

"Oh, you charmer," I teased, though inwardly I really was quite pleased. It had taken me a long time to get used to the idea that a guy as movie-star handsome as Owen—and a powerful wizard on top of that—was into me, when I'd always thought of myself as ordinary in a forgettable way. Owen was a certified genius, so it was unlikely that he was wrong. I still wouldn't turn heads on the street unless I put on my lingerie-model illusion, but I didn't need to if Owen liked what he saw.

"Rod's right, you really are a natural. I don't know if you're picking magic up so quickly because you've been around us enough to absorb some things or if you inherited more from your grandmother than you realized, but your progress is rather astonishing. You've already mastered the basics, and soon we should be able to figure out where your particular talents lie."

"Not that it'll do me much good if no one can know I *have* talents," I grumbled.

"The further we get from that incident, the less likely it will be for people to suspect your new powers might also mean my powers are back."

That perked me up. "How much longer, do you think?"

"I don't know. A month or two, maybe? By the time we figure out your strengths and start specializing your training, certainly."

"So, maybe a few more months in marketing?"

"Let's say the first of next year."

It was October, so I thought I could survive that long. "Do you have any idea what my strengths might be yet?"

"It's hard to tell from the basics. You do seem to be pretty analytical with the spells, so you might be able to help me in Research and Development."

"I think I could cope with that. And I happen to be on the boss's good side." I smiled at him. "In fact, I think I might already have him wrapped around my little finger." I wasn't normally a flirt, even with my boyfriend, but having magical powers had done wonders for my confidence levels. I hadn't realized how unequal I'd felt in this company and with Owen. My previous magical immunity had been special and valuable, but being magical was something else entirely. Now I felt powerful. Being able to make myself look like a lingerie model had somehow made me feel like one, even when I wasn't using the illusion.

"Since I'm not your boss yet, would it be improper for me to invite you over to dinner tonight?"

"Considering that my grandmother is cooking it, I think it counts more as a family thing. Is she driving you crazy yet?"

"No, not at all. It just feels weird for me to come home to a home-cooked meal when it's your grandmother doing the cooking."

"I'm sure she won't be around much longer. Just be sure to remind her how well my lessons are going so she'll know she doesn't have to make sure I learn to use my powers the right way."

We reached the point where we had to go our separate ways to return to our respective offices. "Okay, then, I'll see you after work," he said, taking my hand for a quick squeeze before heading off.

I walked with a jaunty spring in my step back to my office, feeling like I should have a perky pop tune following me on the soundtrack. Not too long ago, I'd hated my job and had despaired of ever finding my place in the company. Now I was having a blast learning to do magic.

True, I still hated my job, but that job was now a cover story, so it was less painful to face. I didn't know where my eventual place would be, but still, *magic!* That made it a lot easier to get out of bed in the morning.

I bounced into my office and asked, "Were there any messages for me?"

My assistant, Perdita, looked me up and down, smirking ever so slightly. Only then did I realize that returning to my office after a long "meeting" with a bounce in my step, a glow about me, sparkling eyes, and a flushed face probably gave entirely the wrong impression, especially since my boyfriend worked at the same company. I immediately imagined that she was picturing Owen and me in a janitor's closet somewhere, and that mental image made my face flush even more, which made me look even guiltier. I wondered if I could get Rod to give me a signed note saying that it really had been a meeting with the Director of Personnel. After all, training did count as a personnel matter.

"No messages," she said, raising one slanted elven eyebrow.

"Good, thanks," I said. "We're making real progress on that magical training program we're putting together. I mean, Rod and I are putting together. That'll be our next big launch." Feeling my face grow warmer and warmer—which was infuriating, since I didn't have anything to feel embarrassed about—I made a beeline for my private office.

Then I realized that something was odd. Perdita had said only two words to me, which was very much unlike her. In fact, those had been the only two words she'd said to me all day. She hadn't said anything when she'd arrived that morning, and she'd only nodded an acknowledgment when I'd left for my training session and told her when I'd be back. Normally it was impossible to stop the flood of words from Perdita, and she drove me crazy from offering to do things for me.

I stopped and turned back. "Is everything okay?" I asked.

She shrugged and didn't quite meet my eyes. "I'm fine," she said before bending down to focus on the doodle-covered notepad on her desk.

I knew that was the international sign for "no, things are definitely not okay," but it was also the international sign for "I don't want to talk about it," so I decided not to push. "Well, you know my door is always open," was all I said before I went into my office. I figured she must have had a fight with her sister or been spurned by her latest crush. She'd probably snap out of her mood by the next morning.

One nice thing about spending several hours a day in those training session "meetings" was that I was a lot less bored heading an ancient near-monopoly's marketing program. I wasn't any busier, but I had fewer hours to fill. Even with stuff to do, I was tempted to practice magic tricks during breaks between tasks, but since Perdita was a very reliable member of the grapevine, that would be like telling half the company.

She left for the day without a word, which worried me, and I must have still been frowning when Owen came by to pick me up to go home because he asked, "What's wrong?"

"I think I pissed off Perdita."

"I would have thought that would be really difficult to do."

"Yeah, me too. I wonder, did I forget to have her conjure some coffee for me this morning?" Finding magical approximations for coffeehouse concoctions was one of Perdita's prized specialties and her biggest value to me, other than her ability to send and receive gossip. "I'll need to be more careful about that. It's not just about not doing magic around others. I also can't change my habits."

"I'm sure it has nothing to do with you," Owen reassured me as he helped me put on my jacket. "She may have just had a bad day—probably a fight with her mom." From what Perdita said about her mother, I got the feeling she was a lot like mine, in which case I sympathized.

As we headed out of the office building, a voice on the awning over the entrance said, "Psst, you two!"

We looked up to see Sam the gargoyle, MSI's head of security. "Hey, Sam, what is it?" I asked.

"Watch yourselves, okay?"

"I don't need to watch myself," Owen said. "I'm *being* watched." He gave a friendly wave to his unseen surveillance team. Since I'd lost my magical immunity, I couldn't see them anymore because they tended to veil themselves magically, but Owen knew he was being watched by official and unofficial monitors from various groups who still weren't convinced he wouldn't turn evil and try to take over the world with dark magic.

"That's not what I meant," Sam snapped with uncharacteristic tension that made me wonder if there was something in the water or perhaps a city-wide spell making usually cheerful people into grouches. It wouldn't be the first time someone had tried casting a broad spell like that. "Just be careful. This is a big city, you know."

"The crime rate here is actually a popular misconception," I pointed out. "Things happen, but if you stay in the right neighborhoods, you're safer than in a lot of cities. We'll try to avoid the crack dens."

"Hey, just lookin' out for two of my favorite people. What, you don't like me carin' for you? Be that way and see if I do it again." I waited for a second for the "just kiddin', doll" I was sure would come, but he flapped his wings and resettled himself so that his back was turned to us.

Owen and I exchanged an uncomfortable glance and departed. "Maybe we should check the top of the Empire State Building," I said as we walked to the nearby subway station. That was where the bad guys had broadcast the last spell to hit the whole city. "Someone's put up a grumpy hex."

"Or maybe something *is* going on."

"Something's *always* going on. And, let's face it, we like it that way."

Once we were in the station, he took my hand and I closed my eyes for a second to enjoy the little magical tingle that sent through me. I'd been able to sense the presence of magic even when I was immune, but now that I had power, myself, I'd learned to pick up on nuances. There was something about the way Owen's magical field meshed with mine that sparked something. I didn't know if it was because we were magically compatible or if it was because Owen had drawn on my latent power in the past, but it was extremely sexy, whatever it was. We'd made a good team when I was immune and he was magical, but there was a lot to like about sharing magic with him.

"I wonder if we could find a garden club for Granny to attend every so often," I mused out loud after we'd boarded a train and were standing close together. It was a real pity to have this magical connection and no chance for solitude. I had three roommates and my grandmother had moved in with him. We had more privacy on a rush-hour train than we had at home, since no one on the train noticed or cared what we were up to.

"In Manhattan?" he asked, raising an eyebrow.

"There are gardens. Community gardening is very big, and there are rooftop and container gardens. She could teach them a lot of things, I'm sure."

"Maybe we could get the boss to invite her out for dinner."

"Bite your tongue!" I snapped, getting queasy at the idea of my boss and my grandmother getting cozy. They already seemed to like each other more than was comfortable for me.

"They don't have to date. They could just spend time talking shop."

"But what if something *did* happen and she decided to stay permanently? Even if she moved out of your place, she'd still be around, meddling."

"Okay, then, garden club it is. We'll do an Internet search and ask around the office tomorrow."

I couldn't help but smile at the idea that he wanted alone time as much as I did. I was still grinning when we reached Union Square and left the train. My grin faded when he whispered, "Don't turn around, but try to look around casually the first chance you get."

I gulped. "You mean Sam was right about watching ourselves? Does he have some kind of precognition?"

"I don't know. It's hard to tell if you're being followed in a place this crowded, but I have a funny feeling."

He led us on a more roundabout than usual route out of the station. The area around the park was still pretty crowded with commuters leaving the subway station, and we stuck to the busier Park Avenue to head uptown instead of cutting over to Irving Place, like we usually did. Eventually, though, to get to Owen's home we had to go down one of his neighborhood's quiet side streets, where there wasn't a lot of traffic— vehicular or otherwise. It was the kind of neighborhood where I didn't mind walking alone at night. When I saw in the rearview mirror of a parked car that a small group of young men had followed us, I realized that today was apparently different.

They looked like gangsters. That is, they looked like gangsters in a high-school production of *West Side Story*. They didn't much resemble the current breed of street toughs that you almost never saw in the vicinity of Gramercy Park. In spite of my nerves, I had an overwhelming urge to bend forward and snap my fingers menacingly as I walked down the sidewalk. Then we passed another car's mirror and I caught a glint of metal in the reflection. These guys were armed, so I doubted they were going to limit themselves to intimidating us through virtuoso choreography.

"Do you remember that shield spell you learned today?" Owen

whispered.

"Yeah. You think they're going to attack us with magic?"

"There's magic nearby."

I felt it, too, I realized. "You're sure it's theirs?"

"It's strongest in that direction."

"You'd probably do a better job with that shield. It's your spell, and you're more powerful."

"I can't."

"I thought me using magic would give you away, too."

"They're watching me. They're not watching you, so they may not notice. If there's a magical attack, your shield should be hidden in the overall surge of power." He must have felt me tense because he gave my arm a reassuring squeeze and said, "You can do it. You fought off everything Rod and I threw at you today, and it always looked like immunity at work."

"But those guys have knives. That spell won't fight that."

"I think those are just for show. If they've got magic, they're not going to bother getting close enough to stab us."

I heard laughter behind us, the sound of a bully who's spotted someone weaker he can prey upon, and then the others joined in, feeding on each other's cruelty. We were still nearly a block from Owen's place.

"What if they know who we are and think we're immune to magic?" I hissed at Owen. "Then they won't use magic on us."

He turned to look at me in horror at that realization. The sound of footsteps behind us grew louder and faster. I braced myself for the attack.

CHAPTER TWO

I wasn't sure what we could do to save ourselves. Would it be better to stand our ground and try to fight or to run for our lives? We were so close to Owen's place... where Granny was, I realized. My grandmother had come to New York from Texas because she'd sensed I'd need her help soon. Surely she'd notice if I was in mortal danger little more than a block away. We hadn't yet covered mental communication in my magic lessons, since that was supposedly a more advanced skill that only a few wizards could do, but I figured that a mental cry for help wouldn't hurt. I put every bit of thought and feeling I had into mentally calling out for my grandmother.

Then I couldn't bear waiting any longer for the attack and spun to face our attackers. All my thinking and crying out for help must have taken only a split second because they weren't quite yet on us. Their steps faltered when they saw me facing them, like they hadn't expected that. I nudged Owen to get him to turn around, too, as we backed against the nearest wall. "What do you want?" I demanded of the fresh-faced, retro street gang.

Their answer was to fan out to surround us on three sides and look menacing, but they didn't get much closer to us. I felt magic move with them, surrounding them, and I thought I saw hints of the blurring around the edges that indicated an illusion. In my public guise as a magical immune, I wasn't supposed to see illusions, so how was I supposed to react to these guys? What was really there? If they'd been ordinary street thugs, I'd have known what to do. A clearly magical situation without a clear agenda was more challenging. Having magical powers was cool, but my magical immunity had been so much more useful in situations like this because I knew what was really happening.

They still weren't doing anything but acting like they wanted to scare us. They weren't making threats or demands, just leering at us as they sauntered around us like cats toying with a pair of mice. Well, if what they wanted was to intimidate or scare us, the way to ruin that was to refuse to act intimidated or scared, no matter how intimidated or scared I really was.

I folded my arms across my chest, rolled my eyes, and stifled a yawn. "Is there something we can help you with?" I said, giving my tone a veneer of civility on top of irritation.

Owen looked at me like I was nuts, then got the hint. "I'm pretty sure dinner's waiting on us, and her grandmother won't be happy if we're late," he said. "So, if you don't mind, can we cut to the mugging part of this encounter?"

Our assailants gave each other surprised glances. I wasn't sure what they expected us to do—maybe scream in terror? I'd seen a lot more frightening things than this in my time among magical people.

"Is this part of your hate club?" I whispered to Owen. "Are they trying to goad you into fighting them so they can say you're evil?"

"There's no telling," he whispered wearily. Frowning, he added, "I think they're elves. Their magic feels elven."

"So I was right, those are illusions!"

"Good work."

"Tell Rod. I want credit."

One of our would-be attackers lunged toward us with his knife, but didn't come close enough to do any harm. "Eek," I said so he wouldn't feel bad about not being scary enough.

And then it was as though someone had sent them a signal, and they all charged forward. This time, it looked like their aim was to do more than scare us. "Run!" Owen urged, and we ran through a gap they opened when they attacked.

A loud crack of lightning stopped us in our tracks. I realized it wasn't generated by our attackers when they pulled back, too. Then a small figure came out of the haze of smoke lingering from the lightning and rapped a cane on the ground. "It's dinnertime," Granny said in a voice that wouldn't accept arguing. She'd heard me! We hurried to her side.

At the same time, a trio of gargoyles swooped down from the tops of nearby buildings, two men dressed all in black appeared as though from thin air, and a bicycle messenger rounded the corner at full tilt, heading straight for the street gang. The attackers turned to run, but the biker was on their tail and the gargoyles chased them down from above. The men in black soon joined in the scuffle.

"What in the devil is going on?" Granny demanded of Owen and me.

"That's what I want to know," Owen said, moving toward the altercation. Granny and I followed him.

"You okay, kids?" Sam asked as he left the scrum and landed on top of a sign near us.

"Was this what you were warning us about?" I asked him, ignoring his question. "Did you know we were going to be attacked? Were we bait for some kind of sting?"

The men in black had bound the wrists of two of the elven gang members, and the bicycle messenger was protesting loudly. Hearing this, Sam left us, shouting, "Hey, this is our collar! It's my sting! You just happened to be here 'cause you're spyin' on Palmer, here."

One of the men in black replied, "This falls into Council jurisdiction."

Sam snorted. "Yeah, you leave us to do all the dirty work on our own most of the time, but then when you feel like it, it's suddenly your jurisdiction."

"We're not under the jurisdiction of any of you," one of the captives protested. "We answer only to the Elf Lord."

Granny tapped me on the arm. "While those idiots fight it out, let's get home. Dinner's getting cold, and there's no point in us standing around. You did your part by drawing them out, apparently."

The MSI security team and the Council surveillance team didn't seem to notice us leaving, they were so caught up in their argument. I figured if they needed us, they knew where to look. It was a relief to get safely inside Owen's heavily warded home and sit down to my grandmother's homemade pot roast with all the trimmings.

"What was all that about?" I asked after eating enough to mollify Granny. "Sam seemed to know it was coming."

"That's what it looked like," Owen agreed. "I don't think the Council guys were supposed to be in on it, though."

"And elves?"

"Maybe they think I've got that brooch or they think I destroyed it and they're out for revenge. I understand there are rumors all over town about what happened to it."

"Eat!" Granny ordered, pointing her fork at his nearly full plate.

"*I* destroyed the brooch," I said. "Maybe I should put out a press release."

"It's probably best that not too many people know what really happened," Owen said, then he noticed Granny's glare and dutifully put a bite of roast in his mouth.

"I wonder what Sam's plan was if you hadn't shown up, Granny," I said. "I guess you got my message just in time—you *did* get my message?"

"Loud and clear. But what are you people teaching her?" she demanded of Owen. "That was the worst mental call for help I've ever heard."

"It worked!" I protested.

"We actually haven't taught her that at all," Owen said with a proud smile at me. "She must have figured that out for herself."

"Then teach her properly before she needs to do it again. My ears are still ringing." Then she turned back to me. "What *have* they been teaching you, if not how to properly call for help?"

"Today we worked on some defensive shields that should mimic the effect of being magically immune."

"Hmmph," she muttered, and I knew I was in for a magical lesson, Granny style, as soon as the table was cleared. She and the MSI people had very different approaches to magic, since theirs was more analytical and based on rigorous study over the centuries and hers was more of a folk art handed down through generations of people who were mostly isolated from other magic users. I hadn't even known that there was magic in my family until earlier in the year, and then it turned out that my mother's side of the family tended to be either wizards or immune to magic. I had one brother who was a wizard and one who was immune.

By the time Owen called a halt to the post-dinner magical workout, I felt as drained as if I'd just done an intense session at the gym. I wondered if magic counted as cardio. "I'm getting totally mixed signals on magic, between Rod and Granny. Who am I supposed to believe?" I asked him as he walked me home.

"Whichever works best for you," he said with a shrug. "The only 'right' way in magic is the way that works with the least power and without hurting anyone. A lot of it is trial and error. Your grandmother does have some interesting approaches. With the lower levels of available magical energy to draw from in your hometown, she's really good at making efficient use of resources. I've incorporated some of her techniques into my research."

"If you tell her that, she'll be impossible."

"Which is why I haven't told her," he said with a wry grin. "If something comes of it, though, I'll owe her royalties."

We reached my front door, and he kissed me good night before saying loudly, "I don't have any evil scheming planned for the night, but I'd appreciate the escort home, if you don't mind." With a smile, he added, "I might as well take advantage of the hassle. See you tomorrow."

When I got upstairs to my apartment, Nita, my one roommate who didn't know about magic, was sitting on the sofa with a big bowl of popcorn in her lap. "Oh, good, you're home," she said without moving her eyes from the television screen. "Marcia's working late and Gemma's out."

"I had dinner with Owen." I joined her on the sofa. She was watching one of those romantic comedies where people fall in love in a montage set to a pop ballad. The couple went on a picnic in the park, went boating on the lake and nearly fell in, danced on a rooftop in the rain, and stared dreamily into each other's eyes across a restaurant table.

I couldn't help but sigh wistfully. That was what being in love in New York was supposed to be about, not fighting off gangster elves and then having dinner with my grandmother while being lectured on how to do magic. Owen and I had yet to manage one normal date that was even remotely similar to the kind of things you saw in movies. The closest we'd come was when we were hanging out as friends before we started dating. I guessed it came with the territory when part of your job was stopping bad magic.

But we weren't on the front lines right now, other than apparently being targets. We should finally have the time to work on the romantic side of our relationship and see what was there without the adrenaline of constant danger or the closeness that came from developing battle plans together. I thought about planning a picnic for the weekend, but then I'd have to pack enough to feed Owen's official monitors, the various factions who were also watching him, and now possibly the MSI security people and the elves who were out to get us. Was just one nice, romantic day out too much to hope for?

"It's a lie!" Nita said, and I turned to her in surprise, wondering if I'd been projecting my thoughts unwittingly.

"What is?" I asked.

"This whole romantic autumn in New York thing. It's like there's an entire industry devoted to selling us this story, and then does it really happen? No! If you try to suggest any of this stuff to a guy, he accuses you of having seen too many movies. Apparently, no one but tourists goes boating on the lake in Central Park. Or is that just what they say when they don't want to pay for it?"

"You *have* seen too many movies."

"Well, yeah, but that doesn't mean it can't be at all true. Have you ever done any of this romantic New York stuff?"

"We went ice skating in Central Park last Christmas," I said. And I fell through the ice, which was supposed to be impossible since the rink wasn't a frozen pond. "Otherwise, no, not really. Work's been crazy, so most of our dates are lunches at the office."

"I think that's the way most people date in this city." She sighed. "They're *so* doing it wrong." I couldn't help but agree as we watched the rest of the movie together. I had an amazing, gorgeous guy, so where was my romantic comedy life?

*

When Owen and I got to the office the next morning, I was eager to interrogate Sam about the previous evening's events, but he wasn't at his usual place on the building's awning. "He's avoiding us," I accused.

"You know he had to be under orders, and he obviously did try to warn us as well as he could."

"Then I guess we can't go demand that the boss tell us what's up."

"I'm sure he'll tell us soon enough."

"I hope he lets us know before we get attacked by elves with knives again."

"Elven blades are dangerous," he agreed. Then we reached my hallway and he said, "I'll see you for our afternoon training session."

As I approached my office, I hoped Perdita had gotten over whatever had been bugging her the day before. I wasn't in the mood to tiptoe around sensitive feelings. I felt a lot more like stomping on things.

She was already at her desk, which was unusual for her, but she merely glanced up at me, then looked down again. Normally, she'd offer me coffee, at the very least. Often, she'd bombard me with gossip and questions before I made it all the way through the door. "Good morning," I called out more cheerfully than I felt, but she just nodded and continued pretending to work. I hadn't given her a project to work on, so I knew her busyness was fake. Giving it up as a lost cause, I went on into my office.

I'd almost made it to my desk when she called out, "Um, Katie, could I talk to you about something?" She sounded troubled and more serious than normal.

I turned back and went to the office doorway. "Sure. What is it?"

She took a deep breath, as though steeling herself for something unpleasant. She wasn't going to resign, was she? Sure, she was a ditz and a klutz, but I was getting used to her, and she often had good ideas. I'd hate to think that I'd driven her away. I hoped I was a good boss. I'd had enough horrible bosses for me to make a conscious effort to not repeat those mistakes. "There's something I think I should show you," she said, not meeting my eyes.

I went over to her desk and sat in the guest chair beside it. "Okay," I said, as reassuringly as I could. "What do you have to show me?"

She glanced around, like she was making sure no one was nearby to eavesdrop, then leaned forward and opened her lower desk drawer. With another glance around and then a big gulp, she pulled a piece of paper out from under a stack of manila envelopes. "This," she said, shoving the paper at me like it was on fire. Then she screwed her eyes shut, as though she expected me to hit her once I saw it.

It was a flyer photocopied onto colored paper, the kind of thing political groups hand out around Union Square. "ARE WIZARDS OPPRESSING ELVES?" the flyer asked in huge block capitals. Underneath, it listed the evidence in bullet points, with each line in a different font. I cringed at the first one, which claimed that wizards had stolen and then destroyed the Knot of Arnhold, the ancient magical brooch treasured by the elves.

Actually, I'd been the one to destroy it, though I hadn't been a wizard at the time. And, technically, we hadn't stolen it from the elves. Their own leader had stolen it to use it in a scheme, then it was stolen from him and sold, and *then* we'd stolen it. It was a complicated story, but it had been necessary for saving the world because the Knot had been united with a nasty gem that probably would have led to World War III if I hadn't thrown it on the electric third rail of a train track during a massive scuffle. The fact that I got magical powers out of the bargain was beside the point. I wasn't named in the flyer, but Owen was, I noted, and his heritage was highlighted. I wondered if that explained the attack on us.

There were other gripes, including an accusation that wizards were abducting elves who dared to speak out. The flyer concluded with a call for elves to disassociate themselves from wizards, stand up for themselves, and fight back. It looked like Sylvester, the Elf Lord, was still up to his old tricks and using propaganda to do what he hadn't been able to do with enchanted jewelry. "Thanks for showing me this, Perdita," I said.

She cautiously opened one eye. "It's not true, is it?"

"Parts of it are," I admitted, "but they rather severely missed the point. There's a lot more to it than that." She opened her other eye, but she didn't seem to relax much. I asked, "Are the elves taking this seriously?"

"Some are. A couple of my friends quit this week. My mom is griping at me about finding a new job." Then she gasped and hurried to add, "Not that I would. I like it here. But, yeah, even some of those who didn't like the Elf Lord before are starting to listen." She twirled a red ringlet around her finger before whispering, "To be honest, I feel kind of like a rat for showing that to you. I mean, I'm turning against my own people."

"Not all your own people," I reassured her. "There are free elves who don't want you to be ruled by a lord of any kind, and they're the ones working with us to keep your people from being even more under Sylvester's control."

"I'm not sure my family would see it that way."

"Don't worry, they won't know where we got this. There are a lot of elves working here." At least, there had been. If this flyer represented elven sentiment, that might change soon. I stood. "Mind if I take this?"

"Please do."

"Thank you again for trusting me." I started to leave the office, then turned back. "Could you hand me an envelope?" She did, and I sealed the flyer up in it. There were a number of elves working in the sales department, where my office was. It was safest not to let anyone see me carrying it from my office, lest they suspect Perdita of bringing it to me.

I headed straight up to the boss's office, where, as usual, he was waiting for me. It's a little disconcerting to have a boss who manages to anticipate your every move, but when your boss is Merlin—yeah, that one—it comes with the territory. You even get used to it. On the upside, I never have to wait for him to see me.

"I take it you have a concern, Miss Chandler?" he said by way of greeting as he gestured me to a seat in front of his desk.

I handed him the envelope. "Apparently, this sort of thing is going around the elven community," I told him.

I watched his face as he removed the flyer from the envelope and read it, but his expression gave nothing away. He murmured a soft, "Hmmm," as he laid it on his desk.

"Is that what last night was about?" I asked.

Instead of answering me, Merlin picked up his phone and called Sam, Owen, and Rod to come to his office. He made one more call to Earl, the young elf who'd been instrumental in letting us know what Sylvester had been up to with the Knot.

Once the gang was gathered, Merlin threw the flyer in the middle of the conference table without comment. They all leaned forward to get a good look.

When Owen read it, he paled. "I suppose this explains last night," he said dryly. Then he looked up at Merlin. "Did you already know about this?"

"There have been rumblings," Merlin admitted, "but we didn't know anything concrete."

"It was apparently enough for you to use us as bait," I said, not even trying to mask the irritation in my voice.

"We had our eyes on you the whole time, doll," Sam assured me. "We were hopin' the elves would show themselves."

"And now we know why they were after me," Owen said with a weary sigh. *Poor guy,* I thought. He already had people from the magical world watching his every move to make sure he wasn't evil. Now he was on the elves' Most Wanted list.

"Have you heard anything about this?" Merlin asked Earl.

Earl squinted at it, then shook his head. "Not in my circles, but I'm kind of persona non grata around Sylvester's people these days. This looks like his style, though. He's trying to create a common enemy and deflect the blame so people will forget that he was secretly hiding the Knot all along and was planning to use it to solidify his power."

Rod picked up the flyer and studied it. "This explains a lot," he said with a grim nod. "I've had more resignations in the past week than in the previous two months, and they were all elves. I was starting to research whether I had some toxic supervisors to deal with."

"More like a toxic Elf Lord," Earl said with a disgusted grunt.

"They're leaving MSI like rats leaving a sinking ship," Rod said with a shrug. "I don't know if that means they don't want to associate with us or if they want to be well out of the danger zone when something happens."

"Do you see this as a real threat?" Merlin asked. "Are we going to see more than mischief from this?"

Earl cleared his throat to speak, then glanced around before saying tentatively, "I've heard …" He trailed off, realized we weren't going to interrupt or disregard him the way his previous boss had, and started again. "I've heard rumors of people disappearing. Elves, I mean. Those who speak out against Sylvester. I don't know anyone personally who's gone missing, but people talk."

"Has Sylvester got some kind of elf Siberia going on?" I asked.

Earl glanced around nervously, then winced as he said, "Actually, they're blaming the wizards for the disappearances, and your people arresting those guys last night just played into that rumor."

"It wasn't our people," Sam grumbled. "Those Council goons pulled rank."

"They played us," I said. "I wonder if that's what it was really all about, staging an attack they knew we'd anticipate to goad us into arresting their people, and then there's proof that the disappearances are our fault."

Merlin sat lost in thought for a moment, then nodded as though he'd come to a decision. "Sam, I'd like you to put together a team to investigate any disappearances that might be related to the company. Earl, please use your underground connections to learn as much as possible. Mr. Gwaltney, provide the names of missing elf employees to Sam, and check in with our remaining elven employees. Please keep me informed of your progress."

I cleared my throat. "Is there something you need me to do?"

He gave me a fond smile. "I think you deserve a break after all you've done recently. Please focus on your magical training." In other words, I was a lot less valuable to the company when I couldn't spot disguised elves or hidden activities.

"Maybe I'll see if I can come up with a way to get out the message that we aren't out to get the elves—of course, without admitting to destroying the Knot or outright saying that Sylvester's the really evil one. Unless, that is, we get some concrete proof."

"Yes, that would be good," Merlin agreed.

That would probably mean having Perdita tell her friends the rumors were false. I wondered if maybe we should throw a big "elf day" party, but then I remembered that our track record for marketing events was iffy. Our enemies tended to use them against us.

Since Owen didn't have an assignment either, I hoped we could try to have a normal, romantic date, after all. For once, we weren't the ones in charge of saving the world.

*

When it was time for my afternoon magic lesson, I bounced into the schoolroom, as myself this time. "What do you have for me today, teacher?"

"Well, you've mastered illusion, shielding, physical manipulation, and you're getting the hang of food and beverages," Rod said.

"Maybe we should do some introductory communication," Owen said. "We don't want to blow out anyone's synapses the next time she's in danger, and that's one thing she can do without revealing that she can do magic." I caught his eye, and he blushed slightly. I suspected he was thinking the same thing I was, that psychic communication between us could be a lot of fun.

Rod glanced back and forth between us. "Something happened?"

"Granny said it was too loud when I called for help last night," I explained.

"Okay, then, magical communication, it is," Rod said. On the room's whiteboard, he outlined the steps, which weren't too different from what I'd done instinctively, though I could see where I'd gone wrong. Then he had me send him a message.

He squinted in concentration, then shook his head. "I could tell you were there, but I couldn't decipher it. Maybe you were trying too hard not to be as loud as you were last night. Just relax and let it flow."

I tried again, mentally raising my voice this time, but he shook his head. "No, you're still whispering."

Owen got up from where he was observing and came over to us. "Try me," he instructed. "As close as we are, that should be easier. I practically get your signals anyway, without you trying."

I was tempted to send a risqué message, then decided instead to suggest we go on a picnic that Saturday if the weather was nice. I waited for his shy smile in response, but he just said, "Okay, you can send now."

"I was!" I insisted aloud. "What am I doing wrong?"

"You may not be doing anything wrong," he said soothingly. "This just may not be where your talents lie. Or you may have exhausted that part of yourself last night. It can be like exercise—if you did something strenuous yesterday, you can't expect to be at your best today."

"Let's go back to something easy you know you can do," Rod suggested. "To start with, try erasing the board."

I focused on the eraser and thought the spell that put it under my control, then willed it upward to where Rod had written the communication spell. It moved, but not as briskly as it usually did. It seemed a little more sluggish, and it took more effort. I had beads of sweat on my forehead and upper lip by the time the board was clear. I couldn't tell if the guys noticed how hard I was struggling.

"See, you can still do that," Rod said. "We'll come back to the communication later. How about something fun? Remember that time Owen and I made it snow indoors?"

I smiled at the fond memory from not long after I'd joined the company. "And that was real, right? Because I could see it."

"Yeah, it was real, though you can also get a similar effect with illusion." He wrote new instructions on the board, then demonstrated by creating his own snowfall. Delicate flakes danced in the air, and now that I knew what to look for, I could sense the way he directed the magic. It was so vivid that I felt cold, even though I knew it wasn't real snow.

Then it was my turn. I ran through the spell, then imagined a magical Christmas Eve snowfall and directed it to appear. Instead of dancing flurries, I got more of a Texas snowfall, with big, wet, gloppy clumps of flakes, and even those vanished before they hit the ground. Soon, the whole snowfall petered out, no matter how hard I tried.

"What is *wrong* with me?" I cried out in frustration.

Owen put his arm around me. "Hey, everyone has bad days, and you used more power than you realized last night. You may not have aching muscles to feel, but your magical muscles are probably stiff and sore today. We should have thought of that and given you the day off."

"Yeah, that's a good idea," Rod chimed in. His smile was encouraging, but I caught the worried glance he and Owen exchanged. I wondered if my earlier successes were merely beginner's luck.

CHAPTER THREE

I was well rested and a little less cocky when I arrived for my next training session. Maybe I'd been more tired than I realized. I'd created a complex illusion, used magic to call for help, and then survived some extra drills with my grandmother. No wonder I'd struggled.

But now I was ready to go. "Hit me with your best shot," I told Rod.

He shook his head. "No, let's warm up first."

"You can sprain a magical muscle?" I asked.

"No, but magic is all about confidence. It's about believing that you can shape the universe to your will, and no matter how powerful you are, that can't happen if you don't believe it will. So, it's best to start with something you know you can do and work up from there." He looked around the room, then pointed to the mug sitting on the table in front of him. "For starters, could you please reheat my coffee for me?"

Heat was easy. It was one of the first things I'd learned. It was all about exciting the molecules. I focused my energy and sent a zap into the mug, then for good measure I cloaked the mug in a blanket of warmth. I felt the familiar surge of power go through me, doing exactly what I wanted it to, and I relaxed. The previous day had just been a fluke, after all. I still had it. "Your coffee, sir," I said with a flourish toward the cup.

Rod reached to take the mug, then flinched when he touched it. "Yeah, you got it hot, all right," he said. More cautiously, he curled his fingers around the handle, raised the mug to his lips, and took a tentative sip. Then he frowned.

"What's wrong?" I asked.

"The mug's hot. The coffee, well, not so much. Did you focus on the liquid?"

"Yeah, I did. That was the main thing. The outside was just to keep it warm longer. It was an idea I had."

"That's a good idea," Owen put in encouragingly.

"It didn't work, though?" I asked. That was supposed to be an easy spell, the kind of thing they taught kids as soon as they were old enough not to burn themselves.

"Maybe you just aimed wrong," Rod said. "Both spells seem to have hit the mug, not the coffee." He put the mug down. "Get a little closer and try again."

This time, I wasn't quite so sure of myself, so the magic felt sluggish. If it had been visible, it would have swirled around the mug, dipping toward it but missing a few times. Finally, I got it inside and kept it steady long enough that I thought I'd done the trick. "Try it now," I said, panting ever so slightly.

Rod picked it up, took a sip, then grinned. "There you go! Good work."

I sighed in relief, but I wasn't sure it counted as good work if doing such an elementary task wore me out that badly. Wasn't this supposed to get easier along the way? I'd seen enough eighties movies with training montages to know how it should work. I was supposed to start out struggling, but I'd keep at it and finally have the big breakthrough that would have my trainer grinning until I totally surprised him by outdoing him, and then it would be time for the big competition. Maybe what I was missing was the inspirational power ballad.

*

I was so frustrated by my magical failures that I barely remembered to be worried on the way home from work. I was too busy griping to Owen about how difficult magic had become for me. "Maybe it was just beginner's luck and I really am not cut out to be a wizard," I said. "There's a reason I didn't get an owl when I turned eleven."

It took him a second to catch the reference because he didn't think in pop culture terms, but then he grinned and said, "You weren't magical when you were eleven. You are now, and there are always ups and downs when you're learning something new. But if it'll make you feel better, I'll run some tests tomorrow. It's possible that something's blocking you."

"You mean the elves might have done something to me?"

"I doubt it because I'd hope I'd be able to sense it, but our enemies have tampered with your abilities in the past."

Fortunately, no elves attacked us during our commute, which confirmed my theory that they'd set us up so wizards could be blamed. If the elves were really after Owen, things would be very different.

I didn't even notice that instead of inviting me over for dinner, Owen merely steered us straight to his place. It was becoming such a habit that an invitation wasn't really necessary, and I didn't blame him for wanting to minimize the amount of time he had to spend alone with Granny. I wondered if there was a polite way to ask her how long she planned to stay. Owen kept insisting that he didn't mind, and he seemed to be telling the truth. He'd never known his own grandparents, so maybe he was enjoying having a grandmother fuss over him.

I, on the other hand, had nearly reached my limit. I'd moved to New York in part to get away from my crazy family. If they followed me here, I'd have to move back home to get away from them again.

As we finished up the last bites of apple pie, Granny fixed me with her steely gaze and said, "So, what's the problem?"

"Problem?" I asked, blushing at the thought she might have picked up on my desire for her to leave.

"Did you hit a snag with your training?"

How did she know this stuff? "I was tired yesterday, so it didn't go so well."

"You did better today, though," Owen hurried to add.

It didn't fool Granny. "Okay, honey, out with it," she said.

I glanced at Owen before saying, "I started off so well. It was easy. And now, it seems like it's more of a struggle."

"Well, you've moved beyond the basics. It's going to be harder. Anything worth doing takes time and effort to learn."

"But that's the thing—it *is* the basics I'm having trouble with now." I heard the frustration in my own voice. "The things that were easy earlier in the week are a lot harder now, if I can even do them at all. I think I'm losing my touch," I finally admitted. Owen's expression was both shocked and concerned.

"Let's see what we can do about that—after we do the dishes, of course," Granny said matter-of-factly.

The dishes went quickly with all three of us working, and then we adjourned to the living room. Owen took a seat to the side so he could observe. His worried look unsettled me. "I'm not going to spontaneously turn into a frog, or anything like that, am I?" I asked him.

He quickly adjusted his expression as he said, "I can't think of any reason you should."

"There is precedent in your department."

"He was meddling with dangerous spells. You're doing the basics."

"It's probably just bad technique that you were taught," Granny said. "Try it my way."

Using Granny's techniques did have slightly better results than my office training session that afternoon, but the simplest spells still left me feeling like I'd singlehandedly fought a great magical battle. In spite of their assurances, I *knew* something was wrong.

"You tell Rod that you're doing things Granny's way from now on," she told me when I called a halt to the exercises and got ready to go home. "How you city wizards get anything done at all is beyond me."

"We do get lazy and complacent with all the magical energy in the environment around here," Owen said, which I thought disappointed her. She'd been gearing up for a big argument. I suppressed a smile. Owen might have found the best way of encouraging her to return home in not rising to her challenges.

*

The next morning, I was still haunted by the thought that the elves might have done something to me. My ability to use magic had totally changed after that attack, and I doubted it was a coincidence. I thought I might ask Perdita some general, innocuous questions about elven magic when I got to work, but she wasn't yet at her desk when I arrived. I took that as a good sign because it meant she was getting back to normal. Showing me that anti-wizard flyer had probably cleared her conscience.

When she still hadn't shown up by noon and hadn't called in sick, I started to worry. There were times when I wouldn't have been surprised if she forgot what day it was and thought it was the weekend, but with a spate of elf disappearances and resignations, I wasn't ready to dismiss it so easily. I called her cell phone, but the call went straight to voice mail, so I left a message for her to check in with me.

I hadn't heard anything by the time of my afternoon training session, so when I arrived at the classroom, I asked Rod, "Did Perdita resign? You would tell me, right?"

"She didn't show up today?"

"Nope, and no call from her, either, which is odd. She's good about letting me know if she's going to be out or unusually late. I left her a message, but she hasn't called back."

"I didn't get any paperwork on her. I can't start investigating job abandonment until she misses two more business days without notice."

Had she put herself at risk by showing me that flyer? And how would anyone know she'd done that? I hadn't told where I got it, and no one had been around when she showed it to me.

Owen showed up a moment later carrying a box full of gadgets. "Sorry I'm late. I was pulling some things together."

"Is that the testing stuff?" I asked.

"Testing?" Rod asked.

"To make sure the elves didn't somehow put the whammy on me," I explained.

"But if the elves don't know you have powers, how would they know to put the whammy on you?"

"How else would you explain the fact that I went from being a natural to being remedial?"

"You really think it's elves?" Rod asked Owen.

"I don't know about that, but I think measuring the flow of magic would be a good idea. The change has been pretty drastic, and I'd like to know why."

"I don't know about you, but I'm fully charged," Rod said. "You don't think the building has dead spots, do you?"

"That's a good theory," Owen said vaguely, which unsettled me. I got the feeling he'd been humoring me about the elves affecting me, but it really did seem like he thought something was wrong. He took a couple of things that looked like small antique brooches out of his box and pinned them to my sweater. He stuck another small metal thing to the middle of my forehead, and I crossed my eyes trying to look up at it. Then he took a crystal object in a metal frame out of his box and set it up on the table, waving his hand at it a few times as colored bars of light went up and down.

"What does that do?" I asked.

"It measures the flow of magic in and out of you." He stuck similar metal things on himself. "Since we got our powers in the same incident, I think it's best to test both of us," he explained as he waved his hand and more colored lights appeared. "And Rod, you'll be our control, since nothing's happened to your powers lately." He rigged up Rod, then said, "Now, all three of us will do the same spells."

Rod ran us through some basics that had become anything but basic for me. Using Granny's version of the spells did help a little. Rod couldn't even argue about me using unorthodox methods, since the results were so obviously better. That didn't mean my results were *good*. I just didn't fail entirely. I was still tiring easily from magic that shouldn't have required a second thought. A glance at Owen didn't reassure me. He was frowning at his device, not in concentration but in concern.

I caught my breath while Rod wrote the next assignment on the whiteboard, but before I could psych myself up enough to do it, Owen cried out, "Stop! Don't do any more magic."

"I knew it! I *am* going to turn into a frog," I said.

"No, you're not," Owen said absently as he focused on his device. "But if I'm right, you're running out of magic."

"Running out of magic?" Rod asked. "How? There's magic all around. We have enhanced circuits in this building."

"But she's not drawing on them."

"So I *am* doing something wrong," I said, heaving a sigh.

"No, I don't think so. I think you're doing the best you can do with what you've got, but you don't have much."

"In other words, I'm a lousy wizard."

"You're not a wizard. That's the problem. I don't think the exploding magical brooch really gave you magical powers. It just activated the latent magic in you."

"But I didn't have magic in me. I'm utterly devoid of magic. That's what being immune is."

"Not exactly. Remember how I can channel power from you?"

"Yes," I said, feeling my face grow warm at the memory. It was really sexy being linked to him that way.

"Well, in you, that magic is inert. I have to activate it to use it. That's a lot of what being a wizard means—having the ability to draw upon the magic inherent in the environment or in people and turn it into power I can use. Nonmagical people just have that power flow through them, so magic can work on them even if they can't use it. With magical immunes, it remains inert and unused, so it doesn't work for anyone unless it's removed from you. What that explosion must have done was activate the power you had in you at the time. When you're using magic, it's flowing out of you, but any new magic flowing in is as inert as it would normally be for you. You'll only have magical abilities as long as you don't use up the activated power. When it's gone, it's gone."

"Is it the same for you?" I couldn't process what this meant for me, but I knew he'd been greatly relieved to get his powers back. Losing them again might be more than he could take.

He shook his head. "No, I'm activating new power, the same as Rod. It really did reboot me by giving me the power I needed to draw upon more power. Granny would say it primed the pump. But since your natural state is immunity and you've never had the ability to activate power, all it did was activate whatever was in you at that time, but it's finite." His eyes softened, and the look he gave me was full of love and compassion, like he'd just given me a terminal diagnosis. "I'm so sorry, Katie."

"You can't teach me to activate power?"

"The technique is part of every spell. You're doing all the right things. You just lack that ability."

"Well, I guess it's a good thing I had to keep the power secret, or I'd have used it up by now," I said, fighting to keep a brave face. It had been bad enough to learn that magic existed but that I had no part of it. Having it and being good at it, then losing it, was worse. I felt like the heroine of a tearjerker TV movie—one of those about a blind woman who gets the miracle operation to restore her sight and sees her husband and kids for the first time, only to learn that the results aren't permanent. My case was less tragic, but it still wasn't happy.

"So, I guess we save it for emergencies?" Rod asked. "We should keep training on a theoretical basis."

Owen nodded. "It'll be more difficult to memorize spells without being able to practice them, but the more you know, the more effective use you'll make of your power when you need to use it."

"What happens after it's gone?" I asked. "Will I be immune again, or just normal?"

"I don't know," Owen said. "This whole thing has been unprecedented. I should get a good paper out of it."

"Owen!" I snapped. He was a real sweetheart of a guy, but when he was in intellectual mode he could be totally oblivious to human emotion.

He had the good grace to blush, and he was fair-skinned enough, in spite of his dark hair, to be a world-champion blusher. "Sorry. I know this is difficult for you, but it is interesting. What I suspect will happen is that when your power gets to a certain level, you'll go through a phase of being nonmagical—enough power for magic to work on you, not enough to do anything. Then after a while even that power will be drained and you'll be back to your usual state."

"How much power do I have left?"

"I'd guess you're down about halfway."

I thought of all the silly spells I'd done just because I could use magic: the illusions, the coffee, making things fly to me instead of reaching for them. Because of those, would I not be able to defend or shield myself in a real crisis? Or worse, would there be a life I couldn't save? "I wish I'd known this to start with," I said with a dejected sigh.

"I should have noticed sooner," Owen said, looking even more downcast than I felt.

"You just said this was unprecedented," I pointed out. "How could you have known to look?" Then I forced a huge smile that I didn't really feel. "On the bright side, once my magic is gone, my grandmother won't have much reason to stick around. She said she needed to be here to help me learn to use my powers. You'll have your house back to yourself again."

I was cheered by that thought, but he didn't look relieved. Me losing my powers wouldn't be nearly as bad as him losing his. For me, magic was a novelty. I wouldn't like it if I got stuck at normal, but I'd spent most of my life thinking I was normal. I understood that intellectually. Emotionally, I wasn't quite there yet. It might take me awhile before I could be honest when I said it.

The worst thing of all was that I didn't know what this meant for my future. I'd already been having a career crisis before I got zapped with magical powers. It had been put on hold until they figured out where I fit in magically. If there was an expiration date on my magic, I was in even more of a limbo. I wasn't useful as a wizard *or* as a magical immune. Part of me wanted to just go for the gusto and burn through my magic so I could get back to normal, but then there was a big part of me that wasn't ready to let go of it yet.

I really hoped Granny had made a chocolate cake for dessert.

*

Although getting to send Granny home was the one upside I could see to my situation, I dreaded telling her. Her only other wizard grandchild was my brother Dean, who'd been an idiot about using magic. I knew she'd enjoyed teaching me and being able to pass on everything she knew. She'd be so disappointed to learn it was only temporary. It would be like telling her I was failing out of medical school.

Owen seemed to sense that I'd want to talk to her alone, so after we'd washed the dishes, he said he was going to play squash with Rod and vanished. I was still psyching myself up to raise the subject when Granny turned to me and said, "Now, what's the problem you wanted to talk to me about?"

"How do you do that?" I blurted.

"It's not magic. It's just common sense. Anyone with eyes could tell you were troubled by something, and that boy hightailing it out of here means you need to talk to me. What is it?"

I decided to just blurt it out, like ripping off a bandage. "Well, it turns out I'm not really a wizard. I just got a certain amount of magic, and it's running out."

I held my breath, waiting for her reaction, but she just nodded and said, "Hmmm."

I babbled on to fill what felt like an awkward silence. "Owen ran some tests, and it turns out that's why it's been a struggle for me. I haven't had as much power to work with. I guess I burned through too much of it in the early stages, and I may have overdone the practicing, so now it's going to run out sooner or later. They want me to stop using magic entirely so I'll have it if a situation comes up where I really need it."

"That would be prudent. And I think this is why I got that feeling I needed to come here. I had no fear that you'd use it the wrong way like your idiot brother did. You have good people teaching you. But having magic and *not* using it, saving your resources for a rainy day, *that* I can help you with."

She got up from the sofa and ambled toward the kitchen, muttering to herself. I followed. "I don't know what ingredients the boy keeps around the house. Other than the books, you'd never know a wizard lived here. But I'll bet he can get them at work, or Merlin'll know where to find them. I was traveling light, so I didn't bring anything with me, and I wasn't going to trust your mother with that sort of thing when I had her send me some clothes."

She reached the kitchen, where she dug around in the cabinets, clicking her tongue in disapproval. "No, I'll have to give him a list to fetch me from work, or I'll have to go to the market next time it's open."

"Granny, what are you doing?" I finally asked when I could get a word in edgewise.

"Why, making you a potion, of course. I know some things that'll help restore your strength, give you a little more energy. It won't stop the decline, but it should slow it."

"But why bother?" I said wearily, leaning against the edge of the countertop. "Why drag this out? I'm pretty much useless as a wizard. I may as well go back to normal. I'm good at that."

She whirled on me and shook a finger in my face. "Now, how do you know you didn't get this gift for some purpose, hm? The good Lord knows what He's doing and has a plan, and that plan bestowed magical powers on you. For all you know, it's just in time to do something no one else could do, so you'd best be ready to make the most of it, whenever that comes. You are *not* useless. I don't know what got into your head to make you think that about yourself. It's probably your mother's fault."

"But I—" I started to protest.

She waved me off. "Oh, I know what you think, that you're so boring and ordinary that no one would notice you. Well, whose fault is that? And it has nothing to do with how much lipstick you wear, contrary to what that silly daughter of mine tells you. I know that no boring, ordinary girl could have caught that boy's eye the way you did. He's no dummy, and *he's* certainly not boring. I suggest you start seeing yourself the way he sees you and work on being the best you instead of worrying about what you're not. At the moment, you're a wizard with enough resources to make a difference when the time comes. Now, go cut yourself another slice of cake while I make out a shopping list."

Chastened, I sat at the tiny kitchen table and cut a slab of chocolate cake. Granny's lecture had cheered me up, but I couldn't help but worry about what might happen that would require my limited magical powers.

CHAPTER FOUR

Perdita wasn't there the next morning, and my call to her went straight to voice mail again, so I sent Rod an e-mail about it. Did she have a change of heart about siding with the wizards or did something happen to her because of her association with us?

It was difficult to focus on work when I was so worried, but I still jumped, startled, when someone knocked on the frame of my office door. I looked up to see a young man with slightly shaggy blondish-brown hair. "Sorry, didn't mean to startle you, but your assistant isn't here, and that's why I'm here. I'm from Security. We're investigating the employee disappearances."

I knew that there were non-gargoyles in the security team, but I hadn't worked with any of them. This guy looked vaguely familiar, and then I recognized him as the bicycle messenger who'd been part of the attempted sting the other night. "Oh, yes, come in and have a seat," I said. "I'd offer you coffee, but that's something my assistant has to do for me."

He waved his hand, and two cups appeared on my desk. "How's that?" he asked as he settled himself in my guest chair. "I don't believe we've met. I'm Dan, one of Sam's undercover experts."

"Yes, I recognized you from the other night. Thanks for coming to our assistance."

He grinned. "Your grandmother had it under control. Not that you were ever in real danger. We had your back." His grin faded, and he said, "Now, about Perdita. How long has it been since you've heard from her?"

"She didn't show up yesterday, so I guess it was at the end of the day before yesterday. There's been no answer when I've called."

"Do you have any idea of her politics?"

"I'm not sure she has any. She's not that serious about much of anything. She did keep working here even after the anti-wizard propaganda

30

among elves began." I hesitated, not sure I should tell him that she was my source, then figured there was no additional harm done at this point. "She shared the flyer about the wizards with me. I know she was nervous about doing that. I didn't tell anyone, and no one was here to see it." I hesitated one more time, then figured that the more the security team knew, the better. "I do know she can be gullible. She fell for some of the Spellworks advertising and rumors last summer, and it took some work to convince her that Owen wasn't evil—even before the word about his parents got out. Just the earlier rumors made her doubt. So it's not outside the realm of possibility that someone told her something that she ended up believing and she's staying away willingly."

He made a note in his notebook. "Do you think that's likely?"

"I'd hope she'd at least ask me about it. She has before, and we've been through a lot since then. My gut says that's not what's happened."

"And I've heard good things about your gut," he said with a grin. "Sam is very complimentary."

"You don't think these missing people are in danger, do you?"

"We have no idea. It's not like we're finding elf bodies in Dumpsters or washing up in the river. We have a few leads, and the more info we get, the better our leads are."

"Thanks."

He flipped his notebook closed and stood. "Thank you for your time, and please let me know if you think of anything or hear anything."

I promised him I would and returned to my fretting. I'd often longed for a break when in the thick of magical battles, but sitting on the sidelines was worse. I couldn't do anything useful, and it wasn't as though I was making use of the time to live a normal life and do all those things I said I'd do if I got the time.

Now that I was on the theoretical training track, Rod had left me to Owen. He was the expert on magical theory and was better at breaking down the theory in a way that made sense even if I couldn't try it out. Because of the time he'd spent without powers, he also had a better understanding of what it was like to study magic without being able to do it.

Since learning about magic without using it couldn't give me away, we met in his office instead of in the secret classroom. He said that way he'd have access to all his reference books, but I figured it also meant he could multitask. I hoped if he got other work done while I was studying, my chances of spending time with him away from work would improve.

Waiting for me was a stack of books with colorful sticky notes emerging from the margins. "I've sorted through some of the more useful theories that underlie most spells," he said. "And here are some spells to learn. You'll have to memorize them without vocalizing them or writing them down. Practice the words and the hand gestures separately and you should be okay." He grinned. "And no, you won't turn yourself or anyone else into a frog if you slip. The only harm done is that you accidentally use up a bit of magic. Let me know if you have any questions."

Learning about magic by sending things flying around the room had been tons of fun. Learning by reading a bunch of old books? Not so much. I forced my way through the theory articles he'd flagged, though it was difficult to pay attention when my mind kept wandering to thoughts of my lost assistant, my vanishing magical powers, and my hopes for weekend plans.

It was with some amusement that I saw the next book in the stack was the *Junior Magic Scouts Handbook*. It looked a lot like my brothers' Cub Scouts handbook, but instead of learning to tie knots and start campfires, the Junior Magic Scouts learned to do basic spells that tied and untied knots and started or quenched fires. "Magic Scouts?" I asked, raising an eyebrow.

"Magical education is purely extracurricular. Some wizards teach their own kids, but most of us go through this kind of program. I should have thought of this earlier. It's one of the best ways to learn remedial spells, and their spells are sound on a theoretical basis."

I noticed that there were notes scribbled in the margins in a childish version of Owen's textbook-perfect handwriting. Even as a little kid he'd been modifying and correcting the text. "Should I learn it as printed or with your version?" I asked, unable to hold back a smile at the thought of little Owen learning magic. I'd seen the pictures at his foster parents' home of a tiny boy whose eyes were owlishly large behind thick glasses.

He blushed and started to answer, but his cell phone rang. He looked at the caller ID readout, frowned, and flipped it open to answer. "Hi, Earl," he said, then he paused, frowning more deeply. "Earl? Hello? Hello?" He moved the phone away from his ear to look at it before flipping it closed. "Strange."

"He may have just pocket dialed you," I suggested.

"But he hasn't called me today, so I doubt he accidentally redialed."

"Does Earl call you often?"

"He's been consulting me some on this case. He's been running into some unusual magic."

A "ding" came from his computer, and he turned to check his e-mail. I took that as my cue to return to my studies. "That's weird," he murmured.

"What is?"

"Earl sent me an e-mail from his phone."

"Does it explain the call?"

"I don't know. There's no text to it, just a photo."

"Of what?" I said, putting down the book and going around his desk so I could look over his shoulder. The photo showed a building—the kind of late-Victorian brick industrial-type buildings that were all over the city.

"Why did Earl send you a photo of a building?" I asked.

"I don't know, but let's find out." He picked up his phone and dialed, listened for a while then shook his head. "No answer."

"That's not good," I concluded. "Do you think he disappeared like those others? He must have found something."

"Or he could be in a dead zone." He dialed again and left Earl a message to call him. I got the feeling he didn't believe the dead zone theory because he then called Sam to update him.

Both of us went back to our respective tasks, but I doubted either of us was really getting anything done. Our heads popped up in unison when Owen's desk phone rang. He answered it and said, "Yes, sir. I'll be there in a moment." He hung up, leaned over his computer keyboard for a moment and clicked a few keys, then said as he rose from his chair, "The photo must be something because the boss wants to talk about it."

I jumped up to tag along with him because while I hadn't exactly been invited, I hadn't specifically been excluded, as far as I knew. At least, Owen made no move to tell me not to come with him.

When we reached Merlin's office, he was studying his computer monitor. "Does this photograph mean anything to you?" he asked Owen, as though he'd been there all along instead of just having arrived.

"I don't recognize it," Owen said.

"And he attempted to call you at approximately the same time he sent this?"

"From what I can tell, yes."

Merlin stroked his beard. "Interesting. I suppose this is a clue, but I can't imagine what it's meant to tell us."

Sam flew in then and alit on the back of a chair. "Still no word from Earl."

"We need to look into this," I said. "Something must have happened if he sent us a clue."

Sam shook his head. "There's no 'us' about it, doll. You're not a part of this one. Neither of you is."

I would have argued, but Merlin's stern glare shut me up immediately. "Sam is correct," he said. "You two have done more than enough this year, and this particular business doesn't concern you."

"But Perdita's my assistant, and Earl wouldn't have been working with MSI if it weren't for us. It's partly our fault if they're in danger."

"Earl was an undercover agent in the court of the Elf Lord, so he was hardly out of danger," Merlin said dryly. "In fact, his association with us may have kept him safer until today."

I didn't have a good argument as to why I should be involved. Even at my most creative stretching of my job description, I couldn't rationalize it. Still, I felt like I ought to be doing *something*.

I waited for Owen to protest, but he just nodded in acquiescence. On our way out of the office, leaving Merlin and Sam to strategize, Owen said, "Do you want to have dinner tonight?"

"We have dinner every night."

"I meant dinner out."

I put my hands on my hips and looked up at him in mock reproach. "Owen Palmer, are you asking me out on a date?"

"I believe that's what it's called when two people spend time together in a romantic fashion. And do you want to?"

I hooked my arm through his. "You had me at 'romantic.' But you have to let Granny know we won't be home for dinner." Then I frowned at him in suspicion. "What brought this on?"

"We've been seeing each other for a while. Is this really so odd?"

"Seeing each other, yes. Going out, no, unless you count crazy quests or going on the lam."

He turned a delightful shade of pink. "Let's try normal life, for a change. Shall I pick you up around seven at your place? Wear something reasonably nice but with fairly comfortable shoes. There may be walking involved."

"Dare I ask what you have planned?"

His grin was borderline wicked. "It'll be a surprise."

*

When he picked me up, I was pretty sure he was wearing the same suit he'd worn to work, just without the tie. Though it was hard to tell with men's suits. As far as I knew, he could have put on a totally different suit with a fresh white shirt. Then again, this was Owen. He'd probably come straight from work.

"How did Granny take it when you told her about dinner?" I asked him as he helped me with my coat.

"She said she had work to do and getting me out of her hair would make it easier."

"I take it you got her those potion ingredients."

"She may be on to something. I know the stuff she gave me back in Texas helped my energy levels. Though I'll warn you, it tasted awful."

"I have no doubt. And it's weird, because she's such a good cook otherwise."

We took a cab to the West Village and went to a cozy, romantic little Italian restaurant with candles on the tables and Sinatra on the sound system. It reminded me of our first real date, though I hoped it didn't end up the same way—with a magical fire in the restaurant that led to a stampede among the customers.

"So, what brought this on?" I asked after the waiter brought us wine and a basket of bread. "I mean, we've been talking about a real date for ages, but it hasn't quite happened."

"I'm not going to jinx us by talking about our track record and hoping our luck has turned, but why shouldn't we go out like normal people, especially when we have a free evening?"

It sounded nice, but the look in his eyes was way too familiar, and it didn't bode well for romance. When he got that look, he was usually about to try something crazy, dangerous, stupid, or all of the above, in order to save the world. He wasn't really a thrill seeker, but he couldn't bear to leave a job undone.

"What are you up to?" I asked.

"Nothing!" he insisted. "Just going out on a date with my girlfriend." For a moment he looked truly contrite. "Am I that bad, that you assume something is wrong when I do the sort of thing that most guys probably do every weekend?"

"I don't know if 'bad' is the word I would use, and we have good reason for not going out much." Namely, the two men in black seated at the adjacent table. The hot celebrity couple of the moment got more privacy out on the town than we did.

He gave me a smile that made my stomach do backflips. "Maybe we could embarrass them into leaving us alone."

"Do you really think that would work?"

He sighed. "I doubt it. But thank you for putting up with me. A lot of women would have bailed on me. I've got a lot of baggage to deal with."

"If I can't stand by you, then who will? And I know who you really are, no matter what anyone else thinks."

He reached under the table to take my hand and clutch it earnestly. "I am so glad I met you."

I squeezed his hand in response. "Me, too. I can truly say that meeting you changed my life."

"For the better?" He sounded like he wasn't sure.

"Most definitely. Yeah, my life has been under constant threat and things have been absolutely insane, but I wouldn't trade it for anything."

He nodded, worrying his lower lip with his teeth like this had given him something serious to think about. "Good, that's good to hear," he said absently. The moment passed when the waiter arrived with our meals.

We actually made it through the entire meal without any crazy disasters or magical attacks, then headed out into the crisp autumn evening. "There's a bakery not too far from here. I thought we could walk off dinner and head up there for dessert," he said.

"Sounds good to me. Lead on."

We walked uptown, got some cupcakes and cocoa at the bakery, and continued strolling. When we crossed Fourteenth, he pulled a small sheaf of folded papers out of his jacket pocket and studied the top page, which was a map. He shoved it back into his pocket and steered us around the next corner.

"Owen, what is this about?" I asked when we'd walked up and down several remarkably non-scenic blocks.

He looked sheepish and said, "I think that photo from Earl came from somewhere around here."

"Oh, you do know the way to a girl's heart," I said, standing on my tiptoes to give him a kiss. "I didn't think you'd be willing to just sit by."

He smiled and blushed as he said, "The cell tower that handled that call is in this area. That may or may not mean anything. Any tower within range may have picked up the call. But I did some online photo searches, and the kind of building in the photo is really common in this neighborhood. So, I figured there was no harm in wandering the neighborhood and seeing if anything looks familiar."

"Excellent idea," I said. "Let's try the next street over."

We walked up and down the neighborhood, frequently comparing the nearby buildings to the printout of Earl's photo. "So many of them are so close, but not quite," I said after we'd been searching at least an hour. "Maybe we're looking at them from the wrong angle."

"We should be able to see it from the angle where Earl took the photo, and wherever he was then, he must have seen something he wanted me to know about."

"Unless, of course, he pocket dialed the photo."

"I don't think that's possible. But even if it was, he couldn't have taken that photo from inside his pocket. He was investigating, and the building isn't particularly attractive or interesting, I'm pretty sure he photographed it for a reason."

"Maybe we should do this in daylight," I suggested after another half hour of searching. "He took the photo in daylight. Things look different in the dark."

"But when it's dark, we may be able to see inside if the interior's lit."

"I wonder what your followers think of all this wandering around."

"I hope their feet are tired." He usually just sounded resigned about the people who watched him for signs of evil, but there was a hint of relish behind his wish. I didn't think I'd ever get him to tell me outright what he felt about it, but I was getting the idea.

Then we rounded a corner, and there it was. "Owen, that's it!" I said, grabbing his arm.

We stopped and he took the photo out of his pocket to compare. "Yeah, that's definitely it."

"So you're going to call Sam, right?"

He didn't answer, but I glared at him until he got out his phone and called the gargoyle. He gave the address, and after a pause he said, "Of course I won't do anything stupid. I just happened to run across it while I was out with Katie and thought you'd want to know." When he'd put away the phone he turned to me and said, "Want to check it out?"

"Wouldn't that fall into the category of stupid things you just told Sam you wouldn't do?"

"I just want a peek. And besides, how much trouble can I get into when I have two of the Council's best enforcers watching my every move? They won't let me get away with anything evil, but I don't think they'll let me come to harm, either."

To be perfectly honest, I also wanted to check things out. "What do you think the building is?" I asked. Strange lights showed through the upper windows. "It's not just some elf rave or underground nightclub, is it? Maybe that's why Earl took a picture, since the cool places don't have signs."

"Can you imagine Earl going to a cool place? Or anyone inviting me to one?"

"Good point." We walked around the block so we could examine the building from all sides. At one point, we flattened ourselves into a doorway when we saw someone approach the building's entry, but they just walked on by. After that false alarm, we almost didn't react in time when someone did go up to the door. There were three in the group, and if I wasn't mistaken, one of them didn't want to be there.

"That person may be in danger," Owen whispered to me. "We should help."

"You think this is where all those elves are disappearing?"

"That person looked kind of like he was being disappeared."

"But what can we do to help?"

"We can bring the Council enforcers down on them."

"Oh, you clever thing."

Once the coast was clear, we started to leave our hiding place, but he pushed me back. "Maybe you should stay here. I'm the one they'll follow."

"I'm not letting you go in there without me. And I'm not standing alone on the sidewalk at night in this neighborhood."

He didn't argue. We reached the door, and I felt the tingle of magic as he unlocked it. "I'm not sensing wards," he whispered.

"Maybe it's a trap."

"Maybe they underestimate us."

I still had a bad feeling as we crept through a narrow, unlit hallway. We'd made it into a vast warehouse-like space when I thought I heard the door open and close behind us. I hoped it was Owen's Council shadows.

If it was, I doubted they'd see anything they could make an arrest over. I didn't see any people or elves, definitely not the person who looked like he was being kidnapped. There was a weird glow at the far end of the room that probably explained the odd lights we'd seen through the upper windows.

"What do you think that is?" I whispered.

"Let's go find out."

We edged our way around the room, sticking to the shadows and keeping as silent as possible, even though I still didn't see anyone we needed to hide from. When we were finally on the same end of the room as the glow, I got a good look at what was going on, and before I could remember to stifle my gasp of shock, everything went black.

CHAPTER FIVE

The sound of an old-fashioned jangling alarm clock woke me from a deep slumber. I snaked a hand out from under the covers to turn it off, then flung the comforter back and sat up, stretching as I yawned. It was time to face the day. I hopped out of bed and went through the morning rituals of washing and dressing, holding a couple of different blouse options in front of myself in the mirror with one hand while I brushed my teeth with the other hand.

And then I was out the door and down the stairs. I waved to the mailman as I made my way down the front steps of the brownstone. "No bills for you today, Katie!" he called out to me.

Strange, I had the oddest feeling that I was hearing bouncy music playing behind me all the while. After fighting off an eerie shiver, I told myself I probably just had a song stuck in my head.

I rounded the corner and popped into the neighborhood coffee shop. "Hey, Katie, I've got your usual ready," the waitress called out. She took the paper cup from the counter and turned to hand it to me, but she stumbled and the cup went flying. I had visions of ending up covered in coffee, but at the last split second, a hand shot out and caught the cup.

"Here you go," my rescuer said, handing it to me. I found myself looking into dark blue eyes, and it seemed as though time came to a standstill. I blinked and saw that the eyes were set in a handsome face topped with dark hair. He was as frozen as I was. And then reality returned with a crash.

"Oh, I'm sorry, Katie!" the waitress said, rushing over to check on me. She blushed to the roots of her curly red hair. "I am such a klutz sometimes. Did I spill any coffee on you?"

"No harm done," I assured her. I turned back toward my rescuer, but he was gone. I felt bad that I hadn't even thanked him. Or gotten his phone number. Or married him. Ah, well, I supposed it wasn't meant to be. I took a sip of the coffee and said, "Just right. Thanks, Perry!"

The sense of background music had faded slightly during that scene, but it returned as I continued down the sidewalk, heading toward work, only a little late this morning. The regulars were already in the park across the street from the store, including the two men who spent their days playing chess there. I paused for a moment with the strangest feeling of reverse déjà vu. Instead of getting the sense that I'd seen something before, I felt like I *hadn't* seen it before, even though I knew I had.

I finished my coffee as I stared up at the bookstore. Three stories full of books, with a bonus coffee shop, had seemed like my idea of heaven when I first went to work there. It was supposed to have been a temporary job, but I was closing in on a year with no sign of anything better on the horizon. With a dejected sigh, I drained my cup and tossed it in a nearby trash bin before heading across the street and into the store.

I took the stairs up to the second floor where the coffee shop was, grabbed my apron from the back, put it on, and adjusted my name tag. "And good morning to you," my coworker—and best friend—Florence greeted me. "I've already got the regular, the decaf, and the coffee of the day brewing. Do you want to take care of the bakery case? The delivery's already come."

"Yeah, sure, I'll do that," I said.

She blinked, frowned, and sniffed as I spoke. "You've got coffee breath!" she accused.

"Do I need a mint?"

"You had coffee on your way to work in a coffee shop? Again?"

I glanced around to make sure there weren't any managers in earshot. "You know as well as I do that our coffee is nasty."

"All coffee is nasty to me. I can't judge degrees of nastiness."

"Don't tell anyone!" I begged as I opened a bakery box and started arranging pastries on the trays that fit in the display case. "But really, we resell second-rate pastries—at a huge markup—and we make terrible coffee, and people still buy it because it's supposedly gourmet and because having coffee in a bookstore makes them feel smart."

She filled an insulated carafe with the regular coffee. "And this store would've gone under ages ago without us. The coffee shop is our biggest profit center, believe it or not."

I stopped working and glanced over at her. "Do you ever feel like working here is giving you bad karma? Shouldn't we be doing something more worthwhile?"

"We're keeping a bookstore financially viable. That makes us deserving of a Nobel prize. We're practically heroes!"

"I guess that's one way to look at it. We're subsidizing literacy. But that doesn't make the coffee any better."

Then we had to stop criticizing our employer as the store opened for the day and patrons came pouring in for their morning caffeine fix. I wanted to stand on the counter and tell them where they could go for better coffee and pastries. If it got me fired, then maybe I'd be forced to find a better job. But I was too busy to give in to the temptation. Those lattes didn't make themselves.

At last, the morning rush ended, and we had a chance to catch our breath before the lunch rush. Florence wiped down the counters while I cleared tables, stacking the abandoned books on a shelving cart. Florence glanced into one of the carafes and said, "There's about a cup left. Do you want it, or should I just throw it out before I make a fresh pot?"

"Is it the regular or the coffee of the day?"

"It's the regular."

"I'll take it." My morning coffee had already worn off, and it was hard to get away for a coffee break when you worked in a coffee shop. I stood behind the counter, sipping the burnt-tasting coffee, while I perused the classified ads in a newspaper a patron had left behind.

"Still job-hunting, I see," Florence remarked when I circled an ad. "Are you going to actually apply for any of these, or are you going to talk yourself out of it again?"

"The result will be the same," I said, sighing.

She snapped me with a towel. "How do you expect good things to come to you when you have that attitude?"

"I don't think my attitude has much to do with it. I'm not even getting interviews anymore. There just aren't any advertising jobs. I've been trying for almost a year."

"And it's become easier for you to stay here. It's a comfort zone."

"Here? Comfortable? Are you insane? Of course I want to get out of here."

She glanced around, as though making sure we weren't being overheard, then bent toward me and whispered, "Well, you might want to start applying again or networking or putting up billboards, or whatever it takes to find something, because I heard we're being sold."

"Sold? To one of the chains?"

"I don't know, but whatever it is, things are bound to change."

"If it stays a bookstore, they'll keep the coffee shop. As you said, we're a profit center."

"But bookselling isn't exactly a growth industry these days. They may just want the real estate."

I groaned and leaned down, resting my forehead on the newspaper. "Just what I needed. Maybe I should accept Josh's proposal and become a housewife. It doesn't look like I'm going to succeed at anything else."

"My, that does sound romantic," she said dryly. "You didn't tell me Josh proposed."

The memory of it was hazy, like it was something I'd dreamed rather than experienced. "Well, it wasn't really a formal proposal. More a suggestion. I think I said something about my job hunt, and he said if I married him, I wouldn't have to worry about it."

She fluttered her hand against her chest. "Be still my beating heart. How did you not swoon and fall at his feet?"

"Shut up!" I scolded her, even as I couldn't help but grin at her theatrics. "I think he was raising the topic. Who proposes out of the blue without having discussed anything about marriage ahead of time? I'm sure the real proposal, when it comes, will be very romantic."

"Yeah, he'll tell you you're a failure, but he's willing to support you."

"That's not what he meant," I insisted, my cheeks flaming. "And I have no intention of letting him support me, but it might be nice to have the pressure taken off the job hunt and to have more time to work on my résumé and go on interviews."

"You'll get the time if the store closes, though that probably won't ease the pressure."

"The store's not going to close," I muttered, returning to the classifieds. And would marrying Josh really be that bad? He was smart, attractive, successful, and he was a decent guy. Heart-stopping romance was the kind of thing that only happened in movies. *And in coffee shops,* I thought, remembering the moment that morning when time had stood still as I looked into those dark blue eyes and felt like destiny had caught up with me.

*

Contrary to Florence's fears, nothing much seemed to change after the sale went through later that week. There was a memo from the new owner saying it would be business as usual for the time being, and life went on. Josh didn't bring up the topic of marriage again, so I started to think it must have been a joke or an offhand remark, not something I should take seriously. And that meant I really needed to find a job.

I was going through my ritual of reading the classifieds during a mid-morning lull while Florence took a break when a voice said, "Job-hunting?"

I looked up to attend to the customer and had that same time-standing-still feeling when I looked into his deep blue eyes. Was he the guy from the other coffee shop? I couldn't even remember his face, so I couldn't be sure. It wasn't a good sign if I was swooning over every pair of blue eyes that crossed my path. I knew that should probably tell me something, but I preferred not to think about it. "Can I help you?" I asked, dropping the newspaper.

"How's the coffee here?" He must have noticed my hesitation because he grinned and said, "And be honest."

"Well, it's not really to my taste. It's kind of, um, strong."

"Burnt?"

"Enthusiastically roasted."

"What about the tea?"

"It's actually pretty good, but it's in bags so you have to brew it yourself. We don't brew tea here. You can see the kinds there in the rack."

"Then I'll have a tea."

While I filled a cup with hot water, he leaned against the counter and said, "I thought books and tea went together, and you know, I can't think of a bookstore that sells real tea in their café. It's just tea bags."

I handed him the cup and he selected a tea bag while I rang him up. "If we upgraded the tea, we'd have to upgrade the scones, and where would that leave us?" I quipped, then realized a second later that I was probably speaking out of turn. I shouldn't be criticizing the merchandise I was selling.

"The scones aren't good?" he asked, raising an eyebrow.

"It's not that they're bad. They're just, well, probably better for keeping the tables level than for eating. I suspect the bakery sends us their day-old stuff and figures we won't notice."

"Then I think I'll skip the scone today," he said as he paid for his tea. He nodded toward my newspaper, with several jobs circled in red. "Are you trying to flee the bad coffee and scones?"

"It's not that. It's just that this was supposed to be a temporary job while I looked for a real job in my field. That's taken a bit longer than I planned." I squinted at the newspaper as I had the sudden feeling that there was something odd there. Was the newspaper classified section *really* the best way to find a professional job?

"How much longer?"

I snapped back to the present, blinking. "Nearly a year. I gave myself a year, and I have three weeks left."

"Then what happens?"

"I guess I give up and leave the city. Or I suppose I could get married and become a housewife."

He dunked his tea bag into his cup and swirled it around. "I would think that finding a husband would be just as challenging as finding a job," he said, watching his tea rather than looking at me.

"Oh, I've already got that covered. I think. It wasn't exactly a formal proposal, but my boyfriend and I have been talking about marriage."

He gave the newspaper another look. "Your field is advertising?"

"Yeah. More on the strategy side than the creative—deciding what approach to take and how to target it rather than actually dreaming up the ads."

"Well, good luck with that," he said with a smile as he walked away, pausing to drop his tea bag in a trash bin.

"He was cute," Florence remarked as she returned from her break and tied her apron back on.

"Yeah, I guess he was. Nice, too."

"And he seemed interested." She raised an eyebrow and smirked.

"I have a boyfriend. Which I mentioned to him, so it's not even like I was flirt-cheating. He was just making conversation. He got tea, and he had to wait for it to steep, so I'm sure he was just killing time." So why were my cheeks burning up?

"Uh huh," she said, then she switched gears. "Did you hear about the mandatory employee meeting tomorrow morning?"

"How early?"

"Eight sharp, before we open."

"Ugh."

"Brace yourself. They're having it here, and they're serving coffee to the crew, so we get to be here at seven thirty to get ready."

"We'd better get to clock in for that."

"That's probably the least of our concerns. The new owner is going to address us, and you know what that probably means."

"He's going to talk about the changes he wants to make?"

"Yeah, like closing the store and doing something more profitable with the space."

"You're such a pessimist."

"Realist," Florence corrected. "This is my third bookstore job. I just wanted this one to last me through grad school."

"We'll be fine," I insisted. I wasn't sure if I really believed that or if I wanted to believe it.

*

I woke the next morning—to that godawful alarm clock—with the sense that I'd had exceptionally vivid dreams of an entirely different life. There had been danger, and there had been moments when I was scared out of my mind, but there was also something nice about it, a sense of accomplishment. I lay there for a moment, trying to recapture the images and feelings, but they dissipated rapidly. The really weird thing was that those images were still sharper than any attempt I made to remember events from longer than about a week ago. I was way too young to have developed Alzheimer's disease, and besides, that was supposed to work the other way around, where the distant past was sharper than the more recent past. I supposed it was normal for the past to grow foggy with time, but I would have thought that a year ago would be clearer than this.

With a sigh, I got out of bed and got ready for work. As I dressed, I thought about how nice this apartment was. It was a full floor in an Upper West Side brownstone, one that hadn't even been carved up into studios. How could I possibly afford this place without a roommate while working in a bookstore coffee shop? Then a blurry-edged memory of finding this dream rent-controlled place popped into my head. Oh yeah, that's what had happened. I put on my coat and headed to the store.

I didn't have time to stop for my unauthorized dose of caffeine, so I was bleary-eyed when I stumbled my way up to the café, where the tables and chairs had already been arranged like a university lecture hall. Great, I thought, one more thing we'd have to fix before we opened for the day. I had started the coffee brewing when Florence showed up, laden with bakery boxes.

"To get them this early, I had to pick them up," she explained.

"I wonder if that means they're actually fresh."

"Gee, I hope not. I have some pictures to hang and I need something for pounding in the nails."

We set out enough plates and cups for all the employees, and I had just enough time to get a head start on serving myself some coffee, which was as bad as I remembered, even when it was freshly brewed. I took off my apron before taking a seat at the back of the café. The rest of the staff came in, with much grumbling and speculation about what we'd learn from the meeting. I wasn't sure which outcome I really wanted. I didn't want to lose my job, but if I did, that might force me to overcome the inertia in my life. I might someday look back on this meeting and realize it was the best thing that had ever happened to me.

The room filled, and the various department managers came in and sat near the front. Once everyone was seated, a familiar man stepped in front of the group and said, "Good morning, everyone. Thank you for coming in early today. I'm Owen Palmer, your new owner."

It was the dark-haired, blue-eyed customer I'd chatted with the day before. I was so very, very fired. I wondered if maybe I'd at least get credit for honesty. That was the only way I could imagine my job being saved. I hoped someone left a newspaper behind this morning. I'd definitely need to review the job ads.

He talked about keeping the store open in spite of the challenging economy and mentioned a few changes to help us be more profitable. Most of it had to do with more creative shelving and how we could take advantage of the fact that we didn't have to abide by top-down dictates like the chain stores. We could shelve books where our customers were most likely to discover them, even in multiple places around the store. It wasn't exactly an earthshattering idea, but it wasn't something too many other stores did. He talked about getting employee input on purchase decisions and offering incentives for hand-selling books.

I tensed when he got around to discussing the coffee shop. I didn't think he'd fire me now, but I prepared myself for a lecture on providing a positive customer experience. "I don't know if you've noticed, but our coffee is lousy," he said. There was nervous laughter from the group, and I cringed. It wasn't my fault, but would he see it that way? "We need to revamp our coffee shop, and we'll be considering new suppliers." I wondered if the revamp would include employees who didn't peruse the classified ads while on the job or openly criticize the coffee to customers. But all he discussed was the quality of what was offered, not the employees. He'd probably fire me privately, in a one-on-one meeting later that day.

The meeting wrapped up, and everyone headed to their respective jobs, or to home, if they had later shifts. Most of the booksellers were already talking excitedly about how to rearrange the sections. Florence and I were less excited, since it was our department that had been singled out as a failure. Not that we disagreed—*we* avoided our own coffee shop—but it didn't bode well for the owner to criticize us.

We hurried to get the café set up for the store opening. In spite of the nasty coffee and stale scones, we had our usual morning crowd. In this city, I was surprised that people hadn't found better options, since I passed several on my way to work in the morning. The whole time, Owen Palmer hung around, lingering over a cup of coffee at the outermost table while he watched the flow of customers.

When the rush had died down and we were getting ready for the morning coffee break crowd, Owen came over to us. "Which of you is the resident coffee connoisseur?" he asked.

"She is!" Florence said, pointing at me and making herself scarce with a wink over her shoulder.

"I guess I am, though I wouldn't call myself a connoisseur. I just drink it," I said. "She doesn't. She doesn't even drink caffeine, if you can believe it—and she's in grad school." I was babbling, giving him information he didn't even want, but I couldn't seem to stop myself.

"Then I'll want you to help me in selecting new suppliers and revamping the shop. We do good business, but I think we could do better if we had better stuff to offer." He frowned. "In fact, I'm not even sure why anyone comes here at all. There's better coffee at just about every corner deli."

"I think people feel like getting their coffee here makes them smarter, or something," I said without thinking, then mentally winced. I shouldn't be shooting off my mouth to my boss. He was just so nice that he lulled me into honesty. He was so good-looking that he addled my senses somehow. Then I wondered if maybe he was that guy who'd made the world go still that morning at the diner.

"Image means a lot," he agreed. "And that's another thing I wanted to talk to you about. Would you mind holding off on your job search for a little while? I think I could use your expertise while we revamp the store. I'm hearing rumors that one of the chains is going to open a branch nearby, and I want to make a big splash before they can get established."

"So you're not firing me?" I blurted.

"Is there a reason I should?" he asked, with a mildly amused smile.

"No, no," I hurried to say. "But you didn't see me at my best yesterday."

"You were honest with me about the product you were selling and steered me to something I'd enjoy more."

"And I was job-hunting on the job," I said without thinking, then winced. What *was* it about this guy? He seemed to deactivate all my filters.

"The way I see it, it's my fault if I can't keep my employees happy enough to want to stay or if I can't recognize talent and make the best use of it. So, this afternoon I'd like you to join me for some meetings with potential vendors and then what are you doing for dinner?"

"Dinner?" I parroted dumbly.

"I'd like to hash out some advertising and marketing ideas. It might be easier to do that away from the store, and if I'm asking you to work beyond your usual shift, I should at least buy you dinner."

He sounded all-business, which dashed the romantic fantasy that had sprung unbidden into my brain. And then I remembered Josh. My boyfriend. The one I had a date with that night. "Oh, tonight. I can't," I said, stumbling over the words. "I have dinner plans already."

"Then maybe we can talk tomorrow afternoon here at the store. My schedule will be a little more open then." He grinned, and a slight flush washed over his cheeks. "I'll buy the coffee, though that's probably more of a threat than an incentive."

"Okay," I said, even as I felt a sting of disappointment that I didn't want to analyze too closely. Getting my head turned by my new boss would be a very bad idea.

But there was just something about him ...

CHAPTER SIX

It was with a surprisingly illicit thrill that I left the store with Owen that afternoon. This was strictly business, but it felt like a first date—a first date with someone I'd had a crush on for ages, which was really weird, since I'd only just met him. I was back to feeling like there was music playing in the background, which made me question my sanity. I didn't think most people went through life with a personal movie soundtrack playing in their heads. I hadn't even turned on the radio that morning, so I wasn't sure where the insidious tune had come from. Maybe from the store's background music?

When we hit the first coffee dealer, the smell of coffee was so strong it nearly knocked me off my feet—in a good way. "I think I'm getting a contact caffeine buzz," I whispered to Owen.

He grinned in response, a smile that lit up his eyes and made my knees go wobbly. He was so very adorable. And he was my boss, I reminded myself firmly. Plus, I had a boyfriend who had brought up the subject of marriage. Wobbling was out of the question. "I may not sleep for a week," Owen said, "which is good because right now, I don't have time to sleep."

The coffee expert at this place took his work very seriously. I felt like I was at a snooty wine tasting and being encouraged to find hints of oak or lemon in the wine, only he was asking us to discern flavors of earth and spices in the coffee. The one time Owen and I dared to glance at each other, we both nearly spit out our coffee from laughing. I didn't know the finer points of coffee, just what I liked and didn't, and that I didn't like supposedly gourmet coffee that tasted like it had been scraped up from the bottom of the coffeepot after sitting for a day or two. This stuff was definitely an improvement over what we'd been serving, but I wasn't sold on it. Luckily, we still had two more places to go.

The rest of the afternoon seemed to go by in a blur—or in a series of quick scenes, all with that music playing in the background. We tasted coffee, made faces, laughed, and compared notes, and all the while, we really seemed to be bonding. I still didn't know much about him as a person, but I knew he was nice, funny, smart enough to retain a lot of information, and he really cared about what he was doing.

As we headed back to the store from the last coffee vendor, both of us vibrating a little from the caffeine overdose, I dared to ask him, "Why did you decide to buy a bookstore? Isn't that the worst possible business to get into these days?"

He thought about the question for long enough that I wondered if I'd been out of line to ask it, and then he said, "I'm not so sure I did it because of the business. It's more like historical preservation, like one of those old-fashioned farms kids can visit to learn about the way life used to be."

"So kids can take a field trip and we can show them these things called books that their grandparents used to read?"

He laughed. "Something like that, but it would be even better if I can do it well enough to make it cool again, even if it is in a retro sense. I can't beat the convenience of buying books online, but maybe I can make it an enjoyable enough experience to lure people in from time to time."

"You're a romantic!" I said, then wished I hadn't. That was probably being a little forward with my boss.

If he thought so, he didn't show it. He nodded thoughtfully, then said, "Maybe I am. I don't know that I've ever found the perfect bookstore, but I have one in my head, the kind of place where you browse for hours. You stumble upon a book you never would have known to search for online, and it ends up becoming your new favorite book and favorite author. You sit in a cozy nook and read for a while until you know you have to take it home, but you can't wait to read more, so you buy the book and then get a cup of coffee and read even more, still sitting in the store."

"And outside it's raining, so it's the perfect day to spend the whole afternoon in a bookstore," I said wistfully. I'd had the same fantasy before I actually went to work in a bookstore.

He turned to me. "How did you know about the rain?"

"It's always raining when I imagine myself in a bookstore. Unless it's near Christmas. Then it's snowing."

"Maybe I should add weather control to my business plan," he said. "If I could make it rain or snow on cue, I might get a lot more customers."

There was something about what he'd said that gave me the strangest feeling of déjà vu, like I could imagine him making it snow, and the image was so vivid that it was like a memory. I glanced at him to find that he was looking at me, a little crease forming between his eyes from his quizzical expression. I got the impression that he'd imagined the same thing.

Then both of us shook it off. "Thanks for coming along today," he said briskly. "I think we agreed on our top three choices, so now we'll see what kind of proposals they offer us. Next we'll tackle the bakery items."

"I think the ones we're getting wouldn't be so bad if we got them fresh."

"But it might be worthwhile to shake them up by considering other vendors. Then we might start getting fresher stuff." We reached the store, and he stopped at the door to say, "Well, I guess I'll see you tomorrow. Have a good time tonight."

"Tonight?" I asked, then I remembered my date with Josh. "Oh, yeah, right, dinner. And I'd better get going or I'll be late. See you tomorrow." I hurried away before I'd be tempted to tell him my plans had fallen through and I'd love to have dinner with him.

*

As I rushed to dinner, I hoped seeing Josh would remind me of why I wanted to be there. But when I saw him, the anticipated frisson didn't materialize. It was like he was nothing more to me than a random stranger who happened to arrive at the restaurant at the same time I did. I supposed he was cute enough—not a heartthrob, but was I the kind of girl who could expect to land a heartthrob? He was essentially the male version of me, the boy next door who probably got the "you're such a nice guy and good friend, like a brother" speech a lot. That made us the perfect match. I knew he'd be reliable and would never stray. What more could I really want?

I had to work up a delighted smile as I approached him in the restaurant foyer. To help with the effort, I thought back to when we first met, but the memory was hazy. How *had* we met? Come to think of it, I could barely remember spending time with him. There were vague images, like a dream or something I'd watched on TV. They didn't feel real. He didn't seem to notice that I'd frozen instead of greeting him with any enthusiasm. He crossed the gap between us, kissed me dutifully and said, "Mmm, you smell like coffee."

I raised my arm to sniff my sleeve. "Do I? Ugh. It probably permeates my whole body. Believe it or not, after today, I'm not sure I want to go near another cup of coffee ever again."

"No, it's good," he said with a laugh. "I like the smell of coffee. Rough day slaving over the coffeepot and espresso machine?"

"No, not really," I had to admit. "My new boss dragged me with him to evaluate new coffee vendors, and that meant tasting a lot of coffee. I didn't know there were so many kinds, and that's not even getting into the fancy flavors." I made it sound like a chore, but I couldn't remember the last time I'd had that much fun. I just didn't want to tell my boyfriend that, and then I felt weird for wanting to hide that from him. "The new owner wants to really upgrade our coffee shop, and the first thing that needs to change is the coffee."

"It *is* nasty."

I bristled at that. It was one thing for me to say it, but I rather resented him saying that about my work. It was irrational, I knew, but I couldn't help it. "I may not sleep for a week after all the coffee I had today," I said, forcing myself not to frown, and then I realized I was quoting Owen's quip.

"So, decaf with dessert tonight?"

"Even that might be too much."

"Then maybe some wine will counteract it."

When we were seated at our table, I had the strangest feeling that I was sitting across from a stranger. I knew we'd been dating for months, but this felt like a first date—the awkward kind of first date where you can't think of anything to talk about because you don't know enough about each other to even start a conversation and asking questions to get to know each other feels like an interrogation.

"What's the new boss like?" he asked me.

I wasn't sure how to answer, even though it was an obvious topic for discussion, because I was afraid I'd gush. "He seems pretty cool," I said with what I hoped looked like a casual shrug. "He's got a lot of ideas about making bookstores interesting, something people will leave their computers to visit."

"Ah, an old fogy, I take it. None of those newfangled e-books for him." He laughed, and I fought back my irritation and my urge to jump to Owen's defense.

"Actually, he's pretty young—around thirty, I'd say. But he is kind of old-fashioned, in a good way. I like his vision of bookstores, and he's asked me to help with some advertising and marketing strategy."

"That should be good for your résumé. Instead of having wasted the past year in a retail job, you can now call it a job within your field."

I bristled again, but crumbled a roll from the bread basket instead of saying anything. "If I get to do interesting stuff, I may want to stay," I said. "I'm not crazy about pouring coffee, but if I get to help on the business side of things, it might become a job worth sticking around for. I really seem to have clicked with Owen."

He choked on the sip of wine he'd just taken, then had a brief coughing fit. "Sorry, that went down the wrong way," he said.

"Are you okay?"

"Yeah, I'm fine." But there was an angry, alarmed look to his eyes that I found oddly chilling. Was he jealous of a boss I'd barely mentioned? I'd worked so hard to talk about Owen in a neutral way. Maybe I'd overdone it to the point it looked like I was hiding something.

He barely spoke through the rest of dinner, and his mind seemed to be elsewhere, like he was mentally cooking up some scheme. It was so unlike him that I was worried, but I got the impression that asking him what was wrong wouldn't go over well. I would have begged off of dessert and said I needed to get home, but he did it before I could. He didn't even walk me home. He merely gave me a perfunctory kiss at the restaurant door and hurried away, like he was late for a meeting. And to think, I'd given up dinner with Owen for that very unsatisfactory date.

*

Before I even had my apron on the next morning, Florence demanded, "I want to know the whole story."

"Josh didn't propose last night. In fact, he got weird and called for the check before I was even done eating and then hurried away like he had to catch the last train home."

She waved a dismissive hand. "Oh, who cares about Josh. What about spending all afternoon with that cutie-pie boss? I'm sensing a real connection between you two."

"He's just using me as a coffee taster, like he thinks that serving so much of it and being willing to admit that what we serve is awful makes me an expert."

"That's all, huh?" she asked, raising an eyebrow. "Didn't you say he wanted to pick your brain for advertising ideas?"

"Well, yeah, but he hasn't done so yet, so there's nothing to tell you."

"And you two didn't talk about anything but coffee all afternoon?"

"I did find out what his vision for the store is. He's kind of a romantic about bookselling."

"Oooh, you said *romantic*," she teased.

"No, he's just got this idea of the perfect rainy day spent browsing a bookstore, and he wants to give that to people."

"Oh, a perfect rainy day spent browsing a bookstore? Now, where have I heard that before? It sounds like you two were made for each other."

I knew I was supposed to bashfully protest, but I paused thoughtfully and said, "It does feel like I've known him a lot longer than I have. I guess I just feel comfortable with him."

"So you won't be circling any classified ads anytime soon."

"If I can help relaunch this store, then that gives me something for my résumé, and that will improve my job-hunting odds, so it's in my best interest to hold off on the job hunt for a while." I slammed the bakery case shut to emphasize that the conversation was over.

It didn't deter her. She merely changed the subject. "Now, what about what happened with Josh?"

"Nothing happened with Josh."

"That's what I meant. Doesn't sound like much of a date."

"It doesn't have to be champagne and rose petals every time we get together."

She crossed her arms over her chest. "Is it *ever* champagne and rose petals with him?"

Again, I had the weirdest feeling that I didn't know. I had a couple of memories of previous dates with him, but they were isolated incidents, not woven into any larger tapestry. "Let's face it, I'm not exactly a champagne and rose petals type. I'm more milk and cookies."

"If he's cookies, then it's the kind we sell here. By the way, we had some leftover sugar cookies yesterday, so I finally got that table by the stairs to stop wobbling."

I felt obligated to defend my boyfriend, even though my heart wasn't really in it. Putting my hands on my hips, I asked, "Do you have a problem with Josh? Last time I checked, *you* weren't dating him."

"But why are *you* dating him? You don't have to settle. There are other fish in the sea. Namely our new boss, Mr. Blue Eyes."

I couldn't meet her eyes because then she'd see that I didn't know. This was all so confusing. I blamed it on a restless night full of crazy dreams in which I'd been chased by magical monsters with a dark-haired, blue-eyed man at my side. Oh no, I'd been dreaming about my boss, I thought, stifling a groan. That had the potential for serious awkwardness.

*

Owen came up to the café after lunch, carrying a stack of binders and a couple of legal pads. "I thought we could go over some marketing ideas, if you've got the time," he said. "We can do it here, and that way you can help if you're needed in the café."

"Sure," I said, hoping I wasn't blushing. Florence's wink didn't help matters. I shot her a glare as I followed Owen to the largest unoccupied table, where he set down his binders and pulled out a chair for me.

After we'd taken seats next to each other, he opened one of the binders and outlined his business plan in more detail than he'd gone into in the all-hands meeting. Then he said, "What I want to do is get the word out about how enjoyable it will be to browse for books here, that sense of discovery from finding something unexpected that you wouldn't have known to go looking for."

I almost forgot to think about what he was saying, I was so entranced by the way he said it. His eyes sparkled and he became animated as he described his vision. I'd teased him about being a romantic, but he really did have a passion for what he was doing. I couldn't help but wonder if that passion carried over to other aspects of his life, and then I had to bury my face in the binder to hide my flaming cheeks. Fantasizing about my boss during a meeting was a new low for me.

"We'll need to draw people into the store so they can discover it for themselves," I said, my voice sounding a little too loud and too high. I fought to get it under control. "When you say it, shelving books in different sections doesn't sound particularly sexy. But when people see it while browsing, they're sure to see how different it is. We'll need events." I mused for a moment, thinking back to my school days when we'd done a class project along these lines. "I know!" I said, looking up. "We'll have a book scavenger hunt! Have a grand reopening party, and one of the activities will be a book scavenger hunt where people have a list of books to find on the shelves. Since what you want to do is more intuitive than the strict chain-store rules, people will see how easy it is to find books."

"That's brilliant!" he said, scribbling notes on a legal pad. "I love it. It's the kind of thing that should get some word of mouth going. And we'll have refreshments from our new, improved café."

We then brainstormed more ideas for the event and how to promote it, and I felt myself shaking off the rust from going so long without working in my field. We were really on a roll and laughing about some ridiculous idea I'd just thrown out when a voice said, "Wow, you're having fun at work."

I looked up to see Josh standing at the end of the table. "Oh, hi!" I said. "What brings you here?"

He bent to kiss my cheek. "Just stopping by to see my girl. Do you have a moment to talk?"

I glanced at Owen, who said, "This looks like a good time for a break."

Belatedly, I remembered my manners. "Owen, this is my boyfriend, Josh. Josh, Owen is the new owner." I didn't know which one of them to watch as they greeted each other, but since I figured I'd know what Josh felt soon enough, I focused on Owen. He seemed perfectly open and friendly toward Josh. I'd have had to stretch to detect even the slightest hint of jealousy. Maybe this was all about business, after all.

Josh, on the other hand, had found his inner caveman. I didn't have to look at him to know he was unhappy. I could feel the tension and dislike radiating off of him. That was weird. I'd never known him to be the jealous type. Then again, I'd never given him anything to be jealous of. At least, I didn't remember doing so in the vague haze of memories of our relationship.

Owen excused himself, taking out his cell phone, as if he planned to use the break to check messages and return calls. I pretended not to notice Josh's animosity and said, "Wow, a daytime visit! I feel so special."

"*That's* your new boss?"

"Yeah. He's got some good ideas. He might even manage to make this place work." I followed his angry gaze toward Owen, who was on the phone at the other end of the store. "Did he beat you up in high school, or something?"

He blinked back to me. "What?"

"You seem to have taken an instantaneous dislike to my new boss. If I didn't know better, I'd think you were jealous."

He opened his mouth, closed it, and shook his head, like he was trying to clear it, then he pulled out the chair at the end of the table and sat. "It has nothing to do with him," he said, not very convincingly. "It's just that I thought you were finally going to get out of this place and stop treading water with your career, and now he comes along and makes you actually *want* to keep working here. He's sidetracking you."

"You know, it wasn't too long ago that you were suggesting I just give it all up and let you take care of me," I pointed out, trying to keep a light, teasing tone in my voice. I tensed anyway, like his answer would be a critical turning point in my life.

"Only because I was trying to take the pressure off. Sometimes I think you sabotage yourself, like you're afraid of success." He took a deep breath and let it out slowly, like he was trying to center himself. "But that's actually not why I'm here. I wanted to apologize for last night. I left pretty abruptly, which must have given you a terrible impression. The truth is, I suddenly wasn't feeling too well and wanted to get home as soon as possible, and it was the sort of thing I didn't want to bring up in a restaurant, if you know what I mean. It wasn't about you, and I didn't want you thinking I'd rushed off angry." He chuckled and added, "Though I guess me showing up here and having a testosterone explosion around your boss probably didn't help matters."

I immediately felt bad for having wondered about him. "Oh, that's okay," I said. "You meant well. And I hope you're feeling better."

"Tons better. I think something I ate didn't agree with me. You didn't get sick, did you? It felt like food poisoning."

"No, I was fine."

"Then maybe it was a bug, and I hope I didn't give it to you. Can I make it up to you tonight?"

"How about tomorrow night? You probably ought to make sure you're better, and I already told Florence I'd go to a movie with her tonight."

He'd tensed when I declined, but relaxed and grinned when I mentioned Florence. He looked across the room toward her, caught her eye, grinned, and waved. Anyone who saw her friendly response would never guess that she spent most of her time trying to talk me into dating someone else. I was watching her, so I barely noticed out of the corner of my eye when he nodded ever so slightly to her, like he was sending a signal. Her smile faded and she looked much more serious—like a totally different person—when she nodded in response. If I hadn't known better, I'd have thought they were conspiring against me.

CHAPTER SEVEN

Owen and I spent the rest of the day working on details for our scavenger hunt event, interrupted only by a deliveryman bringing me a bouquet of daisies from Josh. The card with the flowers wished me a good evening out and told me he'd be thinking of me.

"That's nice of him," Owen said mildly. "How long have you two been together?"

I started to answer, then realized I didn't know. The start of our relationship was foggy. "A while, I guess," I said vaguely. A second later, the answer popped into my head. "Nearly a year."

"So it's serious, I take it."

"Yeah, I suppose it is," I said reluctantly. Then I was surprised that I felt so reluctant about it. But it didn't *feel* too serious, at least, not on my part. I barely remembered Josh existed unless I was with him, and I had a hard time remembering specifics of our time together. The only date I recalled with any detail was our last one. Anything happening before that might as well have happened to someone else. I had far more vivid memories of Owen, and I'd only known him a couple of days. I didn't think that was a good sign.

*

As Florence and I prepared to turn the café over to the night crew, she said, "Would you mind if we made it a night in instead of a night out? I think I've had about all I can take of people for one day. Maybe we could pick up some takeout and watch a video. That way we could talk."

"Sounds good to me. Your place or mine?"

"Yours, if you don't mind. It's closer and nicer."

We stopped by the café where I got my morning coffee and ordered burgers to go at the counter. Perry the waitress turned in the order, then leaned on the counter to chat with us. "Looks like you've got a big night of cholesterol ahead, huh?" she said with a grin.

"Usually, tofu's more my speed, but you've gotta indulge every so often," Florence told her.

"Yeah, as much kale as she eats, she can get away with a burger every now and then," I said. "Me, on the other hand, well, I don't know what my excuse is."

"You work very hard," Florence said. "And now the new boss has you doing two jobs."

"Two jobs?" Perry asked.

"It's not that bad," I said. "He's just getting my help with some planning during lulls at work."

"And you should see this boss," Florence added. "Spending time with him is not a chore. I think he likes Katie."

Perry leaned forward across the counter with great interest. "Ooh, he does?"

"He does not," I said, rolling my eyes. "He didn't show even the slightest bit of jealousy when Josh showed up or sent flowers."

"So you were watching for jealousy?" Florence teased.

"Just so I'd know where things stood. I wanted to see if there'd be a situation I needed to defuse. Things might get awkward at work if my boss got jealous of my boyfriend." I remembered then that he'd asked how long we'd been dating, but that could have just been casual conversation, not an indication of interest, so I decided I wouldn't mention it. I didn't want to give Florence any additional ammunition.

"Order up!" the cook called, and Perry went to get our meals.

"Have a good evening, and I want updates about this boss," she said as she handed us our bags.

At my place, I let Florence peruse my DVD collection while I got dishes and drinks from the kitchen. She was putting a disc in the player when I returned. "I think a good chick flick is just what the doctor ordered," she said as the two of us settled onto the sofa.

The movie opened with the heroine walking to work through her neighborhood as a perky pop tune played and the credits showed on the screen. It was an eerily familiar situation. "Do you ever have days when you feel like that, where you can practically hear the song on the soundtrack?" Florence asked. I turned to see if she was joking, but she looked serious.

"I guess," I said with a shrug. It did look an awful lot like some of my recent mornings had felt.

Then the movie got going. As usual, the heroine had a boyfriend who was obviously wrong for her when the right guy fell into her life. "Sometimes, I just want to smack some sense into these chicks," Florence said, shaking her head in frustration. "Shouldn't it be obvious that this is the wrong guy?"

"I don't know. He doesn't seem *too* bad." I wasn't sure why I was defending him, though. I didn't think I'd want to date him.

"He's boring. I'll tell you what he is: He's the safety net. The comfort zone. He's not going to challenge her, but she's also not going to grow when she's with him."

"Are you trying to tell me something?" I asked.

She raised her hands in mock surrender. "I'm just watching the movie. In real life, though, she'd ditch him in a heartbeat for the heartthrob. She just sticks with him because otherwise it would be the world's shortest movie. Girl meets Mr. Right, realizes it, and dumps Mr. Wrong. The End."

In spite of her denial, I thought she sounded rather personally invested in the situation. Of course, the heroine started spending more time with the leading man, and then they fell in love in a montage of romantic scenes set to a swoony pop ballad. This part gave me shivers because I'd felt like that a couple of times lately. It was the way I remembered my entire relationship with Josh, and it was the way days spent with Owen seemed to go.

"Is something wrong? You look a little pale," Florence said, nudging me.

I shook my head. "I think I've had a few montage days lately. And why is it the good stuff that goes by in a montage? Why can't we dispense with a boring day at work with a coffee montage?"

She laughed, but her eyes looked serious. At the end of the movie, she said, "See, that's how it needs to work out. She realizes her mistake and rushes to make sure she doesn't lose the right guy."

"But does she have to do it in a bridesmaid's dress while riding a scooter?"

"The point is that she does it, no matter how difficult or inconvenient it is. When you know the right thing to do, you just do it."

I quirked an eyebrow at her. "I believe you've made your point. I might miss out on something amazing with Owen if I insist on clinging to Josh, the Mr. Wrong safety net. But life isn't a romantic comedy movie. In real life, the safe guy is the best bet."

"Hey, you're the one who said you're living montages."

"I was joking! Nobody lives montages. We live life."

"If that's what you call it." She helped me clean up, and as she went to go, she placed her hand firmly on my shoulder. "I just want you to have the best. I made some mistakes—been there, done that, got the divorce papers. Don't rush into anything, and be sure of what you want."

"And no riding scooters in hoopskirts."

"Only if you're into that sort of thing. See you in the morning."

When she was gone, I was left mulling over what she'd said. In the movie, the heroine had ignored her friends' advice, and I didn't think I was that type, but I couldn't remember any friends before Florence. I also couldn't remember any boyfriends before Josh. My memories before a week or so ago were blurry and consisted only of a few key moments, but if I tried to push beyond that, I hit a wall. I had photos in my apartment of family members, and I knew they were members of my family, but I couldn't dredge up memories of them other than a few scrapbook pages. It was like I hadn't existed before that morning when Florence told me the store was being sold.

It was like I was starring in a movie and didn't realize it.

Then I shook my head. I'd obviously had too much wine.

*

The next couple of weeks passed in a blur that I remembered only in more montage-like groups of scenes—working with Owen in the store, with lots of little accidental touches that affected us both more than we wanted to acknowledge, dinners and romantic walks in the park with Josh. The strange thing was that I didn't remember these events as though I'd lived them. It was more like they'd been put into my head. I felt as if my movie night with Florence had happened the night before and everything else had just been a dream.

I was starting to wonder if I should maybe seek professional psychological help.

But finally, after much preparation, it was the day before our big event. We closed early, then the entire staff worked together to set up the new signage, re-shelve the books, and otherwise transform the store into the kind of place where book lovers could while away the hours. This time, I wasn't worried about the background music because I knew it was playing on the store's sound system. We had coffee and treats from our new suppliers set out for refreshments, and a party-like atmosphere prevailed.

I approached the science fiction section, sorting through the stack of placards in my hand. "Okay, Earl, here you go," I said, handing the appropriate signs to the section's coordinator, a tall, slim young man with an elven look to him. His ears weren't pointy, but I felt like they should be. "One of those goes on each endcap, and then there are two for the signs that go on top of the shelves. I'll be back around with the shelf talkers." As I walked away from him, I did a double take. I felt like I knew him from somewhere. Then I shook my head. Of course I knew him from somewhere. We'd been working together at the store for ages. He always came up on his break and ordered an espresso.

When the store was all set and the rest of the staff left, Owen and I stayed behind to hide the scavenger hunt clues. I'd been looking forward to this all day, and maybe dreading it a little. Whatever it was, it had my heart pounding and my pulse racing. Maybe Florence was right about my crush on him. It was harmless, though. It didn't have to mean anything.

The music on the sound system changed to jazz standards from the forties, which fit the store's new nostalgic retro look. Then the lights dimmed, and I jumped. "Sorry about that," Owen said as he approached. "I just thought it would be best if we weren't quite so visible from the outside." He held up a stack of colored index cards. "Ready to plant our clues?"

We had a list of books people were supposed to search for, and we went around the store, sticking the cards in the backs of the books and then re-shelving them. Although we'd created the list, we still had to think about where to go and which section would be most likely to come to mind for each book. We ran through the maze of bookshelves like children, and I felt that if I looked out the corner of my eye, I'd see the books coming to life and dancing the way I sometimes imagined they would after a bookstore closed for the night.

"Ah, here it is," Owen said, pulling the next book on the list off the shelf and opening it so I could slip the card in. He closed the book and put it back in its slot, then smoothed the shelf so it wasn't obvious that one book had recently been moved. He glanced at me, then back at the books before saying, "Can I ask you something strange?"

I gulped, wondering what he might consider strange. Would this be a personal question, something about Josh or maybe about the way things were developing between us? "Um, sure," I stammered.

"Have you been having a bad case of déjà vu lately? I mean, seeing people and thinking they're familiar, and then you realize that of course they're familiar because you know them, but that doesn't seem like why they should be familiar?"

"You too?" I asked, a little breathless. "It's been happening all the time to me lately." I hesitated, since this was the kind of thing that might get me sent to a psychiatric hospital, but since he'd started it … "While we're on the subject, do you ever get the feeling that some of your memories are more like dreams, or like time is passing in just a series of highlight images—like a montage in a movie, sometimes even complete with soundtrack?"

He frowned and licked his lips, then said, "No, I don't think I've run into that. But the memories thing, yeah. It's like nothing from before a few weeks ago seems real. And I do sometimes feel like a week or more has passed between the time I go to bed at night and the time I wake up in the morning. I remember the things that happened, but not as though I really lived them."

I laughed, then cut myself off when I realized that I sounded like someone on the verge of madness. "So I'm not crazy, or if I am crazy, then I'm not crazy alone."

"We can share a padded cell," he said with a grin. Then he went more serious again and seemed to be considering what to say next. He took a deep breath and whispered, "There's something else weird going on."

"What?" I whispered in response.

"I think I can do magic."

"Magic?" I thought about saying that was crazy, but was it any crazier than any of the other stuff we'd been noticing?

My tone must have said it for me because he said defensively, "I was in the office and realized that the binder I needed was on the shelf. I wished it would come to me without me having to go get it, and then it flew across the room and onto my desk."

"Maybe the store's haunted and the ghost wanted to help you," I suggested. I didn't know why that sounded like a more plausible explanation, but it did.

"Watch this," he said. "The next book we need is on that shelf over there." He pointed to the opposite aisle. Then he flicked his wrist and the book flew out of its spot and into his hand.

I squealed in shock and jumped backward. "Oh my gosh!" I said when I'd recovered from the initial surprise. My hand trembled as I stuck the card between the pages, and then he sent it back to its spot. "Can you do anything else?"

He held his hand palm-up, and soon a soft glow formed there. The glow formed into a globe and rose into the air above our heads.

"Whoa," I breathed. "I wonder if it's just you or if this is something everyone can do." To test it, I held my hand out the way he had and thought about forming a light. My glow wasn't nearly as bright as Owen's, but it was there. I sent it up to join his. "Oh, wow, I can do magic!" I said with a hysterical giggle.

"I know, right?" He was grinning ear-to-ear. "I guess this makes us wizards. No wonder we clicked. We're two of a kind."

We returned to our task, our magical lights following us as we went from shelf to shelf. I wasn't quite as good as he was at summoning the books to me. I had to be much closer, and it seemed to take more effort— enough that I doubted I'd be using this particular shortcut in day-to-day life. Still, it was cool to play with.

I slipped the final clue card into its book and let Owen send it flying back to its shelf. Then Owen's grin turned mischievous and he raised his hand to point to the glowing orbs. They suddenly shattered like fireworks, showering us with colorful sparks of light. We ran through the store then, light moving all around us in great swirls. He'd bounce some light at me, and I'd send it back to him. It was like dancing, though we hadn't even touched.

He waved his hand in the air again, and a snowfall began. The flakes danced in the air, and I jumped to catch them on my tongue, but they vanished before I could reach them. "You did say you liked browsing in a bookstore on a snowy day," he said.

"But generally the idea is to come in *out* of the snow," I replied. "You should have it snow just outside the windows so people will stay longer."

"That's a good idea," he said. "I wonder what else we can do." With a flick of his wrist, he changed the music on the sound system to an even slower, more romantic piece before he held his hand out to me. "Shall we dance?"

I stepped into his arms, and then we danced in the magical snowfall as fireworks went off over our heads. I wasn't sure if the tingle that ran through my body was from the magic or from being together like this. I had the strangest feeling that I'd have felt exactly the same way without the snow or the fireworks, that it was the man and not the magic that made every nerve ending in my body sing for joy.

"You know," I whispered after a while, "this is probably visible from outside the store. People will notice if fireworks are going off indoors."

"I suppose you're right," he murmured, and the sparks dissipated. The snow kept falling, though. It seemed as though the two of us were alone in our own magical wonderland, where the outside world was nothing but a faint memory. He leaned toward me, and I found myself leaning toward him, breathless with anticipation. When our lips were barely an inch apart, I suddenly remembered where I was and what I was doing.

I wasn't the kind of girl who two-timed. I had a boyfriend. I might break it off with him tomorrow because now I knew what magic really was, but I couldn't kiss someone else until then. It wouldn't be right, and if being with Owen was the right thing, I didn't want to start it off on the wrong foot.

"You know what this snow puts me in the mood for?" I asked, pulling back abruptly and trying to keep my tone light and casual to cover my still-breathless reaction to our near-miss.

"Hot cocoa." The intense look in his eyes as he continued gazing at me told me that wasn't what he was really thinking, but he had picked up on my reticence and was willing to shift the mood.

"You read my mind," I said, smiling in relief. I felt like we had all the time in the world. We had no need to rush things.

The snowfall following us, we made our way up the stairs to the café. We walked side by side, not touching, but close enough that I was conscious of his proximity. I started to head behind the counter, but he shook his head. "No, I think I've got this." A wave of his hand, and two steaming mugs sat on the nearest table. "Your table, miss," he said with a gesture.

I grabbed a tray of cookies left over from the store rearranging party. Our new supplier's cookies were good enough that I didn't think Owen could beat them, even with magic. We wouldn't be using them to level unsteady tables.

After a sip of magical cocoa, I looked at him through the snowfall and said, "What do you think this means?"

"I have no idea. Are we the only ones who can do this? Or can everyone, but no one thinks to try? Has it been like this all along, or is this new?"

"Maybe there's something in the water, or space aliens have experimented on us—that would explain the missing time we've both experienced."

"You know, any other day I might have said that was an outrageous theory, but since I can do magic, I'm not sure I can call anything outrageous anymore. *Anything* is possible."

"Should we tell someone?"

"Who? We don't have a ministry of magic in this world, and I'd rather not end up in some secret government laboratory."

"So, what do we do?"

"I don't know, but we should think about it, and we should definitely keep it a secret for now until we've figured it out."

"Maybe we should use our powers to fight evil," I suggested.

"What evil? We already vanquished the lousy coffee the old-fashioned way. That alone should earn us a medal."

"Mild-mannered booksellers by day, magical superheroes by night," I quipped, trying to sound like a movie trailer announcer.

We finished our cocoa in thoughtful silence, then he said, "It's getting late, and we have a busy day ahead. I'll walk you home."

I started to protest that he didn't have to, but I wanted him to. I tried to tell myself that it was only practical, but safety was the last thing on my mind. There was no sign of the magic that had happened there when we left the store. I felt like I'd left a magical world and had returned to reality, except the reality didn't seem all that real to me either. There was a surreal quality to everything, and I felt more than ever like I'd stepped into a movie. Even the music was there, and I knew it wasn't from the store's sound system.

I was sure that Florence would say this was still more proof that I was staying with Mr. Wrong, my comfort-zone man, when I could have magic—literal magic, in this case—with Owen. And yet I felt weird, like I was doing something wrong, as I walked home with him, close enough to touch, but not holding hands or making any actual contact, except the occasional moment when our sleeves brushed.

We reached my front steps and paused there. "Thanks for walking me home," I said and started to turn to go. "I'll see you tomorrow."

He caught my arm and said in a rough whisper, "Katie." I turned, waiting for what else he might say, but he just stood there, like he couldn't find the words.

I wanted to kiss him, more than anything, but I reminded myself that we'd have plenty of time for that. I didn't want any nagging guilt to mar this perfect evening. I leaned back, away from him, and repeated, "See you tomorrow," before turning and running up the steps. I forced myself not to look back because I didn't think my resolve would hold if I saw him standing there.

The soundtrack playing in my head swelled dramatically, and the music made me want to cry.

CHAPTER EIGHT

It was with decidedly mixed feelings that I headed to work the next morning. I both dreaded and anticipated seeing Owen again. I hadn't thought it possible to hold such contradictory views simultaneously, and doing so made me feel like my head was in imminent danger of exploding. I wasn't even sure it had been real. There was a dreamlike quality about my memories of running around the store, doing magic. What if I had dreamed it? I decided not to say anything to Owen unless he said something to me first. I didn't even try to do magic on my own, but I wasn't sure if I was more afraid of finding out that I couldn't or that I could.

When I got to the store, I slipped upstairs to the coffee shop, hoping to delay the encounter with Owen as long as possible so I'd have a better chance of having my head on straight. I was tying on my apron when Florence arrived. "My, but someone's glowing," she said, raising an eyebrow and smirking.

"Am I?" I blurted, raising my hands to cheeks that suddenly felt like they were on fire. Then I hurried to add, "I just put on a little more makeup than usual, and that had me running late, so I hurried to get here. You know, a brisk walk on a crisp, cool morning is just the thing to put color in your cheeks." And then I realized I'd overexplained so badly that it was obvious I was hiding something.

"Uh huh," Florence said, grinning as she leaned against the counter. "What, exactly, happened here after everyone else left?"

"Nothing! We hid the clues and had some cocoa and then he walked me home." I knew she was talking about romantic stuff, so I didn't feel bad leaving out the part about doing magic together. "Not so much as a kiss on the cheek."

"Disappointed by that, were we?"

"No, it was my decision. I have a boyfriend." A split second too late, I

65

realized that had probably been the wrong thing to say. "Not that it even came up at all. He didn't make a move. I just didn't make a move because of that."

"Mmm-hh," she said, nodding. "So you were thinking of making a move until you remembered your boyfriend."

"No! That's not what I meant!" Rather than dig myself in deeper, I went to work making coffee and arranging the bakery case. "And why are you so invested in this, anyway? If you're so keen on him, you make a move."

"I'm not the one who's feeling the magic," she said.

I nearly whacked my head on the counter from rising too quickly with a stack of paper cups. "The magic?" I asked, my voice rising in pitch and volume. How could she have known?

"You know, that connection you two have. Don't tell me you haven't noticed it. I can practically see the little hearts circling your heads when you two are together."

Actually, little hearts had been about the only thing that hadn't circled our heads the night before. If it had even been real. It had felt like a dream. But if it had been a dream, that might mean it was something I wanted to happen, and I wasn't ready to admit that. I needed to deal with Josh before I started having romantic dreams about other men.

When Owen came to the coffee shop to test the new brew, I knew that it must have been real, unless we'd had the same dream. He didn't quite look me in the eye and he blushed as he spoke to me. Florence watched all of this with great amusement. I'd never convince her that there was nothing going on.

"Let me know how it goes," I told him before he headed down to open the store and start the treasure hunt, my attempt at a bright, cheerful tone coming out a little squeaky. Yes, he was just as cute as I remembered, and my whole body tingled at the thought of the magic we'd made together—literally.

I had to break it off with Josh, I decided right then. Even if nothing ended up happening with Owen, if I could feel this way about someone else while dating Josh, it was a pretty good sign that Josh and I weren't meant to be. I couldn't marry him.

At that moment, Josh came up the stairs into the coffee shop, holding an enormous bouquet of flowers. "For you," he said, presenting them to me with a flourish.

"Oh, uh, thanks," I said. "This is a surprise."

"Well, this whole store revamp thing is a big deal for you, and I wanted to congratulate you. I think I haven't come across as very supportive, but I just want what's best for you. I didn't think that would involve working in a bookstore, but that's my issue, not yours, and I can see how much happier you've been lately."

He was saying all the right things—too right, come to think of it. He sounded like he'd been perusing the self-help section before coming up to see me because his whole speech was right out of one of those "learn to communicate with your mate" books.

While I was still thinking about how to respond, the phone rang, and then Florence called out, "Katie, they want you downstairs to help kick off the treasure hunt."

"Oh, sorry, I've got to go," I said, then remembered that I was still holding that huge bouquet of flowers. Florence reached over and took them from me, and I headed off again.

"Apron!" Florence called after me, and she took the apron from me once I'd untied it. I nervously smoothed my hair as I hurried downstairs.

"We couldn't start this without you," Owen said, now sounding less bashful than he had earlier. There was a small crowd of customers gathered around the table where we were handing out the treasure hunt clues. "Do you want to do the honors?" Owen asked me.

"The honors?"

"Start the hunt."

"Okay, on your marks, get set, go!" I called out. The contestants instantly dispersed. "That seems to be going well," I said. "And I'd better get back up to the coffee shop because it looks like we're going to be busier than usual."

"I'm sorry, I should have hired someone to take your place before now. That detail slipped my mind."

"Take my place?" I asked, suddenly alarmed. Was he angry that I hadn't kissed him the night before?

"I'd planned to make you the assistant manager in charge of marketing and get you out of the coffee shop entirely—that is, if you don't mind. I should have talked to you about that earlier."

"Well, yeah, that sounds wonderful," I said. "But for today, we're swamped. The new coffee is going over really well already. You may have to hire a couple of new people."

He grinned. "We make a pretty good team."

"Yeah, I guess we do." I had that same sense of gravity pulling me toward him that I'd had the night before, and again I resisted it. Before the temptation could overwhelm me, I hurried up the stairs to the coffee shop.

I paused at the top of the stairs when I saw that Josh and Florence were in the middle of an intense conversation. I hadn't thought they knew each other all that well or that they'd have anything to talk about other than making small talk about me, but they seemed to be arguing.

"I thought your assignment was clear," he said to her, and I moved behind a display so I could eavesdrop without being seen. What assignment could he possibly mean?

"Hey, I'm just the sassy best friend in this scenario," she said. "If you knew the source material, you'd know she's supposed to ignore my advice. I'm the person she's supposed to resist, and I've been giving her plenty to resist, trust me. I can't help it if you aren't holding up your end of the script."

"Not holding up my end? What more do I have to do? I brought flowers!"

"I wouldn't call telling her that she might as well give up finding a job and marry you a good campaign for Mr. Right. That's Mr. Wrong behavior."

"That wasn't my idea. That was in the scenario."

"Then you've got a lot to overcome. Someone set you up for failure."

This made no sense. It sounded like they were in on some kind of plan together. I slowly backed away, heading toward the stairs, as Josh said, "I guess I'll just have to reset things. Supposedly, this shouldn't have worked on either of them, especially on her, but it has, so it looks like we had bad information. We can still fix it, and then no harm done."

I'd just reached the stairs and was ready to flee when Josh left the counter and strode over to me. "Hey, there you are, darling," he said with a smile. "How'd your contest go?"

I tried to get away from him, but he moved faster than I did and caught my wrist. "Don't touch me!" I cried out and jerked away from him. I lost my balance and would have fallen down the stairs, but he caught me, and I was too stunned and shaken to get out of his grip. He held me tightly, staring into my eyes, and then I got dizzy. Everything went blurry and dim.

When I opened my eyes, I found myself still staring into his eyes, but I couldn't quite recall what I was doing on the stairs. All I knew was that my heart felt like it would burst from love as I looked at him. "You saved me," I whispered.

He smiled in what looked like great relief and released his iron grip on me to brush my cheek with his fingers and sweep my hair away from my forehead. "Of course I did. Are you okay?"

"I–I think so," I said. "I'm a little dizzy, though."

With his arms around me, he supported me as he led me to the nearest seat. "Maybe you should bring her something to drink," he shouted at Florence, who shot him a glare before pouring a cup of coffee and adding a generous dose of sugar to it. He took it from her and handed it to me, kneeling by my side as I drank it.

"What happened?" I looked up to see Owen standing there, looking alarmed. My head swam again, and the impression I'd had of him as a good friend who'd sparked magic in me shifted. I didn't know where that had come from, but now I knew him as the skeevy boss who'd been making passes at me. I'd nearly fallen on the stairs while trying to get away from him and back to Josh.

"She's fine," Josh said curtly. "I'll take care of her."

"Katie?" Owen asked warily.

I shied away from him. "I'm fine," I snapped. The hurt in his eyes gave me that weird dizzy feeling again, like I was the center of a tug-of-war between two versions of reality. He didn't look like the kind of boss who'd make unwanted passes at his employees during business hours, and he certainly didn't seem like someone I'd be so desperate to flee that I'd trip on the stairs and nearly fall, but that was how I remembered it.

"Okay, then," Owen said with a nod, and he turned away and headed down the stairs.

"I'd better stay with you for a while," Josh said, "just to be sure."

"I'll look after her," Florence said.

"No, I think I'll stay."

I got the impression of conflict between them, but I wasn't sure what it could be. I recalled her warning me about the boss and how I shouldn't get my head turned by his good looks while I had a nice, solid man like Josh around.

I forced myself out of the chair. "I'm fine. I didn't actually fall, so no harm done. And now I have to get back to work." With what I hoped came across as a saucy wink and not a nervous twitch, I said, "You're welcome to hang around awhile, but you'll have to buy some coffee first. Don't worry, it's much better than it used to be."

Without waiting for his response, I headed back to the counter and put on my apron. "Do you want the usual house blend or the special of the day?" I asked him.

"Surprise me," he said, leaning forward, his elbows on the counter. I had a vague memory of Owen doing the same thing, back when I'd thought he was just another customer and I'd warned him about the coffee, but then the image shifted so that he was leering instead of smiling and I was telling him about the nasty coffee to get rid of him. Yes, that was what had really happened. I must have tried remembering otherwise to make it easier to work with him.

Josh hung around for a while, chatting with Florence and me when we weren't busy and staying to the side when we were. After lunch, he said, "Well, I'd better get going. I have some things to do to get ready for tonight."

"Tonight?" I asked, but then the memory came flooding back. "Oh, yes, tonight, that special dinner you've got planned. You still can't give me any hints?"

"Nope. Just wear something pretty." He grinned. "A manicure might be nice if you've got the time."

"A manicure?" I asked, but he was already gone. Then I figured it out.

People would be seeing my fingernails if I were showing off a ring. "Florence, I think he's planning to propose tonight!"

"Yeah, I bet he is," she said dryly.

I examined my nails. "I don't think I have time for a manicure." Holding my hands toward Florence, I asked, "Do I need a manicure? Or can I maybe get by with a quick file and buff?"

She glanced at my hands before gently pushing them away. "You're fine, and I don't think you need the manicure for getting the ring slipped on your finger, just for showing it off afterward. You could get the manicure tomorrow. That is, assuming you say yes and will be wearing the ring."

"Of course I'll say yes. Why wouldn't I?"

She stared at me silently for a while, then said, "Just be sure that's what you want, okay? Think about it long and hard before you go to that dinner, and then don't let anything that happens sway you. Go with your gut, with your first strong impulse, not with any afterthought that might hit you."

"What's that supposed to mean? We've been talking about getting married for ages. This is only going to formalize it."

"I just want you to get what you want—what you deserve," she said, turning away. She looked troubled, with frown lines between her eyes, tension around her mouth, and, if I wasn't mistaken, tears in her eyes.

"Florence, what is it?" I asked, catching her arm before she could move away from me. "Is there something you know that you aren't telling me? You haven't seen him with another woman, or anything like that, have you? I can take it, whatever it is, and I'd rather know now before I make any major decisions."

As she faced me, Florence seemed to be in real pain—agony, even. She took a deep breath, started to say something, then squeezed her lips shut and shook her head. After a long pause, she said, "I just don't think he's good for you. Don't ask me why I think that, but I do. That's all. I want you to think for yourself."

I blinked, taken aback. "Who said I wasn't thinking for myself? It's not like he has me under an evil spell, or anything like that." Then I frowned. "You've never liked him, have you? You've been against him from the start. But I *do* like him, and I believe I'm intelligent enough to make my own decisions."

For the rest of the day, we spoke only enough to get our work done, which made for an awkward working environment. It would have been a relief to go downstairs to help award the prizes to the treasure hunt winners, but that meant facing Owen. I kept a wary distance from him the whole time and tried to avoid looking directly at him. The impression of his attention being unwanted had faded, but being around him gave me that unsettling feeling of teetering on the brink between two realities. When I saw him heading toward me, I escaped upstairs. Even Florence's iciness was preferable to that.

My shift ended with the end of the contest, and after I'd put away my apron and turned the coffee shop over to the evening crew, I tried to get out of the store without running into Owen, to no avail. He'd been waiting for me and pulled me aside. "What's wrong, Katie?" he asked, looking so hurt and confused that my heart broke for him for a moment, until I remembered what he'd done.

"You dare to ask that?" I snarled.

"You're angry because I gave you a promotion without checking with you first? You can turn it down if you don't want it."

I remembered that conversation, and in that memory, we'd been acting like friends. I hadn't seen him as a threat, hadn't found his attention unwelcome. I'd liked him. My stance on him wavered. "No, that's not it ..." I said vaguely, trying to recapture what the problem was.

"Then what is it? Last night, I thought we had something. I mean, we did *magic* together. It was the most amazing night of my life. And now you won't even look at me. Do you have regrets? Not that there was anything to regret. I guess I can see being a little freaked out by the magic. I'm still trying to wrap my mind around it. I almost thought I'd dreamed it, and with the way you're acting, maybe I did. Don't you remember it?"

"Magic ..." I whispered as images sprang to mind. Sparks and snowflakes danced through the air, and I'd felt so alive. But it had just been a dream, hadn't it? The dream had reflected my fears of the power my employer had over me. Then again, he'd also dreamt it. That had to mean it was real, right? Unless maybe his dream was about his power over me and we just happened to use the same imagery in our dreams about the same subject. "I have to go," I said, pushing past him. "I have a date tonight. *With my boyfriend.*"

He stepped out of the way, raising his hands in surrender. "Okay. If that's the way you want it, I can understand. It's up to you. I'd just thought ... I'd hoped ..." He shook his head. "I thought you were different." Then he walked away before I could make my own dramatic exit.

I should have been happy to have an end to that particular dilemma, but my heart was heavy as I headed home to get ready for my big date. At the end of this evening, I'd be engaged. This was what I'd wanted for so long. Once we were married, I wouldn't have to work in the store anymore. I'd be free.

Funny, that wasn't supposed to leave me weighted down with gloom.

*

That evening, I was dressed up in my best little black dress and high heels with my hair up and my nails buffed when Josh came to pick me up for dinner. He wore a tuxedo and had yet another bouquet of flowers for me, this time red roses. I had that same burst of love for him when I saw him that'd I'd had on the stairs that morning, and all the gloom dissipated. I loved him and wanted to marry him. That was the only thing I'd ever wanted. I threw my arms around him and kissed him.

"Well, that's more like it," he said, and I got the strangest feeling he was talking more to himself than to me.

A cab waited for us at the curb and whisked us off to a fancy, romantic restaurant. This was the kind of proposal I'd hoped for when he'd made the first offhand remark about getting married. It had all the right ingredients, right out of a diamond commercial. I wondered when the big moment would come. Probably with dessert, I decided. That seemed to be the traditional way of doing it. Would he just get out the ring and kneel, or had he set up some fancy presentation where the ring would be in a piece of cake or a glass of champagne? I could barely focus on the meal from thinking about what was to come.

But then as the meal wore on, my enthusiasm gradually waned, even though we were surrounded by soft music and candlelight. I found myself looking across the table at him and getting that old feeling that I was looking at a stranger. I'd forgotten about that in all the excitement. Had I been excited about him proposing, or was it just excitement from being proposed to? Was this what Florence had meant about trusting my gut, focusing on my feelings instead of on the situation? It was so confusing, like I was feeling two completely opposite things at the same time. How could I be madly in love with Josh and wanting to marry him while still thinking of him as a stranger I didn't particularly like?

I remembered other things as the evening continued. Just before that moment when he'd rescued me on the stairs, there had been something I was upset about, and it had to do with Josh, not Owen. I hadn't been fleeing up the stairs from Owen, I'd been fleeing *down* the stairs from Josh after hearing him talk to Florence. She'd said something about Mr. Wrong and Mr. Right, and she'd been talking like these were roles we were all playing.

Then I realized what all this reminded me of: that movie Florence had selected for us to watch. There was the safe guy and the right guy, but the safe guy wasn't even truly safe. He was someone to settle on, but there were warning signs and red flags about what life would be like with him. A marriage with him might not be bad, but the heroine could never really be herself while she was with him. There would always be a part of herself she'd have to deny, and that would be tragic. Choosing the right guy might feel risky, but the payoff would be huge.

The waiter brought out a small cake with sparklers on it, and the sparklers triggered another memory, of sparks dancing in the air as Owen and I ran through the bookstore. The memory was just as vivid as these sparklers in front of me. It hadn't been a dream. It had been real. I'd wanted to kiss Owen after that, more than I'd ever wanted to kiss Josh—or anyone else. He wasn't Mr. Wrong, the skeevy boss who could help my career at the cost of my soul. He was Mr. Right. I could have magic, so why settle for less?

Just as I realized that, Josh got out of his seat, knelt in front of me, and opened a ring box.

At first, I was frozen. I wanted to say or do something before this went any further, but I couldn't. I couldn't even hear what he was saying over the pounding of my heart and the rush of blood in my ears. When his lips stopped moving, I heard myself say, "I can't," and then my feet made the decision my brain couldn't. I got up and ran from the restaurant.

The store was still open, so I hoped Owen would be there. I supposed it wasn't utterly essential that I talk to him now. He'd be there tomorrow, and I could talk to him then. But something drove me to get there right away. I knew who was right for me and I didn't want to waste a moment. After the way I'd left him, I didn't want to give him a chance to dwell on the way I'd acted toward him. If I gave him too much time to think about it, he might come to hate me, and I couldn't bear that.

I tried flagging down several cabs, but they all passed right by me. A motorcycle messenger stopped and said, "Do you need a lift? You look like you're having an emergency."

I knew I wasn't supposed to trust strangers, but this was a crisis, so I said, "You know the bookstore on Seventy-third?"

"Yeah, I won the treasure hunt there today—hey, that's where I've seen you before. Hop on."

He looked familiar enough that I decided to go for it. I hiked the skirt of my dress up to my thighs to climb on behind him, and he handed me the spare helmet that was hooked to the seat. I held on to him for dear life as he tore down the streets, weaving in and out of traffic. I kept my eyes squeezed shut, sure we were going to crash at any moment, and before I knew it, the cycle came to a stop. "Here we are," the driver said.

I dismounted shakily, handed him the helmet, then waved thanks to him as I hurried to the store's entrance. It was more than an hour before closing time, and the store was still full of customers browsing the shelves. Our promotional efforts seemed to have paid off, I noted, but that wasn't my focus. I needed to find Owen. I thought about going to the customer service desk and using the store's public address system but decided that would be overkill. Instead, I headed toward the manager's office with the hope that he'd be in there doing paperwork.

I didn't realize that I'd started jogging—no mean trick in high heels—so I could get there faster until some of the patrons stopped looking at books and turned to stare at me. I forced myself to slow to a brisk walk as I wove through the aisles. When I had to stop to let a couple with a stroller get past, I turned just in time to see Owen coming down the stairs. Before I knew what I was doing, I called out his name.

He froze and frowned. "Katie?" he said. I wasn't sure how much I actually heard over the background noise of the store and how much was just me recognizing my name on his lips. I rushed toward the stairs as he hurried the rest of the way down.

"I'm sorry," I blurted when we met at the foot of the stairs. "I don't know what got into me today. It was like everything that had happened with us was just a dream and reality was totally different. But I was wrong about what was real. I was wrong about Josh. I was wrong about you. You're the one."

This time, I let gravity have its way as it drew us together. Our lips touched, and it was more than I could have imagined. I felt like I was coming awake—truly awake—for the first time in my life.

Both of us suddenly pulled away from each other. "Katie?" he whispered.

"Owen?" I responded.

Then, simultaneously, we said, "Where are we?"

CHAPTER NINE

I felt dizzy and groggy, like I'd been suddenly awakened from a deep sleep and hadn't quite caught my bearings while the dream world I'd just left still had a grip on my brain and the real world hadn't yet come into focus. What was going on here?

Owen looked similarly confused. He clasped my hands in his and whispered urgently, "I think we need to talk."

I blinked, then remembered that we were standing in the middle of a bookstore. A small crowd of shoppers hovered nearby, pretending not to notice us while still watching avidly. But, a *bookstore?* What were we doing in a bookstore?

Owen released one of my hands and led me to the maps section under the stairs, where no one was browsing. "What's the last thing you remember—really remember, when you know it was us?"

I closed my eyes to think, then said, "We went into that warehouse that Earl sent us a picture of. There was something in there, but I didn't get a good look at it before everything went black. And then I was here in the store just now, except I also remember having been here all along. I *think* I know when it started being really me instead of fake memories, but I'm not entirely sure." I knew I was babbling, but I'd just discovered that I'd apparently been living someone else's life without knowing who I really was, so I figured that being freaked-out was perfectly understandable.

He nodded. "Same with me—everything went black, then I was here. What I think we saw was a portal."

"So we're wherever that portal went? Which is apparently the universe of bad romantic comedies. Why couldn't I get Narnia?"

"Romantic comedies?"

"That's what I seem to have been living, which would explain why I kept thinking I heard a musical soundtrack in the background and why my life seemed to go by in a series of montages. It even fit the plot. I had the safe, seemingly nice guy who didn't fulfill me, and then you came along and I was torn. I had the snarky best friend giving me romantic advice—she was pushing me toward you, by the way. I even did the mad dash across town when I realized you were the one for me. It was right out of that movie Nita and I watched the other night. Or however long ago that was. We've been here at least a month, it seems, but with all those montages, it's hard to tell." I was babbling again, but it was better than screaming, which was what I wanted to do.

Someone entered the map section and browsed for a few minutes, forcing us into silence. I tried taking a few deep, cleansing breaths since I was afraid I was on the verge of hyperventilating. I'd been kidnapped and my mind had been messed with. I didn't know where I was or how long I'd been there. It was a lot to take in.

The shopper was still pondering two different tourist maps of the city, and I got the feeling he was memorizing the information so he wouldn't have to buy one. Owen must have had the same thought, for he rolled his eyes and gestured with his head. We slipped out of the alcove below the stairs and headed for his office. By this time, the small crowd that had watched our romantic moment had dispersed.

As soon as we were safely inside with the door closed, I flopped down into a chair and kicked off my high heels. "Now, where are we, really?" I asked. "I'm pretty sure we're not in the real New York."

Owen leaned against the edge of his desk. "No, we're not. I know every bookstore in the city, and this isn't one of them." His voice grew wistful for a moment. "Though I kind of wish it was. We must be in the elven lands."

"And where's that?"

"It's, well, you weren't too far off when you said Narnia. It's another magical world that exists on a different plane."

"You mean there's a whole fantasy world in some other magical dimension—and it looks a lot like our New York, but without the magic?"

"I don't think this is the way the whole world looks. It was probably created just for the people they took out of New York. The elves have ways of pulling your fantasies out of your head and giving them to you. And of making time do funny things."

"*You* wanted to live in a bad romantic comedy?" I asked in surprise.

"I sometimes wish I could run a bookstore and not have to worry about saving the world or being suspected of being the next great evil. I might have been thinking along those lines that night. That's what they seem to have given me. But is this what *you* want?" He sounded surprised and skeptical.

"I wouldn't say that I *normally* want this kind of thing," I said, feeling a little uncomfortable about having my psyche exposed like this. "I was just thinking about it, so I guess it was at the top of my mind when they hit us with the whammy. Like I said, Nita and I had just watched a movie like this, and maybe for a moment I thought life might be easier if it went that way. But why do this to us? Is this their idea of torture?"

"Lots of people have been disappearing, so maybe they've been getting inconvenient people out of the way."

"Or people who've seen something they shouldn't." I thought back on my time in this place, then said, "Perdita's here—she's the waitress at the café I pass on the way to work."

"Earl runs the science fiction department, and I think my Council watchdogs have been playing chess across the street."

"I wonder what fantasies they're living out, and what they know that got them sent here."

"You have to admit, this is a brilliant concept for a prison. If you think you're where you belong and if you're living out your dreams, will you try to escape? Your brain might even resist the truth because it's not something you want to know. You'll try to escape from a miserable prison, but not your dream life."

"Then why did we remember?"

He smiled and gave me a look that made me melt. "Maybe our real life *is* our dream, when it comes down to it. This world tried to keep us apart, and we resisted that."

"And the kiss sealed the deal. How very fairy-tale."

He nodded. "It was the ultimate contrast between the fantasy and reality, and it brought it all back." I had to smile. Leave it to him to take the magic out of magic. In my mind, though, the kiss broke the evil spell, no matter what he said. "I suspect your waning magic had something to do with it," he continued. "They wouldn't have been able to insert you into this reality if you hadn't been susceptible to magic, but then using the magic on you used up some of your magic, which made the spell on you weaker."

"Our magical games last night probably didn't help that. Or did help, I suppose. That may be what allowed me to resist." That thought sparked a realization. "I don't think everyone here is a prisoner, though. Some of the people we've been interacting with must be the guards, so to speak. I overheard Josh and Florence talking about something to do with a scenario—they must have been talking about the romantic comedy thing. It sounded like they were part of a setup and were conspiring against me. I was trying to get away from them when Josh caught me. He must have hit me with a stronger spell."

"*That* was why you turned against me."

I cringed. "Sorry about that, but I suddenly remembered you as the boss who was coming on to me and my feelings for him got a lot more intense."

"He must have been trying to keep us apart. Us finding each other again probably wasn't part of their plan."

"Florence seemed to be in on it, too, from the way she talked to Josh, but she kept trying to push me away from Josh and toward you. She told him it was because I was supposed to resist her, but I think she was giving me clues all along. In fact, when we had a movie night, she picked that same movie Nita and I watched and pointed out the pattern." I groaned. "I should have seen it then."

"You were under a spell. I'm not sure you were capable of seeing it."

"I'm so glad all that wasn't real, though. I can't imagine a universe where I'd have dated someone like Josh." I couldn't fight back a shudder. "When they gave me fake memories of dating him, they left out the pertinent details, like why."

"I think the spell was supposed to keep you happy enough not to ask pesky questions like that."

"The next question is, how do we get out of here and get back home? Do you know how to get out of the eleven lands?"

He ran his hands through his hair, rumpling it rather adorably. "I don't know a lot about this. It's not the sort of thing they talk about with outsiders. I've just read a few mentions, and it comes up often in folklore. We may be in a constrained area within their realm. There's a lot we'll have to figure out to have any idea how to get out or if we even can."

"What about all the other people who are stuck here? Should we try to break the spell on them?" I grimaced. "I hope I don't have to kiss them. I've already kissed my share of frogs."

He gave me a wry smile. "I don't think that would do any good—and I'm not just speaking out of jealousy. What we'll need to do is come up with some way to generate enough cognitive dissonance to jolt them out of the spell. Reminding them of something from the real world should work because it will create too much contrast between what they're experiencing and what they know to be real. From there, it should snowball. We can wake up the people we know enough about, and then they can find and work on the people they know."

"And then prison break?"

"Then I hope some of them remember more than we do about what was in that warehouse. I suspect that will be key to knowing why we're here and maybe even how to get out."

"So I guess the first order of business is to wake up as many people as possible and see what they know about what the elves are up to," I said. "In the meantime, we'll have to be careful. We don't want to clue the bad guys in on the fact that we know, or they might hit us with another whammy."

"Right, we'll have to try to act like nothing has changed."

I made a sour face. "That doesn't mean I have to go back to Josh, does it?"

"No, you made that decision while still under the spell. Maybe they'll relax if they think we can get together without it breaking the spell. We'll just have to act like we're the bookstore owner and the employee who've fallen in love and who have no idea that they're wizards trapped in a magical construct."

"I'm not sure how we should act, then—or if they'll know. The movies usually end soon after that kiss, after I've dashed across town to find you and tell you I love you. If anything happens beyond this point, it flashes forward to the wedding, and I don't think that's a logical next step. I mean, I just had another guy proposing to me an hour ago."

"That would be rushing things," he deadpanned. "But maybe we should quit worrying too much about being movie characters and just act like normal people. We should be okay as long as we don't do anything that doesn't fit this reality."

"Do you think the elves are spying on us remotely, even when we're in private, or only when we're in public?"

"If they can spy remotely, we can expect to be put in more secure custody at any moment because they'll know we broke the spell. I think they'd have already done something about us discovering magic if they'd been watching us all this time."

"Good point."

He checked his watch. "It's almost closing time. If I'm being normal, I'll make a pass through the store and close out all the registers. Then we should probably do something appropriately date-like. Want to go out for a drink?"

"I could *really* use a drink."

"Drink it is, then, after we close. You're welcome to hide out in here until then."

I shook my head, stood, and stepped back into my shoes. "Nope. I'm not letting you out of my sight. I'm too afraid that the next time I see you, you'll be a mild-mannered bookstore owner again."

I was nervous about leaving the store after we closed because I wasn't sure what we'd find outside, now that the spell was broken. Was whatever magic that made this place look like New York tied to the magic that gave us our false identities? It looked the same when we stepped outside, but then as I scanned the area while waiting for Owen to lock up, I noticed something very different. There were elves all around us—elves who actually looked like elves, pointy ears and all. They all wore gray outfits that looked like something in a science fiction movie from the era when they apparently thought bland jumpsuits were the clothing of the future. Some of the elves in gray stood near us on the sidewalk. Others were across the street. Nobody who passed by them seemed to notice them. And they were definitely watching us.

I put my arm around Owen's waist and leaned my head against his shoulder while he was still facing the store and whispered, "We're being watched, and I don't think we're supposed to be able to see them. Josh must have alerted the powers that be that I was resisting the spell."

He put his keys in his pocket, put his arm around me and murmured, "All we have to do is look like we've just discovered we're in love with each other."

"And have no idea that we're in some kind of fantasy elven concentration camp. That'll be the hard part. I think we can handle the other."

"If we're convincing enough with the other, we shouldn't have to worry about convincing them we don't know." He tilted my chin up and kissed me like he hadn't kissed me in ages. "Just getting into character," he whispered.

"Well, it worked. You've made me woozy."

We headed down the sidewalk with our arms around each other, gazing at each other as if we were the only two people on the planet. We stopped for quick kisses at each intersection, then laughed and ran across the streets holding hands when impatient motorists honked. The whole time, I saw the gray guys out of the corner of my eye. It didn't seem like all of them had followed us, but there were enough of them.

The bar we found was a relatively quiet, elegant place rather than a raucous neighborhood pub, but it was still too loud for intimate conversation. Between the music on the sound system—the kind of music that would have been called "soft" if the volume hadn't been turned to maximum—and the sound of dozens of conversations in a small space, there was a dull roar of background noise that made it necessary to shout from inches away in order to be heard. The gray guys followed us inside, but they didn't find a table or order drinks. They just stood nearby.

Owen got wine for the two of us, and then we leaned against the small open spot near the end of the bar. He did a slight double take as he looked at me, and for a moment I wondered if he'd been re-enchanted while ordering drinks. Instead, he grinned and said, "That's a really nice dress, by the way."

I looked down at it, remembering the important date I'd dressed for in another lifetime, and said, "Thanks. I have no idea where I got it."

With the self-consciousness from being watched and from needing to shout, I didn't have to conjure up the feeling of being on a first date. It was just as awkward as any "he's a great guy, but he just needs a little confidence" blind date I'd ever been on. As we drank wine and shouted superficial inanities at each other, I noticed that the gray guys were drifting away, apparently convinced by our act. When we were down to one observer, we left the bar.

We walked arm in arm toward my nearby apartment. The gray guy was still with us, but far enough away that we could whisper without being overheard, unless he had magically enhanced hearing. "You know, none of this is quite perfectly New York," I said as we walked through streets that looked right but that were all wrong. "It's all slightly similar, but not the same."

Then I knew what it reminded me of. "It's like those movies or TV shows that are set in New York but filmed in Toronto or on a backlot in Hollywood. You get the establishing shot of New York, and then the street scenes look New York-ish, but a New Yorker would know that those locations aren't anywhere in the city. This neighborhood could play the Upper West Side in a movie, but I'd bet you'd never find any of these places in the actual Upper West Side." I groaned and added, "So not only did they stick me in a bad romantic comedy movie, but it's also a low-budget one!"

"Elves are notoriously frugal," Owen said with a grin.

When we reached my charming brownstone apartment, we paused at the foot of the front steps, like any couple saying good night at the end of a first date. "This is one thing I wish I could have in the real world," I said, gazing up at the building. "I'd never be able to afford this. I wonder what it really looks like." And then I realized something that made me gasp. "You mentioned that because of my current condition, I have enough magic for the spell to work on me. Does that mean that if I'd been immune, they wouldn't have been able to bring me here?"

"They might have been able to bring you here, but the spell to mask your identity wouldn't have worked. You would have known who you were the entire time, and you'd have seen this place the way it really is."

I nodded slowly. "So, when we wake these people up and they realize what happened, they'll know I'm not magically immune anymore. And that means ..."

I didn't have to complete the sentence. All the color drained from his face as he said, "My secret will be out."

CHAPTER TEN

Owen shook his head with an exasperated sigh. "I can't believe I didn't think of that. I'm so used to being magical that I totally forgot that the wizards think I'm immune right now. That does put a wrinkle in things."

I clutched his arm urgently. "So maybe we should learn more about the situation before we start waking people up—if we even have to wake them up. Maybe we could get them home somehow, and that will break the spell, and then they won't have to know about you."

"I don't think that'll work. Too many of them have interacted with me, so they'll know I was affected, and I think it looks worse if I don't do something about it as soon as possible. I'll just have to be up front about it and take whatever consequences come." He took a deep breath, then set his jaw and said firmly, "In fact, I think we should revive Mac and his partner first."

"Owen, that's insane! It's like telling them, 'Oh, by the way, I got my powers back awhile ago.'"

"That's going to be a problem," he agreed. "And maybe I should have been honest all along instead of hiding it. But I think it's a show of good faith if I revive them first and bring them in on this. They may know more about the elven realms than I do, and they may know more about what happened to us, since presumably they were taken because they saw it happen. Mac's a good guy, and he's known me most of my life. I believe I can trust him to be fair." He gave a hopeful smile that would have been more convincing if it had gone all the way to his eyes. "And maybe saving the day here will help change my image. Either way, it means I can quit hiding, even if they still don't trust me."

"Do you have a memory you can use to revive Mac?"

"I've got a few things he might recall from when he visited my parents when I was a kid. He'll have to wake his partner because I don't know him well enough, and I'll leave that decision to Mac. I'll just have to try to find a way to get Mac alone to talk to him."

"Well, if you're sure ..."

He took a deep breath and appeared to force his shoulders to relax. "I'm not saying I'm sure this is a great idea, but I don't seem to have much of a choice."

I realized we'd been talking for quite a while and wondered what our watcher thought. A long chat at the front door after a date shouldn't be too strange, I hoped. I impulsively leaned in to give Owen a kiss on the cheek, like I was saying good night. We both paused for a moment, then kissed on the lips, lingering ever so slightly. "I don't think you should come inside," I said, quite reluctantly because I didn't want to be alone or let him out of my sight. I wasn't even sure where he lived in this world. "Like I said earlier, I was being proposed to by someone else just a couple of hours ago, and we don't want them to think we're privately plotting."

"I'm curious as to whether this guy stays here with you or follows me," he murmured as he nuzzled my neck and made me wish I hadn't just announced that he shouldn't come up. "Turn back like you're watching me go and see what happens. Then once you're inside, try veiling yourself and look out the window."

After one last kiss, he turned to leave and I headed up the front steps. I paused at the front door to turn back and didn't have to fake a besotted grin as I watched him go. I had to fight to keep that grin when I saw that the gray guy stayed on the sidewalk in front of my building. It made sense that I was the one being watched when I was the one who'd resisted the magic, but that didn't make me any more comfortable about it.

When Owen was out of sight, I unlocked the front door and went up the indoor stairs to my apartment. Once inside, I changed into sweats before attempting Granny's veiling spell and peeking out the window. The gray guy was still out there, but he didn't seem to be watching my place with an intense focus.

Sleep seemed impossible, but I turned out the light so my watcher would think I was going to bed and therefore not likely to do anything suspicious for the rest of the night. I settled onto my bed in the darkness and leaned back against the pillows. The fact that I could do so and feel it made me sure that this apartment wasn't an illusion, even if it was a fantasy. Building an entire replica of pseudo New York seemed like overkill, so I was sure some of it had to be illusion. But how much? For my apartment to be tangible, the building had to be real, but how many of the residents were real people, either prisoners or guards? Were the extras in this movie real people or just illusion, and were there enough people here to fill out every building? Would they bother to finish out the insides of buildings even if no real person lived there?

There was one way to find out. I tiptoed to my door and then up the stairs. I didn't recall ever seeing a neighbor coming downstairs or hearing any noise above me. When I reached the upper landing, I paused and listened for any signs of life coming from that apartment. There was no stereo or TV on, but it was late enough that most people would be in bed.

Feeling like I was violating all kinds of social mores, I put my hand on the doorknob, then I squeezed my eyes closed in dread as I turned the knob. It did turn, and the door eased open, so either nobody lived there or my neighbor didn't lock his door and I was about to be really embarrassed.

When nobody shouted at me, I opened my eyes and was surprised by what I saw. It was an empty shell of a room, not as finished as an "unfinished" apartment, since it didn't even have rough features like interior walls. It was just a space that happened to be enclosed. It did still have windows, and I imagined there were illusions on those windows to make it look like a normal apartment from outside, but just in case, I dropped to the floor and crawled so my watcher wouldn't be able to see me.

I couldn't see much in the dim city light coming in through the windows, but I didn't think there was much to see, just a lot of nothing. The exterior walls looked like the back side of a movie set, and I had to be careful as I crawled because the floor joists were bare, the plaster of my ceiling showing in the open spaces between them. Although crawling was slower than walking, I soon felt like I'd gone beyond where the wall of my apartment should have been. I glanced at the windows and saw that they were a slightly different size and in a slightly different position. The open space must have extended into the next building. I suspected it might go on until there was some reason it had to stop, like the end of the block or an inhabited apartment.

I wanted to keep exploring, but the risk of getting stuck somewhere and not being able to get back to my place without being caught by my watcher was too great. As I crawled back toward the door, I wondered how much of this prison was just an empty shell, a Hollywood-style backlot to create street scenes. But even if most of it was empty, building something like this seemed like a huge undertaking requiring a lot of resources, either physical or magical. That had to mean that what they were keeping secret by bringing us all here was equally huge.

*

I could hardly wait to tell Owen what I'd discovered. We ran into each other again on our way to work, right in front of the store. I wouldn't have thought it would take much effort to play the newly-in-love couple, but I was so conscious of being watched by the gray guy who'd followed me from my apartment that I couldn't relax into the role, even if it was entirely genuine.

We kissed awkwardly, then I blurted, "You'll never guess what I found last night!"

His lips twitched in a not-quite-suppressed smile. "Most of these buildings are empty shells?"

"Oh, you too, huh?"

"Great minds think alike. We should probably explore more when we get a chance. It could be useful to have a way to move between buildings. Though we'll have to be careful while we have a shadow."

"Ooh, that sounds so secretive, like we're in an underground movement. I feel like I should get a jaunty beret, like the French Resistance."

"You don't want to tip our hand, do you?" Although his tone was teasing, I noticed that he kept glancing toward the park across from the store, where Mac and his sidekick were in their usual spot, playing chess.

"Should we talk to Mac now?" I asked, following his gaze.

Owen studied them for a long moment, then said, "Let's wait a little while, enough to appear normal. If you seem to come out of Josh's spell and then we're immediately having intense conversations with people we usually just exchange pleasantries with, it would look suspicious."

"You're not getting cold feet about your plan to bravely face the consequences, are you?"

"No, but we should be methodical about this." He frowned in thought for a moment, then said, "Let's take lunch to the park, and I'll challenge him to a game."

"Okay. It's a date, but you can always back out if you change your mind."

"I won't," he said firmly, but he didn't look happy about it.

*

When I went up to the coffee shop, I wasn't sure how to approach Florence. She'd conspired with Josh, and yet she'd steered me toward Owen. I figured if she was playing the sassy best friend role in this romantic comedy, she'd want to squeal over me finally taking her advice and getting together with Mr. Right. I tried to psych myself up into a good morning-after glow as I reached the top of the stairs and headed for the counter.

"Well, look at you!" she said with obviously faked enthusiasm. "Someone's all aglow this morning. Last night must have been spectacular. Let me see the ring."

"There is no ring."

She looked truly stunned. "He didn't propose? Then what's the glow about?"

I had to fight not to smile. "I turned him down."

"You did *what?*" It came out in an outraged-sounding yelp, but her eyes lit up and she was unable to restrain a grin.

I tried to remember how the movie had gone so I could sound convincing, since I figured I'd need a better reason than "the spell broke" to explain why the whammy Josh had apparently put on me hadn't worked. I tied on my apron and straightened the knot to buy myself time to think, then said, "Well, I thought that a lot of my reservations had to do with how unromantic he was the first time he brought up marriage, like it was some chore he was doing to help me. But then when he did the all-out proposal, complete with ring, sparklers, and kneeling, and I *still* felt the same way about him, I knew it was wrong."

She gave up fighting the grin and beamed ear-to-ear. "Even with the sparklers?"

"Yeah, even with the sparklers."

"What did you do next?"

"I left. I can't believe I did it, but he was kneeling on the floor and everyone was watching, and I just said, 'I can't,' and left the restaurant, and I headed straight to the store to catch Owen before he left. You were right. He was the one, and he has been since we met. Everything just clicked with him. It was right."

She leaned forward like she was in the audience at the exciting part of a movie. "And what happened?"

I didn't have to fake a blush. "Well, I told him what I felt, and we kissed, and it turns out he felt the same way, too, and then we went out for a drink and he walked me home."

She used her apron to wipe imaginary tears from her eyes. "Oh, I just love a happy ending."

"Don't make fun of me," I warned.

"I'm not!" Then she gave me a saucy grin. "Did the earth move for you? Did it change the way you saw everything?"

I had to think quickly. Was it just the way she sounded, a friend looking for juicy details, or was she testing me to see if the spell had broken? If the latter, was that so she could help us or so she could report us to her superiors? She seemed truly happy for me, and I doubted that my getting together with Owen was part of the elves' plan, but she could have been playing her role to the hilt. It was too risky to trust her, so I merely smiled and said, "It was nice."

"Nice? That's all you've got to say? Don't let him hear you say that. He'll take it as an insult."

"That's between us. 'Nice' is all you need to know—and don't you *dare* ask him."

"Oh, I'll get it out of you sooner or later," she teased. "But I really am happy for you."

*

In spite of his brave talk about facing Mac head-on, Owen was pale when I met him with sandwiches from our café to take to the park. "Are you sure you want to do this?" I asked.

"No," he admitted, "but I am sure it's the right thing to do. Let's just hope this works and that he's fair about it. I'm sure he will be." I didn't think he sounded too convinced, but he strode across the street like he was on a mission, and it was clear he wasn't going to talk himself out of it or let me do so. I followed him, feeling a lot less confident than he was acting.

Mac and his Council enforcer partner were at their usual table, playing their usual game of chess. I had to wonder what fantasy they were being allowed to live out that they wouldn't want to escape. Sitting in a park and playing chess all day didn't sound like my idea of an ideal life. Then again, living out a bad romantic comedy film hadn't been high on my list, either. It had just been what was on my mind when they'd taken me. Maybe we'd interrupted a good game of chess by going out to dinner that fateful night.

As luck would have it, the park was fairly full and the only spot where we could sit was at the other end of the picnic table where Mac and his buddy were playing. Owen greeted them, then asked, "Do you mind?" as he gestured at the empty end of the table.

Mac nodded and said, "Go ahead."

Owen and I sat and started eating our lunch. We made self-conscious small talk, trying to sound normal and innocent. That's more difficult than I would have thought. You usually don't even think about the things you say when you're having lunch with someone, and you don't care what random semi-strangers might overhear. We chatted for a while about how good the sandwiches were and how we were glad the food in the café had improved. There was some discussion of the changes being made in the store and how they were working. All the while, Owen kept tabs on his target out of the corner of his eye.

He abruptly steered the topic back to food. "The smoked gouda in this sandwich is an interesting choice," he said. "It goes well with the ham."

"It's the bread that gets me," I said, following his lead. "I'm so glad we found that bakery. I'd swear it's right out of the oven." Then I noticed Mac's buddy glancing at our sandwiches as we ate and I thought I knew what Owen was up to. We went on praising the sandwich ingredients, and I then extolled the virtues of the cookies that had been delivered that morning. "It smells like we baked them ourselves," I said. "You know there's chocolate in the house. It's *divine*."

Now the buddy looked like he was about to start drooling. Mac was focused on the game, but he seemed to be stuck, unable to decide what move to make next. Owen glanced over at the board and said helpfully, "That knight has room to move."

Mac blinked, seemed to see what Owen had seen, moved a piece, and not long afterward won his game. His buddy leaned back, stretched, and said, "I think I'm going to take a lunch break. Want to join me?"

"Nah, I brought a lunch."

When the buddy was gone, Owen said, "Would you like a new opponent?"

"Why not?"

Owen threw away the trash from his lunch and took the seat across from Mac. I knew nothing about chess, so what they were doing made no sense to me. Their first few moves went rapidly, with Owen moving a piece and Mac responding immediately, and then Owen moving again, seemingly without even having to think about what to do. Then Mac paused and leaned back, frowning at the board. "I'm having the weirdest sense of déjà vu," he said. "I could swear I've played this exact same game before."

"That's interesting," Owen said mildly. I wondered if he was doing this on purpose, playing a game he'd played before with Mac. "Did you win that one?"

Mac's brow creased, and he said vaguely, "I don't remember."

"Then I guess we should keep playing." Owen indicated the board, and Mac leaned forward to make his move.

The moves went rapidly back and forth again for a while, and then they slowed down as each of them thought about his moves—though I got the feeling Owen was only pretending to think and knew exactly what he was going to do. During one pause, Mac asked, "Who taught you to play chess?"

"My father—foster father, actually, but he was the only father I ever knew. He started teaching me when I was just a kid. That was what we did in the evenings for fun."

I watched Mac carefully to see how he reacted. He rubbed his temples, then he shook his head, like he needed to clear it. "Some fun for a kid," he said, making his move.

"I was a strange kid," Owen said with a shrug. "I thought it was fun. What I really liked when I got a little older was when my parents' friends came over and I got to play against them. I'm not sure they liked it so much, though, being beaten by a scrawny little kid with thick glasses. I had to sit on a phone book to reach the board. I think my father thought that was the fun part, watching his friends react to the way I played." He moved a piece, then said, "Check."

Mac looked like his attention was barely on the game, and he didn't even react to Owen's move. I didn't know anything about chess, but I knew that

Owen's "check" was bad for Mac. He stared at the board for a long time, and I got the impression that he was really seeing a different board from a different game.

Owen went on like he hadn't noticed. "The first time I asked to learn to play, I must have been about five. I'd started kindergarten, but they quickly moved me up because I was bored. I was so little, and those kids were so much bigger than I was, and I kept beating them in everything, so they hated me. I had an older friend who tried to defend me, but my parents were worried we'd get in trouble for fighting, so they got me a dog." He paused as Mac finally made his move, made his own move in response, then continued.

"They figured that the dog would scare off anyone who tried to hurt me on my way to and from school. It was a small town, so no one minded that this dog would walk me to school and then run home, and he always knew when to head back to the school to get me. He must have heard the bell and knew it was time. Anyway, that dog was very protective of me, and one day I was playing in the front yard after school when one of my parents' friends came over. The dog didn't know he was a friend, and I had to call him away. It was probably the first time I'd seen an adult look scared."

Mac froze, his eyes distant, and Owen glanced at me before going on. "Later, the friend and my father were playing chess, and I watched the whole time. I think that made the friend almost too nervous to play because that meant the dog was there, also watching him. After that, I asked my father to teach me to play."

Mac blinked, then whispered, "Owen Palmer?"

"It worked," I murmured under my breath. I'd been kind of hoping it wouldn't, in spite of what big-picture implications that might have had.

"Don't react," Owen said softly to Mac. "We're being watched."

"Watched? By whom? What are you up to, Owen?"

"I'm not up to anything," Owen protested, visibly fighting to keep the appearance of cool. "I'm as much a victim here as you are." He quickly described the situation as we understood it, then asked, "What's the last thing you remember from the real world?"

"You and Katie went into that warehouse, and we followed you. I didn't think it was anything, but McClusky's a hard-liner and didn't want to risk letting anything slide. There was a portal open in there, and then some elves came into the room and grabbed you two. We moved to intervene, and I guess they got us because after that, the next thing I can recall is being here." He paused, looked at Owen, then at me, and said, "Wait a second, altering consciousness ..."

Before Mac got around to connecting the dots on his own, Owen plunged ahead. "Yes, it works on us. Something happened when we destroyed the brooch, and now neither of us is magically immune. In Katie, it's very likely temporary. She's already losing her powers, and that's why the spell seems to have been weaker for her. She fought it, and that allowed her to snap both of us out of it. I'm still not totally certain what it means for me, but I haven't used magic outside the office since then."

"You hid it well," Mac said dryly. "So the elves have us captive, huh? I guess we saw something we weren't supposed to."

"That's what we think. I was hoping you saw more than we did."

"Just a portal. Who else is here?"

"We've seen a few people we know from MSI who'd gone missing," I put in. "There had been a lot of reports of missing elves, so I imagine they're here, too."

"And you say memories break the spell?" Mac asked.

"Bringing up a vivid memory from the real world seems to work," Owen said. "For us, it was an accident that we simultaneously came up with something that reminded us of each other." He turned pink and left out exactly what that something was. "My story from when I was a kid worked for you, so I hope that's all it takes for us to wake up everyone else. You'll have to bring your partner out of it, since you know him best."

"But be careful," I added. "There are people we think might be monitoring us. If they notice we've remembered, they might do something."

"If you're worried about that, then you'd better act natural now," Mac said. "There's a guy across the park who's watching us."

I was facing away from our possible watcher, and my back itched between my shoulder blades at the thought of being observed. It took all my willpower not to turn around to see who it was. I was afraid that even using the compact mirror trick to see behind me would be too obvious. "Is he an elf wearing gray?" I asked.

"Yeah. You've seen him?"

"Even before the spell broke last night, I did something that I shouldn't have been able to do if the spell was working—probably because I'm losing whatever magic I had. They've been following me since then. I'm trying to convince them that one part of the spell may have broken, but the big spell is still okay."

"What do you think they'd do if they knew you'd broken the spell?" Mac asked.

"Probably put us back under it," Owen said with a shrug as he moved a piece on the board. I didn't know enough about chess to know if it was a real move or if he was maintaining the pretense.

Mac frowned. "I'm worried that they're keeping such close tabs on you. We should probably have a contingency plan. I wonder if it would help to write down a memory and then keep it in a place where you're bound to see it, even if you forget who you are again." He moved a piece on the chessboard.

"That's a good idea," Owen said, countering his move. "We should all do that as soon as we can."

Mac nodded acknowledgment and continued authoritatively. "The first step is getting information. We need to find this end of the portal that brought us here. We need to find the boundaries of our prison. It would help if we knew what they're hiding. And then maybe we can find a way to get out or send a warning. If we can revive the people we trust, we can get more done."

"We'll revive the ones we know, and I think they'll know which of the other elves should be on our side," Owen said. I was a little surprised that he didn't resist Mac taking over, but then he'd known Mac since he was a little kid, so it probably seemed natural to Owen to defer to him. "We'll take every opportunity we can to see what else we can learn."

"Okay, then." Mac nodded toward the board. "Finish the game. I'll try not to be a sore loser. I'll deal with McClusky. You want me to tell him all that I know?"

"If we're going to work as a team to get out of here, I think he'll figure it out, so you may as well be up front about it," Owen said wearily.

Mac looked even more somber as he said, "And you know I'll have to report this when we get back."

Owen went a little pale, but he nodded. "Of course. I guess I'll deal with that when we get back." He made a move, then said, "Checkmate."

"And just in time, too," Mac said out loud as McClusky arrived, sipping from a paper coffee cup and nibbling on a giant cookie.

"Did the kid beat you?" McClusky asked.

"It was a good game," Owen said diplomatically.

"You were right about these cookies," McClusky said around a mouthful.

"Come over any time," I said. "You have to try the brownies, too."

"See you around," Mac said with a wave as Owen and I headed toward the store.

When Owen still hadn't commented even after we reached his office and closed the door behind us, I said, "That went well."

"As well as can be expected," he said with a solemn nod.

"What's wrong?"

"Wrong?"

"You don't seem happy."

"We're prisoners with no obvious means of escape and I've just let the magical authorities know that my powers have been back for a while without me telling them. The best-case scenario isn't exactly rosy."

To distract him from his bad mood, I said, "Since it worked to break the spell, I'm going to assume what you said to Mac was true. But did you really have to have a dog to protect you on the way to and from school?"

"The dog wasn't to protect me."

"He wasn't?"

He blushed slightly, a hint that my tactic was working. "The first time the bigger kids got to me, I panicked and lashed out with my powers. I had very little control over them then and didn't even do it consciously. There was no serious harm done—at least, nothing that didn't wear off after a while—but the bullies were in danger until I learned to use my powers. James and Gloria figured that if I had a big dog at my side I wouldn't be frightened, and everyone would be safe."

"Did it work?"

"After a few dog bites. The bullies were kind of slow to learn."

I hated to bring up business again after relaxing him, but we needed a plan. "What next?"

He frowned, thinking, for a moment, then said, "Act as normal as possible. And we should probably avoid talking to anyone else we know is a prisoner for the rest of the day."

"Do you know how hard it is to *act* normal? Just the fact that you're acting keeps it from being normal, by definition. *Nothing* about this situation is normal."

He took my hand and gave it a reassuring squeeze. "Of course it isn't. Maybe a better way to phrase it is 'unchanged.' What would be normal in this scenario?"

"Well, we've just fallen in love and found each other, and we're in romantic comedy world." I tried to remember every sappy movie I'd ever watched with Nita. "I think we're due for a montage where we walk around the city, generally acting like we're in a perfume commercial—stuff like holding hands, acting like you're oblivious to the rest of the world, or else seeing the world in a new way now that you're in love. Doing spontaneous things like buying flowers or getting a street musician to play our song." I felt my face growing warmer as I listed all the things that I'd imagined in those moments that had probably led to me getting stuck in this scenario to begin with. "Talking, laughing, splashing each other in fountains, pausing to kiss in picturesque places."

"That would be the perfect cover for exploring the dimensions of our prison. Good idea, Katie. You may have to cue me, though."

"Oh, come on, you can't be that hopeless," I teased. He sure knew how to burst a girl's romantic bubble.

"I'm not that spontaneous."

"Remember, we're *acting* normal, not *being* normal. And speaking of normal, since we haven't hired someone to replace me in the coffee shop, I'd better get up there. Florence is really grilling me about you, by the way. I think she's working for them."

"Then this is your chance to convince her. But before you go …" He slid a notepad and pen across his desk. "Write down a memory powerful enough to jolt you out of the spell, just in case."

I scribbled a few lines about growing up in Texas, since that was something that hadn't come up in this scenario at all, and put it in my skirt pocket. "See you after work," I said as I left the office.

The gray-suited elf was in the store, lurking among the shelves. I fought to keep my eyes from focusing on him as I passed him on my way to the stairs, then forced myself not to turn around when I heard footsteps behind me.

"Sorry that took so long," I said to Florence when I reached the café. "We've got to hire someone new for the coffee shop so I don't have to juggle this and the assistant manager thing. Owen's already giving me the info dump."

"I bet that's not all he's giving you," she said.

"We just went to lunch and then had a meeting," I protested, willing myself to blush and forcing myself not to look at the gray guy lurking in the background.

"A meeting, hmmm," she said with a smile. "About what?"

"Well, what to do tonight did come up, but otherwise we were talking about progress at the store."

"So, that's what you're calling it these days," she said with a wink. She seemed louder and more cheery than normal, probably because of the gray guy.

I was about to reply when she gasped ever so slightly, then gulped. I turned around to see Josh standing at the top of the stairs. "Awkward!" Florence singsonged under her breath.

CHAPTER ELEVEN

"Oh, no," I moaned. Then I noticed Josh acknowledging the gray guy and realized Josh had to be one of the prison guards. He must have been assigned to watch me. No wonder he'd been keen to keep me close. I must have really messed up his assignment.

Josh came toward the counter, and I clutched its edge until my knuckles went white. "Katie," he said stiffly, then without moving his gaze from me, he said, "Could we get some privacy?"

"Hey, I work here," Florence sassed back at him.

"Over here," I said to Josh, moving away from the counter—but not so far that Florence wouldn't be able to hear if she concentrated hard enough. The gray guy moved with us, and I tried not to look at him. "What is it, Josh?"

"You owe me an explanation," he said.

I couldn't say what I really wanted, so I tried to look contrite as I said, "I'm sorry for leaving you in the lurch like that, but I just couldn't—"

He cut me off. "Couldn't what? Give me an answer?"

"You mean saying 'I can't' and running off wasn't answer enough for you? I thought it was pretty clear. But in case you need it more specifically, no. My answer is no."

"No, you won't marry me, or no, you don't want to be with me?" His tone shifted from angry to gentle. "Because we don't have to get married now. We can take more time to work things out. You not wanting to be engaged doesn't mean we have to break up."

"I mean no to all of the above. I knew it wasn't what I wanted, so I had to get out of there." It sounded weak, but I wasn't sure how I should play this scene. In a romantic comedy scenario, the story dictated that I do something big and dramatic instead of talking about it like a normal person would. In the movies, we didn't get to see Mr. Wrong in the aftermath of the dramatic exit unless something hilariously humiliating that he totally deserved happened to him. We just saw the heroine happy with Mr. Right. Unless …

With a sinking feeling, I realized that this was supposed to be the scene where the heroine reconciled with Mr. Right after making the biggest mistake of her life in ditching him temporarily for Mr. Wrong. If I was still under the spell, I'd realize the error of my ways and apologize, and then we'd have a romantic reunion where all was forgiven. I didn't think I could pull that off.

Instead, I dredged up every scene I could recall of the heroine explaining herself to Mr. Wrong before rushing off to be with Mr. Right. "It was an epiphany," I blurted. "I looked at you there with the ring and the sparklers and the music and all that, and although it was everything I thought I wanted, I knew it wasn't right for me. You were doing the right things, but you just weren't the right guy. You're going to make some lucky girl very happy, but you need to be free to find her." I thought that sounded suitably noble, even if I did have to fight my gag reflex to say it. I didn't hate him like the prison guard that he was. I was giving him up so he'd have a chance to find happiness.

He made a good show of acting distraught, waving his hands in the air and making a pained expression. "Did I do something wrong, something that made you upset?"

"No, you did everything right. It's not you. It's me." I had to bite the inside of my lip to keep from laughing. I didn't think anyone ever actually said that.

"There's someone else, isn't there? Your boss."

"Don't you think it's a bad sign for us if I could be attracted to anyone else?"

He reached for my hand and grabbed it, holding it too tightly for me to pull free without making a scene, and this wasn't supposed to be a scene. I felt the tingle of magic grow around me, and my thoughts went hazy. He was putting the whammy on me again. Was it the little whammy to make me like him or the big one to make me forget who I was? Or would the little one not work without the big one? I desperately tried to hold on to any memories I could of my true self. I remembered kissing Owen, being part of magical battles, working in my family's store back home—all the things that weren't supposed to be a part of this world. My name was Katie Chandler, I was from Cobb, Texas, and I worked for Magic, Spells, and Illusions, Inc. I wasn't part of this world, and I wasn't in love with Josh, or whatever his real name was.

"Come on, baby, how can you resist me?" he purred, making sad eyes at me.

I didn't know about magic, but that was enough to break any spell.

"Seriously?" I asked, raising an eyebrow. "You're resorting to puppy dog eyes? That, right there, is why we're not right for each other. You want a girl you can win stuffed animals for at the fair, and I am *so* not that girl. We don't even have the same idea of what's romantic." For instance, his whole romantic proposal scenario left me cold. I didn't want to be surrounded by strangers for what was supposed to be a private moment. If I knew Owen at all, if he ever did propose, it would just be the two of us there. He wouldn't make a big production out of it.

"So, it's really over, then," he said. "You won't give me another chance?"

Had I ever been this whiny and needy about a breakup? Maybe in high school—at least, I hoped that was the only time. "Yes, it's over. Thank you for the good times, but I think it's best if both of us move on, really. I've got a new job at the store, and I'm really enjoying it here now. I don't need you to take care of me."

Ever so slightly, Josh glanced at the gray guy, and I saw out of the corner of my eye that the gray guy nodded. "Okay, then," Josh said, backing away, but still holding onto my hand. "If that's the way you want it."

It occurred to me that if I'd stuck with Josh while retaining my memories, I might have had a chance to learn something. But I wasn't that good an actress. He'd have probably figured me out before I learned anything useful. "It is the way I want it," I said firmly.

He gave my hand one last squeeze, and I blinked as another wave of magic hit me. I had a moment of haziness, and then my head cleared. "Well, then, have a nice life," he said.

"You, too," I added, smiling fondly. He glanced over his shoulder, like he was looking for someone, but no one was there, and then he left.

As soon as he was gone, Florence exhaled loudly and said, "Good riddance to bad rubbish. If you hadn't sent him away, I would have."

"I guess I should have said something more before I ran off last night," I said sheepishly. "When a guy asks a question like that, you owe him a real answer."

"I can picture him kneeling in that restaurant with you already out the door."

I winced. "How humiliating!"

"Couldn't happen to a nicer guy. Now, let's get this place ready for the afternoon coffee break rush."

The rest of the afternoon, I had the nagging sense that there was something I was forgetting, something I was supposed to do. I must have been pretty obvious about it, since Florence asked me at one point, "Did you leave the iron on, or something?"

"What? Why do you ask that?"

"Because you've got that look."

"Oh. I guess there is something I've forgotten, but I can't remember what it is. I suspect there's some errand I was supposed to run today, but in all the excitement, I've totally forgotten. When my electricity or telephone gets cut off, I suppose I'll know, huh?"

"Ah, new love. It makes fools of us all," she said with a melodramatic sigh, but in spite of her teasing tone, she looked serious.

"Yeah, when you go straight from having one guy propose to realizing you're in love with another guy, it really messes with your mind."

"But in a good way."

I kept that strange feeling the rest of the afternoon. At the end of my shift, Florence told me, "Now, you go down and see that adorable new guy of yours. Do you two have plans for tonight?"

Plans, there had been something about plans, hadn't there? "Just going out to dinner," I said with a shrug. But I couldn't shake the feeling that I'd forgotten something important.

"Well, have a good time, and in case you were wondering, you did the right thing. You made the right choice."

"You're sure?"

"I'm sure. I hope you are."

"Yeah, I guess I'm sure."

"'Guess' and 'sure' don't usually go in the same sentence. But I bet when you see him, you'll know, and there won't be any 'guess' about it."

I hovered in the doorway of Owen's office when I got downstairs, watching him work. His dark hair fell across his forehead as he bent to study the document on his desk, and my fingers itched to go over to him and push it back. He looked so at home in the office cluttered with books and papers. He belonged there, and I belonged with him. Florence was right. Now I was sure.

I rapped lightly on the door frame. "Ready for dinner?" I asked.

"Just a second. I have some things to finish. I do still have a store to run, or at least look like I'm running," he added with a crooked smile. "Come in, and shut the door behind you so we can talk."

"Of course you're running a store," I said as I shut the door. "Why would you need to look like that's what you're doing?"

He glanced up at me then, frowning. "Katie? Is something wrong?"

"Josh showed up, demanding an explanation. That was about as pleasant as you might imagine."

"Josh showed up?" he asked warily.

"Oh, you don't have anything to worry about. I broke up with him definitively. He didn't take it too well. He tried to talk me out of it, but I know he's not right for me."

"Is anything else wrong?"

"Other than that, things are fine, and I think I shouldn't have to worry about him anymore."

"Do you think he knows anything?"

"Well, obviously he knows about us—he'd already figured that out. I didn't think there was any point in hiding it."

Owen got up from his desk and came around to stand next to me. "There's nothing else you think he knows?"

"What is there for him to know? It's not like it's any of his business."

He placed his hand against my cheek and leaned down to kiss me, then straightened and looked at me like he was waiting for something. "Mmm, that was nice," I said. "I hope there's more of that to look forward to this evening."

"Katie …" he said, his voice sounding strained.

"Yeah? What's wrong?"

"Don't you remember the other plans we had for this evening?"

"We talked about dinner. Any other plans remain unspoken or implied, but if you want to spell them out, I'm game."

I didn't understand the alarm in his eyes. I'd never had a guy look that disturbed after a kiss before. Was my breath bad?

"Katie, check your pocket," Owen said, his voice rough with emotion.

"Why?" He was starting to worry me.

"Just, please, do it. Check your pocket."

He sounded so upset that I figured it wasn't worth arguing about. With a shrug, I reached into my pocket and found a folded piece of paper. "Oh, that's probably what I've forgotten," I said as I pulled out the paper. "It must be my to-do list."

When I unfolded the paper, I saw that it was covered with my handwriting, but it wasn't a to-do list, and it wasn't anything I remembered writing. "My brother Dean figured out he was a wizard, and he used his powers to break into all the stores on the Cobb town square," it said. That was not was I was expecting to see, but even so, something clicked in my head, then everything went hazy and cleared again. As soon as my head felt clear, I started shaking violently in the aftershock. I looked at Owen and whispered, "Whew, that was a close call."

"You're okay now?" he asked. "You remember?"

"That we're being held in some wacky elf prison? Yeah, I remember." I sank into the nearest chair before my legs could go out from under me. "It's a good thing you made me write that down. But why didn't the kiss work? Isn't that supposed to be what works in fairy tales? It worked before."

"It may be that our relationship is now the same in both worlds, so it's not enough to do the trick anymore. A memory from your family involving magic was a great idea. It has nothing in common with this reality."

I studied the life-saving piece of paper in my hand. "Do you think I'll need a new one?"

"I hope we don't need it again." Even so, I refolded it and put it back in my pocket. I looked up to see that he was still frowning at me. "I take it Josh really was here?" he asked.

I rubbed at my temples. Snapping out of the spell had given me a headache. "Yes, and it went just like I told you, only he must have hit me with the whammy when I didn't fall under his sway. He seemed convinced I'd give up and go back to him. And maybe I should have."

"What?" It was an outraged yelp.

I hurried to reassure him. "Not for real, but if I pretended to be with him and to ignore you, then he'd never suspect that the spell had broken, and if he's in on it, maybe I could have learned something."

He shook his head. "No, it would have been too hard to stay convincing."

I couldn't help but smile. "Yeah, that's how I rationalized it, too. I'm not sure my stomach is strong enough to pretend to be into that guy. There is one thing I noticed, though. One of those gray guys was watching him, and Josh seemed to consult with him a couple of times. Now I'm sure we're not supposed to be able to see them. When I went back under the spell, I didn't see him there anymore, and I don't think he just vanished. So if you run into one, don't look at him directly. I wonder if the gray suit is a uniform, like the enforcers in black."

"It'll make our lives easier if it is. Do you think Josh will be a problem?"

"Probably not. I still liked you when I was under the spell. I still sent him away after he put me back under the spell. Nothing changed other than knowing who I really am. Maybe they're satisfied that the spell is holding now that he's reinforced it. But I wonder why no one's working on you that way. You're usually the real danger, and they have to know by now that you've got magic back, since this place worked on you."

He frowned. "Maybe it's because you're the one who's resisting and going against their plans, so they know they have to work harder to keep the spell going. If you hadn't resisted their plans for you, I don't think I'd have ever snapped out of it."

"So losing my powers is actually a good thing. That's nice to know." I said it sincerely, but it came out sounding sarcastic. I supposed I had mixed feelings about it.

"Do you feel up to our perfume-commercial recon mission?"

"Should we do it, or should we lie low after that close call?"

"If we do it right, it should look like we're lying low. They'll expect us to go on some kind of date. But you may have to prompt me for what I should do."

We made one last pass through the store and made sure the evening shift was up and going, and then we hurried out the front doors. He surprised me by picking me up with his hands at my waist and spinning me around. I laughed, and then when he set me down, I leaned my head against his shoulder. "I guess you have seen a perfume commercial," I whispered.

"Nope, but I have seen a few movie trailers."

"Good move. Very convincing." Then as I looked over his shoulder, I saw that we weren't alone, and this time it wasn't just an elf in a gray suit. It was McClusky, who was harder to spot without his usual black enforcer uniform. "And it looks like we have an audience," I whispered.

"Another gray guy?"

"No, McClusky. I guess Mac broke the spell on him."

He groaned. "What do they think I'm going to do, try to take over this world with my evil magic?"

"I don't see Mac, so maybe it's just McClusky's paranoia. You don't have anything to hide from him. We're doing what we said we would do."

He let out a deep breath in a long sigh, and I felt his muscles relax ever so slightly before he released his hold on me. He took my hand, and we ambled down the sidewalk. "So, flowers next?" he murmured. At the next corner store, he paused to buy a bouquet, then presented it with a flourish. I didn't have to fake my delight. As cheesy as it was, it was also really nice. I buried my face in the flowers and had to fight off a sneeze when I accidentally inhaled some pollen. The near-sneeze made both of us laugh. I wasn't sure if we were acting out a romantic comedy movie trailer or the opening credits to a television situation comedy.

It sort of killed the mood when Owen then went back into spy mode, whispering in my ear, "Since this neighborhood seems to correspond with the Upper West Side, we shouldn't be able to walk too far across town without reaching the river. By my calculations, we've only got a couple of blocks in this direction before we hit Riverside Park."

"You know just what to say to a girl," I whispered back. I was beginning to fear that we weren't fated to have a time when there *weren't* life-or-death circumstances. I was already cherishing the romantic moments we had before the spell broke.

My heart began beating faster as we neared the next intersection. There was the park across the street, and on the other side of it should have been the river. There wasn't an easy way across the river from this point, so I suspected the river worked as the wall to our prison. The trick would be testing that wall without going for a really nasty swim.

When the light changed, we crossed the street and hurried through the park, attempting a romantic frolic. I tried for a lighthearted giggle, but it came out as more of a mad cackle, so I decided to be romantic in silence. We reached a point where we should have been able to look out over the river, but we kept going through more and more park. "I don't get up to the Upper West Side that much, but is Riverside Park this wide?" I asked.

"Not here, I don't think," Owen said, "but there's something about this that looks familiar."

"I think it's supposed to be Central Park, but it's whatever green space plays Central Park in movies and TV shows that aren't actually filmed in New York."

"Yeah, while I haven't explored every inch of it, this is one of the parts of the park where I've been a lot, and none of this is quite right," he agreed.

We kept walking through the not-Central Park, then suddenly we came out of the park and into the city, as though we were leaving Central Park and heading into the Upper West Side. We stood on the sidewalk with traffic whizzing past us as we tried to get our bearings.

"Okay, that's weird," Owen said. "It's like we're in a loop instead of having clear boundaries. Which makes sense—if we bumped into a barrier, we'd notice it, even if we were under a spell, but while under the spell we might not notice that we keep coming back to the same neighborhood, no matter how long we walk."

"Which means we can't get out of here," I said with a sinking feeling.

CHAPTER TWELVE

"We haven't tried going up or downtown," Owen said, sounding like he was trying to reassure me as much as himself. "Maybe that's where the entrances are."

We crossed the street and kept going, back into the Upper West Side. When we hit the Broadway-like street, we turned and headed up it. As we walked, we paused every so often to look at the menus posted outside restaurants and acted like we were having trouble deciding where to eat. We made it past the street where my apartment was and kept going uptown, but then somewhere around Ninetieth Street we found ourselves back around Lincoln Center—or a vaguely Lincoln Center-ish complex with a fountain in front of it.

Owen proved he'd listened to my description of romantic things to do by giving me a playful splash from the fountain. I played along by squealing and running, but he caught me and pulled me close to him.

"So we've got a prison that's around twenty blocks by maybe four blocks," I said into his ear. "How depressing."

"But it means we have less ground to cover to find that portal." He tensed momentarily, then said loudly, "So, in all that walking, did you find a place you wanted to eat?" I saw an elf in gray lurking nearby and forced myself not to look directly at him. McClusky was also there, but I wasn't worried about him since we weren't up to anything evil.

Leaning against Owen and snuggling under the shelter of his arm, I sighed and said, "Don't hate me for insisting on all that walking to look at every restaurant in the neighborhood, but that first Italian place we saw looks good. It's a nice night. Maybe we can get a seat on the sidewalk."

"Okay, Italian it is."

"But I do have a list of other places I want to try later." I attempted a flirtatious eyelash flutter. "There were a couple of interesting-looking spots for breakfast." His blush made me smile in spite of the tense circumstances.

We got a sidewalk seat at the restaurant, and at first I wished we'd sat inside because Mr. Gray stood on the sidewalk right next to our table—pedestrians moving past him without apparently seeing him—but then I realized that had been Owen's strategy. Sitting outside made it look like we didn't think we had anything to hide, but it meant we were onstage the entire time, playing out the scene of a first real date.

The acting was kind of fun, though, and before long, I was able to make myself forget my role. It was a rare chance for us to have a semi-normal date. Since the elves were probably controlling just about everything and maintaining the illusion that this was a world without magic, the odds were slim that there would be any magical chaos. As long as we could forget Mr. Gray and McClusky, who'd taken an adjacent table, we could enjoy a rare romantic meal with no worries. We leaned on the table and stared into each other's eyes, sipped red wine, fed each other tidbits from our plates, held hands under the table, talked, and laughed.

Conversation was the hard part. We couldn't talk about anything that might give away the fact that we knew who we were, so we couldn't talk about work the way we normally did when we went out. There was the store, of course, but since we'd supposedly met there and spent all day working there together, that was only a starting point for the conversation. Instead, we had to talk about ourselves in a way that Owen and I never really had before, as close as we were—no mention of work, of magic, or of the strange things we'd been going through.

"What did you want to be when you grew up, when you were a kid and before you had to think about practical things?" I asked him.

"I wanted to be a professor, like my dad. I thought that meant reading books all day and talking about them. I was the weird kid who liked doing research in school. What about you?"

"I wanted to work in a business. I didn't really know what that meant, but I wanted to do something where I would wear a nice suit and carry a briefcase to work in an office with a view in the city. I wasn't sure what people like that did all day, other than talk on the phone and sound important, but that was what I wanted."

"Wasn't there anything you liked doing, though?"

"I don't know." This was getting as uncomfortable as it would be on a real date, but if I couldn't talk about it with Owen, I might never work out my career issues. "I never thought about it that way. I was so busy, I didn't have time for things other than school, chores, and helping my parents with the store. I was in the band in school, but I never wanted to be a musician. I liked reading books and seeing movies, but I couldn't think of any jobs doing that. I mostly just liked helping a business run well. This may be why finding the right job for me has been so challenging." That was true in both this reality and in the real world. My real-world struggles may even have provided the fake world's situation. Romantic comedy heroines were seldom on top of the world, doing exactly what they'd always wanted to do.

"But you did have some music in your background. What do you like to listen to?"

I groaned. "This is so embarrassing. Yeah, I played the flute, but I don't really listen to music. I'll have the radio on in the car, but since I don't drive here, I don't listen to music all that much. I'm guessing, based on what you play in the store, that you like jazz."

"Yeah, when I listen to music. I usually prefer silence, but jazz can be restful and complicated at the same time. I don't play music at home very often, but I sometimes like going out to listen to jazz."

"Then we should go do that sometime." That was, if we ever got back home. Or did this world have jazz clubs?

"We should. It's a date." His smile made my heart flutter. I was so used to him that it was easy to forget how cute he was. He was just Owen. Him smiling at me that way reminded me all over again of the first time I'd noticed him, when I'd mentally called him "Mr. Right." This conversation was also showing me how little we knew each other. I knew who he was as a person, having seen him through all kinds of dire situations, but I didn't know any of these basic things about him that usually came out in early dates. We'd already fought a magical battle together before our first date, which made small talk seem beside the point. Now, Mr. Gray's lurking presence was forcing us to go through the "getting to know you" phase.

I took a sip of wine and asked, "What's the best vacation you've ever taken?"

"My parents were very big on educational travel. We went to historical sites and museums in the area and around the world."

"That sounds like your idea of fun."

"It was. But the best one was when my dad was doing research at a museum in England when I was about ten, and he took me with him as his assistant. He treated me like a peer, and though we didn't see much outside the workroom in the bowels of the museum on that trip, it was probably the most fun I've had on a vacation." He grinned. "I bet your vacations were a lot more normal than that."

"We didn't take a lot of vacations when I was a kid. When your family has a business, there isn't much time off, and the summer break was our busy season. We went to San Antonio during Christmas break a few times, and my friends and I did it again during college." There hadn't been many details, and of course no magic, but otherwise my romantic comedy character's background had been a lot like my real one, so I hoped nothing we said raised any red flags for the gray guy.

Owen didn't say anything about taking a vacation together, since supposedly he and I had only just met and that would be rather premature for a first dinner date, but he looked into my eyes and gave me a slight smile, and I knew he was thinking about the way he'd been promising that we'd go on vacation when everything settled down, only it never seemed to.

He drank some wine, then seemed to pull together his courage and asked, "Have you ever been in love before?"

That was a biggie. Being with him had eclipsed everything else I'd experienced, making me reevaluate my past. "Once, when I was in college," I finally answered after taking a big swig of wine. "At least, I thought it was for real. Now, I don't know. But it was really serious at the time. We were talking about getting married when we graduated. And then he met someone else during Christmas break our senior year and changed his mind. He told me when we got back to school for the spring semester, right when I was expecting him to propose."

"Ouch," he said with a wince.

"Yeah. I went through that semester in a fog. Fortunately, I already had almost all the credits I needed to graduate and just had a few classes I needed to focus on. That's the main reason I didn't come to the city when my friends did after graduation. I think a part of me was still hoping he'd come to his senses and want to get back together again, and I wanted to be nearby when he did. Then one day it was like someone flipped a switch, and I suddenly didn't care anymore. It was all gone."

"That was when you came to New York?"

"I was looking for a fresh start, I guess, and I felt like I'd held myself back for too long, so I needed to work overtime to make up for it." I wasn't sure I wanted to know his answer, but I felt it was only fair that I should ask, "And you?"

He studied his plate, pushing the tines of his fork through the sauce. "I don't think so, not really. I did date some in college, but I don't get close to others easily. I might have had feelings, but it was difficult for me to show them, and by the time I got the courage to show or tell someone how I felt, she'd have given up on me and drifted off. That's why it's good we met at work. That way, I had a chance to get comfortable with you before you'd expect me to say or do anything."

"I never imagined someone like you would be into someone like me."

He seemed genuinely surprised. "Really? Why not?"

Embarrassed now, I focused on the piece of bread I was shredding into crumbs. With a shrug, I said, "Because guys generally don't notice me that way, so I don't expect them to, especially not guys who look like you and who are successful. You could have anyone you wanted, so I don't expect you to want me."

The look he gave me nearly stopped my heart with its intensity. "You should see what I see."

It was a good thing I was sitting down or I might have swooned and hit the ground from the way he said that. I was dying to ask what he saw, but that would have been fishing for compliments. I settled for blinking back tears.

Fortunately, he said without prompting, "You're intelligent and perceptive, and you're really lovely in a way that goes straight to your soul. I don't have to worry about you losing your looks because no matter what changes on the outside—the color of your hair, your skin, your size—it won't change your essential loveliness."

Impulsively, I leaned over and kissed him. "And that's why I love you," I whispered. "One of many reasons. But, wow."

He turned bright red and abruptly changed the subject. "Do you want to get dessert?"

"Not now. Maybe we'll stumble across a place that looks good on our way home, and then I'll be hungrier for it." Plus, at the moment my stomach was too busy doing cartwheels of joy for me to imagine eating anything.

We left the restaurant snuggled together, his arm around my shoulders. "I think this has been the best first date I've ever been on," I said. Well, aside from having a creepy audience the whole time, but at least the restaurant didn't burn down and a fight didn't break out. Even better, McClusky seemed to have given up on catching Owen doing something evil and had left after he finished his dinner.

"It was good, wasn't it? We'll have to do it again. Not the first date part. We can't do that again. But another date, yes." He sounded as flustered as I felt.

We walked in the general direction of my apartment, and then at one corner he stopped, turned to face me, and kissed me. Just when I was getting into it, he whispered in my ear, "We must have done a pretty good job of convincing him we're not a danger because our friend is heading in a different direction."

"Time to turn the tables?"

"You're reading my mind."

We lingered a few moments more, then turned and headed down the crosstown street Mr. Gray had taken, keeping far enough behind him that he wouldn't spot us. The streets weren't terribly crowded, but there were enough people out to allow us to blend in, though I wondered if they were real or illusion. Surely there weren't that many people imprisoned here. If they were illusions, would he know the difference between the illusions and us? We might have been more conspicuous than we thought.

But he didn't seem to notice us as he turned to go uptown. We were getting close to the prison's boundaries, where we'd looped back to Lincoln Center, but he didn't slow down. At the last crosstown street, he turned again and headed into a tiny park on the corner, one of those Manhattan pocket parks filling the gap where a building once had been. There was a tall fence around the park and a gate that closed and locked behind him.

"Maybe this is the way out," I said, grasping Owen's arm.

We hurried to the gate. Owen made short work of the lock, and then we slipped into the park. The gateway to the park was approximately at the prison's boundary, but we didn't find ourselves back in Lincoln Center. We were in a park that should have been barely the size of a single brownstone, but instead it was a vast, lush garden. It was as dark in there as it had been in the city, the trees casting mysterious shadows.

"This must be where their entry point is," Owen breathed. "We're in the elven realms now, their more natural state."

"You mean, this is the prison gate? The way out?"

"The way out into the elven realms," he specified.

"But wouldn't that be where the portal is?"

"Presumably, but I don't think they'll let us just wander around until we find it." As if to prove him right, we came out of a stand of trees and nearly ran into a bunch of the gray guys, who seemed to be having a meeting. I felt a slight tingle of magic as Owen must have veiled us just in time before any of them turned our way. We scuttled behind some bushes, then crept our way to the park entrance, staying hidden as more gray guys joined the meeting.

Only when we were safely on the other side of the gate and well away from that block did either of us breathe normally again. "Okay, that was a close call," I said with deep feeling.

"Yes, but worth it. We seem to have found the way out of the prison and into the elven lands, and maybe that was a guard shift change meeting."

"Does that do us much good?"

He shrugged. "It's information, and the more we have, the better. We know a spot we should probably watch, and if that was a shift change, then that's a possible weak spot in their schedule that we might be able to exploit. I'll have to report this to Mac in the morning."

He took my arm and we started heading for my apartment. "Are you okay with reporting to him?" I asked.

"Why shouldn't I be? He works at the Council level, so he outranks me, and he's more experienced at this kind of thing—not that anyone's really experienced at being held prisoner in another realm, but I'm mostly a laboratory guy. And I think everyone else will be more comfortable with someone other than me in charge. I'll probably come out of this better if I'm a good little soldier instead of trying to be a general. It's a chance for me to maybe earn some trust."

I squeezed his arm. "It'll be okay, I'm sure. Anyone who really knows you has to know you're not even remotely evil."

He didn't say anything else until he kissed me good night at my front steps, and I got the feeling he'd be up late thinking and planning—or worrying. As tired as I was, I didn't go to bed until I'd written out a few more memories and stashed them in places I was sure to run across them but where no one else was likely to see them, just in case they searched my place when I wasn't there.

*

The next morning, Owen and I had agreed to meet for breakfast at Perdita's diner so we could talk before we went to the store, where we seemed to be under tighter surveillance. The gray guy wasn't outside my apartment, so we must have convinced him—or bored him to death—on our date the night before. I arrived first. "Your usual?" the still-enchanted Perdita greeted me.

"No, Perry, I need breakfast this morning."

"Then have a seat." She gestured toward a nearby table.

Owen joined me a few minutes later. When I looked across the table at him, a memory struck me. "It was you that first morning, saving me from one of Perdita's spills, wasn't it? I should have known then. You'd think that would have snapped me out of it immediately."

"Yeah, it was me, and I should have known, too. There was just something about you. It reminded me of when I first saw you for real." We both kept our voices low as we talked, since we had no idea who among us might be the guards assigned to keep an eye on us instead of other prisoners or part of the scenery.

"That's what it was like for you?"

"Yeah, it was."

"Oh," I breathed. "Because time sort of seemed to come to a halt for me, like there was nothing else in the universe."

"Yep, that was it."

I got a lump in my throat. "Really?"

"Yeah, really. That's why I could barely talk to you when Rod and I met you for that interview. I felt like I was finally meeting my celebrity crush, and I was terrified of making a fool of myself."

I gazed at him with an adoring smile, warm from the sensation of falling in love all over again. I could thank the elves for that much.

Perdita came over to pour us coffee and take our orders. She glanced at Owen, then at me, then back at Owen, then she grinned and said, "So, you did listen to Florence."

"Yeah, I did," I said.

"Good. I'm glad. Now, I'll have these out in a moment for you."

When she was gone, I whispered to Owen, "I thought she was on the verge of something there."

"It's probably best not to snap her out of it in public. We don't know who might be watching."

"Are we sure we want to snap her out of it at all? She's not very good at being stealthy. She makes a great diversion, but she can't hide what she's thinking."

"But she knows everyone. She'd probably have access to half the prisoners here."

"Then we should save her for when we want numbers. Right now, we need information."

He nodded. "That's a good point. If we break the spell on her too soon, everyone will know about it."

Perdita returned a moment later to refill our coffee. "Your breakfast should be ready in a sec." With a smile, she added, "I'm so glad you listened to Florence. You two just seem right together, you know?" She started pouring coffee into my mug, and then she frowned and blinked. Coffee spilled over the rim of my mug as she gaped at me.

And then she snapped out of whatever wonderland she'd zoned off to and jumped out of the way, the coffee carafe slipping out of her hand and shattering on the floor. "Oh, sorry Miss–I mean Katie. Let me clean that up for you." But instead of reaching for the towel tucked into her apron, she waved her hand and made the coffee disappear from the table. That seemed to finally sink in, and she gasped and blurted, "Katie, Owen, what's going on here?"

So much for breaking the spell only in private or for not bringing Perdita in until we knew more. This was a rather spectacular display of spell-breaking. I was sure that everyone had turned to look when the carafe broke. I just hoped they hadn't seen her magic away the spilled coffee.

Owen reacted while I was still thinking. He leapt out of his seat and caught Perdita like he was afraid she'd faint, then moved her to his seat. "Take deep breaths," he told her loudly enough for those around us to hear.

Another waitress rushed over to see what happened and called out for a busboy to come clean up the broken carafe and the remains of the coffee. "Are you okay?" she asked Perdita.

I jumped in before Perdita could answer. "She probably needs some fresh air. I'll take her outside." I got up and went over to her, took her by the hand, and said firmly, "Come on, Perry, let's go outside for a second."

She looked up at me, opened her mouth to speak, then saw the expression on my face and let me lead her out of the diner. As soon as we were outside, she gasped, "What is this place? What's happening?"

"Hush!" I urged, glancing around to see if anyone was watching or listening before I briefed her. "Seeing Owen and me together must have broken the spell for you," I concluded.

"Oh my God! What do we do? How do we get home? My mom will be so worried. That is, if she isn't here, too. What if they took my family because I showed you that flyer?" She sounded so hysterical I worried that I'd have to slap her out of it.

Instead, I grabbed her shoulders firmly and said, "Calm down! If they know the spell's broken, they may try to hit us again with it, and then we may not be able to break it. What's the last thing you remember before you ended up here?"

"I was on my way home from work. I got into the vestibule of my building, and then nothing. I was suddenly working in a diner, only I thought that was where I'd always been."

"Don't worry, if you don't recall running into your family here, they probably aren't here," I said, as gently as I could in this urgent situation. "This seems to be a pretty small world. You have to go on playing your role, pretending that nothing has changed. Can you do that?"

"But I'm a terrible waitress. I'm so clumsy."

I couldn't fight back a wry smile. "That actually hasn't changed here."

She stopped hyperventilating. "Oh. Yeah, you're right. I *have* been a terrible waitress. Why did they make me a waitress?"

"I don't know. I don't know why they did half of what they did. Have you ever thought about being a waitress?"

"I've sometimes thought that would be where I ended up if I screwed up another job, and then I'd be even worse at being a waitress than I was at anything else. And I was worried that if the elves and the wizards stopped dealing with each other, I'd lose my job."

"Well, that's apparently where your subconscious placed you in this world. The elves *are* up to something, but here, all the prisoners are on the same team, wizard or elf. For now, though, you have to go on like nothing is different. Assume everyone around you is in on it until we know more and can come up with a plan. Can you do that?"

"There are so many people here that I know!"

"Yeah, that's what I figured, and we'll take care of them when we know more. But just go on for now, okay?"

She took a few deep breaths, then nodded. "Okay. I can do this."

I patted her on the shoulder. "I know you can. Now, are you ready to go back inside?"

"I guess. Your breakfast is probably ready."

Back in the diner, the floor had been cleaned and the other waitress had put our meals on the table. "You okay?" she asked Perdita.

"Yeah. I don't know what came over me." She grinned and added, "Maybe all the grease I've inhaled in here just came out of my pores and made that coffeepot slip out of my hand. Sorry about that, Katie, Owen."

"No problem," Owen said with a thin smile.

When the diner staff had left us to our meals, he whispered, "How did it go?"

"She's freaked out, but I gave her the scoop. Now I just guess we'll have to see if she can pull it off."

"Maybe I should enchant her," he mused.

"Let's see what she does. She does know a lot of people and could be helpful for passing messages here. I don't see any of the gray guys." I groaned. "And I forgot to warn her about them."

"If you warned her, she'd pay more attention to them."

"Good point. And now we know just how tenuous that spell can be. All it took for her was seeing us together."

Perdita seemed to be pulling off the deception as we finished breakfast. She didn't do any obviously amateur stuff like winking at us. Her persona here was close enough to her real self that there weren't any obvious differences. If she could just remember not to use magic, I thought she'd be okay.

And if not, she'd blow the whole thing wide open.

CHAPTER THIRTEEN

Mac and McClusky were at their usual spot in the park when we arrived at the store. Owen winced and said, "I'd better report on what we found and what's happened."

"Do you have to?"

"I don't want to give them anything they might take as a danger sign, like withholding information, and I don't know how much McClusky saw. Maybe if what I say matches what he saw, he'll relax a little." He ambled over, with me in tow, to watch the game in progress. McClusky's suspicious glare told me he still wasn't convinced about Owen.

"We may have found the way into the elven realms last night," Owen said softly.

Both Mac and McClusky looked up sharply. "Instead of there being barriers, the neighborhood loops back on itself," Owen explained, "but we followed one of the gray guys to a park at the boundary, and it was bigger than the boundaries. There were a lot of those gray elves gathered there."

"But you didn't find the portal itself?" McClusky asked, nudging one of his pieces onto a different square.

"I thought the chances were slim that we'd be able to get anywhere near it, you know, with all those guards present." A little bitter sarcasm slipped through in his tone, but I still thought Owen was showing admirable restraint in not ratting McClusky out for following us—or in not socking him in the jaw.

"Owen's right, I can't imagine that they don't have the portal heavily guarded and warded. I doubt we'd be able to just get away that way," Mac said. "But I'm thinking there's more of us in here than of them. They're counting on us not fighting back or trying to escape. If we get enough people snapped out of the spell and working together, we might be able to overwhelm them and force them to let us go. Start reviving people, but keep it quiet, and make sure they keep it quiet. We'll operate as cells for now. Each person should only know those he revived, not anything beyond that. Unless you broke the spell on someone, assume in all interactions that the person is still bewitched."

Owen stiffened, like he was about to protest, and I could tell from the look in his eyes that he didn't agree with this plan at all. But then he nodded acknowledgment and slapped Mac on the back, as though congratulating him on the game, before we headed for the store.

Once we were in Owen's office, I said, "You don't think overtaking the guards is the best plan, do you?"

"I don't see how it can work. Even if we're in charge, they can keep us here indefinitely if we can't get to the portal."

"What are you going to do?"

"Keep trying to find a way out that doesn't involve violence. If I can do that before Mac plans his prison riot, then things won't have to get ugly. I doubt the elf prisoners will go along with that plan, anyway. It would mean turning on their own people, and no matter how unhappy they are with Sylvester's regime, I don't see them going after other elves unless they absolutely have to, or trusting any plan put together by wizards. Remember how Earl had to be deep under the influence of the Eye of the Moon before he was willing to attack Sylvester."

"Speaking of Earl, should we snap him out of it now?" I asked.

"Might as well."

He called Earl into his office for a meeting, presumably to discuss how to market his section. As Earl sat in front of Owen's desk and discussed which series was most popular, I studied him, trying to recall everything I could about working with him. He'd been given a human illusion, so he looked different from the Earl I knew, and that made it harder to dredge up anything that would trigger a memory.

Then I got an idea. "We should come up with a logo to brand our fantasy section," I said. "That treasure hunt was so successful, I thought we could take it a step further and create a logo that looks like an enchanted object, and do a broader treasure hunt for that kind of object—maybe something Celtic-looking."

Owen immediately picked up on where I was going with it, grabbed a notepad and a marker and drew a reasonable facsimile of the Knot of Arnhold merged with the Eye of the Moon, the enchanted brooch we'd been looking for when we met Earl, who was on the same quest. "Something like this," he said, turning the notepad to face Earl.

Earl got a funny look on his face, like he was trying to dredge up some distant memory, and I moved in for the kill. "We could build a narrative around it, like the brooch itself is an ancient elven object that gives the wearer invulnerability."

"We could call it the Knot of Arnhold," Owen put in.

"But it's been lost for centuries, and then it reappears, but it's been merged with an equally legendary gem that gives its owner great power."

"Call that the Eye of the Moon," Owen said.

"And now the brooch has been lost. Whoever owns it could rule the world—after starting a lot of wars. There's a great quest to seek it, but are the seekers looking to use the brooch for their own gain or to destroy it and save the world?"

Earl sat there, looking stunned. His eyes glazed over. I leaned toward him and whispered, "Shut up, Earl." That had been what Sylvester and his cronies used to say to Earl all the time when Earl was working in the Elf Lord's court.

Earl jumped out of his seat, shouting, "Sylvester's opened a portal to the elven realms! We have to stop him!" After his outburst, Earl stood panting for a moment, then he blinked and looked around the office, at Owen, and at me. He blinked again, then said shakily, "Are you who I think you are?"

"Who do you think we are?" Owen asked.

"You're Katie and Owen, but you're not people I know from working in a bookstore. You're wizards with MSI. All of this is wrong." He sank back into his chair like his legs had just gone out from under him. "What is this place?"

"It's some kind of containment zone in the elven lands. I guess you saw something they didn't want you to see."

Earl rubbed his temples with his thumbs and shook his head a few times, like he was trying to clear out the cobwebs. "Yeah, I followed one of Sylvester's men to the warehouse, and I found the portal there. They've got a steady connection to the elven realms. Our people have supposedly been cut off from there for ages. I tried calling you, but I guess they got to me first. We didn't talk, did we?"

"I got the call, but there was no one there," Owen said.

"How did you two end up here?"

"I got the photo you sent, and then we found that same warehouse."

Earl nodded. "Now that I think about it, there are a lot of our people here. This must be where everyone goes when they disappear." He grinned suddenly. "As prisons go, this one doesn't suck. It was almost like being on vacation. I was getting paid to talk about science fiction and fantasy books. But how do we get of here?"

"That's the part we're working on," I said.

"What we're trying to do for now is get everyone snapped out of the spell," Owen added.

"Without tipping off the guards," I put in.

"The guards?"

"It's probably a safe bet that anyone you run into here that you don't know from MSI or from your elf underground is working for Sylvester to keep us here and docile," I explained. "You may also see people who actually look like elves. They wear gray suits and seem to be in charge, but you don't see them at all when you're under the spell. Try to ignore them. We don't want them to know that we've broken the spell, so it's very important that you act as normally as possible."

Earl's eyes widened with worry. "Oh, yeah, there's no telling what Sylvester would do to us if he knew we were on to him."

"It looks like a strong memory from the real world works to break the spell," Owen said. "If you run into someone you know, try to get them alone and then start talking about something that will trigger them, then explain all this."

"That 'alone' thing is very important," I added. "You don't want someone snapping out of it and reacting visibly when one of Sylvester's people might be looking. If one person tips them off, we might all be in danger. And don't do too many in a row. If you spend the day meeting up with all the people you knew back home, it might look obvious. Work gradually, and try to make the situations look as natural as possible."

"Also, we're trying to keep this in cells, so if one group is discovered it might not lead to everyone, so once you revive someone, that person shouldn't tell you who else he's reviving," Owen said.

"Okay, got it," Earl said, nodding. And then his eyes narrowed. "Hey, wait a second, if we've been under a spell, how did you two end up here? I thought you were magically immune."

Owen blushed slightly. "Remember when the brooch was destroyed and we got caught in the backlash? It seems to have rebooted me, and it gave Katie a dose of magic."

"I'm only a temporary and not very good wizard," I said.

"You were good, you had a real knack," Owen argued. "You just have a shortage of power to draw upon."

"Oh, okay," Earl said, taking it in stride. "Am I supposed to keep that a secret?"

"I think they already know," Owen said dryly.

When he'd gone back to the sales floor, I said to Owen, "Between Mac, Perdita, and Earl, I think we've found that there's a way to snap people out of it without kissing them."

His lips twitched with a slight smile even though his eyes looked troubled. "I don't think that would work for everyone, only the people who'd remember kissing you."

"Which would narrow it down significantly, to just you," I said. "Which is fine by me. And now it's time to get back to my pretend job."

Except I didn't go up to the coffee shop. Owen might not have been willing to go against Mac's bad plan, but I wasn't bound by the same constraints. I headed to the science fiction section to talk to Earl. He jumped in surprise when I came up behind him. "Katie, what is it?" he asked, then added in a softer voice, "Is this bookstore business or, you know, other business?"

"Other business." I glanced around to make sure no one else was in earshot—especially not Owen—then said softly, "I need to talk to you about something that Owen can't say to you." My heart was racing, and I felt more nervous about being caught by Owen than by the guards, but I forced myself to forge onward. "You know the wizards are going to be suspicious about him having his powers back, and the Council enforcers who've been following him got zapped here, too. He's working with them in a show of good faith, and he's letting them take the lead. The instructions he gave you are from the Council guys and part of a plan that Owen doesn't agree with."

Earl stiffened. "The wizards are taking the lead on an elven matter in elven lands?"

"Yeah, that's pretty much how I figured your people would react. I think that's what Owen expects, too, but he's in a difficult position. If he goes against them, they'll think he's a dangerous rebel."

"But if the elves resist, then we're just being elves."

I grinned and patted him on the shoulder. "Exactly! I don't know who the elves would want leading the way, but be on the lookout for a leader who makes sense as you go around figuring out who's here. It would be nice if we could remind everyone that while we're prisoners, we're all on the same team, but I'll settle for not doing something really stupid that doesn't take the real situation into account. And, of course, don't tell Owen I said anything to you. Please."

"You can count on me. Thanks for letting me know."

*

I didn't see any lurking men in gray when we left the store after work, but there was no guarantee that none of the other people milling around weren't among our captors, so we put on the usual act of discussing where to have dinner and then wandering until we found a place we could agree on. Unfortunately, the gateway park wasn't near any restaurants, so we didn't have an excuse to just wander by there. We settled for stopping by an ice cream shop after eating dinner and then walking as we enjoyed our ice cream. That seemed like the sort of thing a newly-in-love couple might do.

"So, what's the plan?" I murmured to Owen when we were about a block away. "See if we can get in before the shift change and the meeting and then find the portal?"

"Too risky," he said after catching a drip off his cone with his tongue. "I want to know a lot more before I try going in again. However, I have an idea for surveillance. Do you think they'd put any of the prisoners in an apartment across from their gateway?"

"No, but it would be a good place to house guards."

He nearly tripped over his own feet. "I hadn't thought of that."

"The whole building probably isn't occupied," I hurried to reassure him. "We should be able to find a vantage point for watching the park. That was your plan, wasn't it?"

"Yeah, something like that."

At the end of the block where the park was, we made sure no one was following us, then tried the door at the top of the first set of steps. Owen unlocked it magically, and we found that the entry lobby appeared fully furnished. When we squinted at the upper landing, it seemed less detailed. We headed up there and found that it looked a lot like the backdrop of a stage set. Even the small table on the landing was just an image painted onto the wall. The door on that landing was unlocked.

Past the doorway was blank space like I'd found above my apartment, open through to the end of the building, without interior walls. We picked our way across, walking on the floor beams. When we were across the street from the park, we settled down to watch.

We were about half an hour earlier than we'd been the day before, but soon the gray elves began arriving at the park. They came in ones and twos, but never more than that. I kept a running count. When the flow had trickled off and then ceased, I said, "I counted twenty."

"They started arriving around eight thirty. Do you think you can wait around a while longer?"

Perching on the narrow beam wasn't very comfortable, but I said, "Of course. Let's see how long the meeting lasts and how many come out."

Things were quiet for the next twenty minutes. No one came down this street, which meant we'd have to be really careful when we left. It didn't seem like this was a place we could get away with randomly wandering into too many times. Finally, gray elves began emerging from the park. "I counted eighteen this time," I said. "But I couldn't tell if they were the same ones or different ones. They may as well be clones. And since we're not supposed to be able to see them, we can't exactly pull the 'accidentally spilling ink on him' trick to tell them apart."

Just then, the exterior door downstairs slammed shut, and we both froze. Another door inside the building then opened and closed. It sounded like someone had gone into the apartment immediately below us.

We froze. Meeting each other's eyes, we silently agreed to wait and see if anyone left. Several long moments went by without any sound of doors opening or closing. Sounds of muffled conversation came from downstairs. Did that mean someone had been below us the whole time? We'd spoken very softly and hadn't moved much, and no one had come up to check things out, so I hoped that meant they hadn't noticed anything.

Owen began inching across a beam, and he gestured for me to follow him. It was fully night now, and while there was some light from the streetlamps outside, it was still pretty dark inside, which made it hard to see our footing on the open beams. The last thing we needed was to put a foot through the plaster into the apartment below.

There were apartments below us the whole way across, so we moved with painstaking care. We could walk upright between windows but had to drop to hands and knees while crossing windows, in case there was someone watching from outside. I thought it likely that there would be illusions in the windows making it look like normal life was going on in normal apartments, but we couldn't confirm it, so we didn't take any chances.

By the time we reached the far end of the building, my legs were cramping and my knees felt bruised. Out on the landing, we brushed the dust off ourselves and straightened our clothes. When we got downstairs, Owen made sure the way was clear before we left the building and hurried around the corner toward the more populated areas.

We passed a couple of the gray guys, but they didn't seem to pay us any particular attention. "Are you going to report all this to Mac?" I asked Owen.

"I have to," he said with a helpless shrug. "If I'm ever going to have any kind of life, I have to convince him to trust me, which means no secrets."

He didn't sound at all enthusiastic about it. "You're worried about Mac's plan."

"I think it will expose all of us and risk getting us all put under the spell again. And that's the best-case scenario. It could also get people hurt or killed."

"But you don't dare argue with him for fear of looking like you're taking over, which naturally leads to taking over the world using bad magic."

"Not that he'd listen to me even if he did trust me. I think he still sees me as a five-year-old."

"What would you do if you were in charge?"

"I'd work closely with the elves. Maybe one of them could switch out with one of the gray guys and get inside for some recon—maybe even find the portal and get through. We're at a disadvantage while we're here in the elven lands, so I think the key is to get help from the other side."

"But anyone approaching from the other side is likely to find themselves here."

"That's why we need to get someone through who looks like an insider."

"Earl's too well-known," I mused, "but maybe someone he knows might be able to pull it off." I contemplated telling him that I already had Earl working the elf angle, but I figured Owen was safest if he had plausible deniability.

Not that I liked having secrets from Owen. In fact, I was a little worried about how he'd take it. That wasn't enough, however, to deter me from doing what had to be done to get all of us home without Owen having to defy the Council.

Since it had been my habit while under the spell, I figured it was safe to keep stopping off at Perdita's diner on my way to work. When she saw me the next morning, she rushed over to me. "I used to go out with the guy who delivers our supplies," she whispered. "I think he might be in the underground—he was very political. And then there's a guy who comes in at least once a day who's going out with my best friend's sister. I don't know where he stands, but if he's here, he's probably on our side, right? So, what do I do?"

"Have you ever kissed either of them?"

She blushed slightly and coiled a ringlet around one finger. "Both, actually."

"Give that a shot."

"Oh, like in the fairy tales?"

I started to explain about cognitive dissonance, then remembered who I was dealing with. "Yeah, like that. But be careful. Make sure you're alone, and then explain it and have them revive anyone else they know and trust." I hoped that if her ex was with the underground, he'd know how resistance cells worked, because I really didn't want to try to explain that to Perdita.

"By kissing them?"

"Talking about your life back home works, too. Kissing's just quicker if you had that kind of relationship there but don't have it here. Anything that brings back strong memories."

"Okay, got it, thanks," she said a bit too enthusiastically, then dashed off before I could order my coffee.

After I'd ordered and received my coffee from another waitress, I left the coffee shop and nearly ran into Perdita kissing someone in a delivery uniform. She gave me a thumbs-up behind his back. It looked like we had one more member on our team.

Owen was sitting with Mac in the park when I approached the store. I thought about joining them, then decided that varying our routine a little not only wouldn't look suspicious but might help keep our guards guessing. Besides, I wasn't sure I could keep a straight face now that I knew things that Owen didn't.

Earl caught me as I entered the store. "I've got three more of us," he said. "None of them know any more than I do, though. They were political enemies Sylvester wanted out of the way."

119

"Good job," I told him.

"And one of them's a leader in the underground. He wants to meet with the wizards."

That was potentially awkward. Then again, reviving Earl and getting him started on the others had been part of the official plan. "You should tell Owen," I said. "He'll be in soon."

I went upstairs and hoped Florence didn't pry too deeply into my love life. She was surprisingly quiet this morning, though. Either she'd given up on getting anything interesting out of me or she was giving it a rest. She merely teased me a few times about Owen. I wished I knew where she stood, but I couldn't think of a way to probe without giving myself away.

During the midmorning coffee break rush, I looked up from making lattes to see someone who looked vaguely familiar. I wondered if it might be someone I knew as an elf but didn't recognize in human mode. He didn't seem to recognize me and gave me no subtle signals that he was in on any secrets, so I figured he wasn't one of Perdita's or Earl's converts. The tricky thing about recognizing people here was that not only were they likely disguised, but they were also out of context. He could be someone I saw in the halls at work every day who was a total stranger in an Upper West Side bookstore—and I'd have had the same trouble recognizing him in a real Upper West Side bookstore.

While I made his latte, I mentally ran through all the people I knew at MSI, and I still came up blank. It was an hour later as I was making a fresh pot of coffee that I blurted, "Dan!"

Florence turned to me. "Are you okay?"

"Yeah, why?"

"You just blurted what for you is a pretty harsh curse. Did you burn yourself?"

"No," I said. Then I realized what she'd thought I said and decided to go with it to cover my mistake. "I just spilled something. Sorry."

"You don't have to apologize. I have no delicate sensibilities to offend, since I'm not from the Victorian era. You can even say 'damn' on TV."

"Maybe I should have said, 'Egad!'" I joked. But I was pretty sure that the guy who'd bought coffee was Dan, the new security guy who'd posed as a bicycle messenger in the sting to catch the elf gang.

After the rush, I took off my apron and headed downstairs to see what assistant-manager stuff I needed to do. We had to at least pretend to keep the bookstore running so we wouldn't look suspicious, and that was a full-time job even without worrying about planning a prison break. I couldn't believe that not too long ago I'd been complaining about being bored in my job.

Owen and I finally got a spare moment to meet in his office. As soon as we were alone, I asked, "Do you remember Dan, the new guy in security?"

"Vaguely. He played the bicycle messenger, didn't he?"

"Yeah. He was here for coffee today, so I guess he got caught investigating—maybe looking for us, so he might know more than we do. I hope he comes back, but I don't know how to break the spell on him if he does. Do you know anything about him?"

"I didn't even remember his name. Mac might know him. Our security and the enforcers work pretty closely." He paused, frowned, then said, "And speaking of Mac, Earl just told me the elves want a meeting with him. Well, technically, they want to meet with the wizards, but he's in charge."

"What are you going to do?" I asked, trying to act like this was news to me.

He shrugged. "Pass on the message. Mac's not going to like it, though. He'll see it as a challenge to his authority, and it is—probably one he'll lose, since wizards are vastly outnumbered here."

Cringing, I said, "They may be even more outnumbered. Perdita has recognized people and started breaking the spell."

He grinned. "I guess she's our wild card." The grin faded quickly, and he said much more soberly, "I'll talk to Mac after work." With a weary sigh and an attempt at a smile, he added, "At least I'm improving my chess game. James should be pleased when we get back."

I was surprised that the look in his eyes said, "*If* we get back."

CHAPTER FOURTEEN

When Owen went to talk to Mac, I came along for support. I didn't think Owen would so much as say a snarky word in his own defense, so he needed backup. I tried to feign interest in the game they started playing before they got down to business, but my attention was more on the gray guy nearby. I couldn't tell if he was merely standing guard at his assigned post near the park and bookstore or if he was specifically watching us. It was hard to see where his eyes focused when I had to keep my eyes from focusing on him.

"We've been breaking the spell on the people we know," Owen began, "and they're doing the same for their contacts. But it turns out that some of the leaders of the elf underground are here, and they want to meet with you to discuss strategy."

Mac made a move on the board before saying, "What's to discuss? I've got a plan."

Wincing, Owen said, "I think they want to brief you on *their* plan."

"Why should we care?" McClusky asked.

"It is their world, and I think they have the majority here, since this seems to be Sylvester's elf Siberia," I said.

"I have no idea what they're planning, but we ought to stay in the loop," Owen said.

"Won't a meeting between heads of different factions of prisoners be noticed?" McClusky asked with a scowl.

"It depends on where we meet," Owen said. "Most of the buildings are uninhabited. They only seem to have bothered finishing the apartments that are actually in use by either captives or guards. That leaves a lot of space that's just for show on the outside and wide open inside. You can enter at one end of a block and make it all the way down the block in some places. That means people can come in from various doors. It should look less like a meeting then."

Mac nodded. "Okay, then. Say, tomorrow night at eleven. Tell us where to enter and where to go."

"You're leaving that up to him?" McClusky protested.

"Oh, didn't we tell you, Owen's evil scheme is to wipe out you and the elf leaders so he can become the grand overlord of these few blocks of fake New York," I shot back without thinking. As soon as I realized what I'd said, I bit my lip in contrition.

Much to my relief, Mac chuckled. "She's right. There's no point in getting silly about this. He wants to get home as much as we do. Pass on the message, son, then let us know where you need us to go. You two will be there, of course."

"Us?" Owen asked.

"We *are* outnumbered. I want to have as many wizards there as they have elves."

*

We went out to dinner, maintaining our usual pattern, though Owen didn't even try to pretend like he was on a date in a new relationship. As a matter of fact, this was starting to feel normal for me—us in the midst of a crisis and him distracted by it. I totally understood the distraction, but I did find myself looking back with nostalgia at those enchanted days when we hadn't known what was going on.

"What's up?" I asked when he was unusually silent and distant for a while.

He smiled wryly. "How much time do you have? I'm just trying to think of a way to deal with this that doesn't put me in the middle of an elves versus wizards dispute. I'm not even sure where I stand with the elves. They may be more suspicious of me than the wizards are."

"You might be surprised," I said. "I put Perdita on the case months ago. There were some initial rumors, but she's been countering all of them, and when she spreads something, it goes far and wide. She's got a better reach than CNN."

"So they probably won't elect me their new leader—which is good—but they're not expecting me to try to take over the world." He sighed then. "But since apparently McClusky does think I'm pulling some grand scheme, the fact that they don't hate me on sight will look very suspicious."

"Sorry for butting in earlier, by the way."

"Don't worry about it. I don't think it makes much difference, one way or another. I could get myself killed while pushing his grandmother out of the way of a speeding car, and he'd find it very suspicious that I bruised her."

If he was making dark jokes, then I figured his funk wasn't too deep. To prevent him from sinking back, I said, "Do you have any ideas for a meeting location?"

"I'm trying to decide if we should go for a building near the store, where several of us have regular reason to be, or maybe near where one of us lives. Or should we stay entirely away from anything associated with us?"

"We'll also need to be careful to avoid any space on top of an occupied apartment."

"I was thinking of finding an empty basement, if there is such a thing."

"Oh, good thinking. Then there'd be a floor."

"Are you up for a scouting mission?" he asked with a mischievous smile.

"What do you think?"

We dropped back by the store after dinner so he could check on some things, then we headed toward my place. On the block before we reached my building, Owen glanced around for followers, then led me up the front steps and magicked the front door open. Once we were inside, we found a narrow staircase behind the main stairs, leading down into a basement utility area. Or, where one might have been in a real building. It seemed as though the utilities here were all magical, so there was no need for boiler or furnace. That meant the utility room was one of those blank spaces, and it led into a much larger blank space that filled the basement. "Bingo!" I said.

"This should do the trick," he agreed. "The windows are even mostly blocked, so light shouldn't be visible outside. Now we just need to find multiple entry points."

We determined that the space could be entered directly through the basement apartment entrance under the front steps and from the apartment in the adjacent building, as well as the way we'd come in. Entering from farther down the block required a more complicated route that involved going upstairs and over an occupied apartment before coming down the main stairs where we'd entered. We saved that entrance and another entrance in the middle of the block for ourselves because they were more complicated to explain. Owen made note of the addresses and directions for the other entries so he could give the location to Mac and Earl in the morning.

*

Perdita wasn't quite her usual chipper self when I stopped by for my morning coffee the next day. "Do you have any idea when we're getting out of here?" she asked.

"We're working on some plans," I told her.

"Good, because I'm ready to go home. I like being your assistant more than I like being a waitress. I bet you like your job better than working in a bookstore, too, huh? Or do you even see the bookstore? What is this like for you, since magic doesn't work on you? Or does it? I don't get it. How could they have enchanted you?"

I was surprised it had taken her so long to get around to thinking of that. "I actually got a dose of magic awhile ago. It was an accident. I don't have much, and it's fading already, but I've been trying to learn to use what I've got."

"Oh, *that's* where you were going with all those 'meetings.'" She made sarcastic air quotes with her fingers. "I just thought you were getting it on with Owen somewhere, since you came back all flushed and excited."

I restrained a groan. I'd suspected that was what she was thinking. "I was just excited about practicing magic." I was surprised by how wistful I sounded. Having magic had a lot to do with me being in this mess, though I didn't know what might have happened if they hadn't been able to imprison me this way. They might have locked me in an ordinary cell.

"And Owen? I thought magic wasn't supposed to work on him, either."

"The same accident that gave me magic restored his powers."

"I thought he wasn't evil."

"He's not evil. He's just not harmless. There's a difference. You haven't noticed him doing anything bad in the last few weeks, have you?"

"No." She dragged the word out like she wasn't sure, and I tried not to sigh in frustration. If her reaction was any indication, Owen would practically have to sacrifice himself saving us all to prove he wasn't as evil as his parents.

*

Even though my job mostly consisted of pouring coffee and putting baked goods in paper sacks, it was difficult to concentrate when I was thinking of that night's meeting. Before I left work, I gathered the day-old bakery products that we would have thrown away. I hoped that maybe having some sweets would keep the meeting from getting too rancorous. At least I'd have something to bite on so I'd be less likely to say something I'd regret.

Owen was working late at the store, so I went home by myself and then had to kill hours before it was time for the meeting. I dressed like I was heading over to visit a friend who'd made a late-night breakup distress call and headed out with my bag of cookies and scones soon after ten. That gave me time to be cautious and still get there before everyone else did.

The gray guys had stopped staking out my apartment, and I didn't notice anyone else following me as I headed down the street. When I reached the right address, I went up the front steps and mimed hitting an apartment buzzer before I magically unlocked the door. That took me a couple of tries. It used to be such a simple spell, but now it left me so drained that I had to pause in the vestibule and eat a cookie before I could make it up the stairs to the empty apartment shell.

Picking my way across the floor was a challenge with next to no light, so I was glad I'd allowed myself plenty of time. After the unlocking spell took so much effort, I didn't dare try to generate magical light, and a flashlight might have been dangerously obvious. I was incredibly glad to reach the doorway to the stairwell that led to the basement, where I didn't have to worry about how I walked.

As early as I was, Owen had beaten me. He was waiting in the basement meeting area, a small globe of magical light glowing at his feet. "I wanted to make sure it was still a safe meeting place," he explained. "I might have been able to call it off if it had been compromised."

"I just wanted to make sure I could get through the door on my own," I said.

He immediately looked concerned. "I didn't think about that."

"Relax. I was fine. I can still do that much magic. Cookie?" I held the bag out to him.

"You brought refreshments?"

"I'm from the south. We don't have gatherings without food. I probably should have baked. These are just leftovers from the store."

At about five minutes before eleven, there was a rustling noise near the basement apartment entrance. Owen doused his magical light, and we both froze, holding our breath. A rectangle of grayish light showed as the door opened, and two figures were silhouetted in the opening. I was pretty sure it was Mac and McClusky, but we stayed quiet until they identified themselves.

The door closed, plunging the room back into darkness, and then a magical glow appeared near the floor, where it wouldn't be as visible through the windows, which were up near the ceiling. "We're here," Mac said.

Owen's glow relit, and he said, "Good, you found it."

Mac looked around the empty space. "So, this is what it's like inside all these buildings?"

"From what we can tell," Owen said.

"It would be pointless to build an entire city, inside and out, just for show," I added. "I wonder how much of all this is illusion."

"But there's still enough to physically interact with, which tells me that the Elf Lord's scheme is big enough to make it worthwhile," Mac said. "Speaking of which, any sign of our elf friends?"

"Not yet, but they've still got a few minutes," Owen said.

McClusky scowled, but before he could say anything about elves, I held out my bakery bag. "Cookie? There are also some scones in there." He looked at me like I was insane, but Mac reached over and took a square of shortbread from the bag.

We waited a while longer, and then McClusky gestured for the bag and took one of the giant cookies. Mac checked his watch, then shook his head and said, "This is just like them. It's a power game, you know. They're showing they have the power position by keeping us waiting."

I was surprised to see Owen smile ever so slightly as he said, "Okay, you've made your point. I'd like to get this over with."

At that, the shadows shifted and five elves appeared right next to us, as though they'd been standing barely a foot away that whole time. I couldn't stifle a yelp of surprise, and I wasn't the only one. McClusky started coughing, having choked on his cookie.

I hadn't heard or seen the elves come in. Had they been there all along? Earl was there, but I didn't know the others, and when I got a look at their apparent leader, I forgot about the others. He was in human guise, so he didn't look like an elf, but he did look otherworldly. All elves seemed to look eternally young, but while Earl looked like he really might be a college student, this guy had the look of a thirty-year-old actor who could still believably play teenagers. That is, sexy, mature-for-their-age teenagers, the types who have steamy affairs with their young, pretty teachers on teen nighttime soaps. He also was perfect casting for the role of dashing young rebel leader, with his intense eyes and catlike grace.

It was a good thing it was so dark and the lights were so far away from me, I thought as I brushed a few beads of sweat off my forehead. I wondered if maybe he was using a charisma spell to maintain the upper hand in the meeting because I normally didn't react to other men this way, especially not when I was standing right beside Owen.

The elf leader smiled at all of us—though it felt like the smile was mostly directed at me—and said, "Hi, I'm Brad."

That broke the spell. I bit my tongue before I blurted, "Brad? *Seriously?* Brad the elf?" He'd have looked right at home in a jaunty beret with a couple of bandoliers over his shoulders. He should have been "Jacques" or maybe "Pierre." Brad was the star player on the football team, not a resistance movement leader. The rest of us introduced ourselves, using first names only. I wished I'd thought to give myself a cool code name because "Katie" wasn't any more of a good resistance name than "Brad."

"Now that you've graced us with your presence, I guess we can get started," Mac said, sarcasm dripping from his words.

Judging by the elves' body language, I had the feeling Mac was going to face some resistance, and not the kind he was trying to organize. I didn't know yet if it was the idea of working with wizards or Mac assuming leadership they weren't on board with, but I recognized a certain degree of wariness in the way they viewed the situation. They weren't crossing their arms over their chests, or anything else that obvious, but there was something defiant about the way they stood.

"Who are you to decide that you're in charge?" Brad asked mildly. His tone wasn't challenging at all, but his eyes might as well have had lasers in them.

"I represent the Council."

"The Council only governs wizards. We have our own leadership."

"Your leadership is why we're here. We all seem to have been caught up in your people's power struggle."

"So you admit it *is* our business."

Owen took a slight step backward, giving off clear "I'm not with him" signals.

"Would you just listen to my ideas before we start arguing over who's in charge?" Mac bellowed.

"I am very much interested in hearing your ideas," Brad said.

"Okay, then," Mac continued, "I think our priority has to be getting out of here, and the way to do that may be to take them by surprise. History's full of uprisings where the prisoners attacked their captors."

"And how many of them were successful?" I couldn't help but mutter. I could tell from Owen's face that he was thinking it, but he didn't dare challenge the Council representative. When Brad gave me an appreciative look, I felt like a kindergartener who'd received a gold star for my drawing.

"It sounds like a good way to get ourselves put back under the spell or to get put in a real prison that's not as comfortable," one of the other elves, a pixie-haired woman named Doris, said.

"You want to stay here forever?" Mac asked. "That's a lot longer for your people than it is for mine. How else do you think you're going to get out? We have to force them to let us go, and that means forcing them to listen to us. Now, I figure that anyone here that we don't know is either an illusion or is working for them. The illusions seem to be like the extras in movies. They're just part of the scenery. They don't talk, they don't interact. They just go about their business. Everyone else is probably in on it, working to maintain the illusion. Those are the people we can grab. I'm sure you've all got someone in your day-to-day lives who's like that. If each of us gets one or two, then we'll have taken out most of their people, and then we can fight back."

"What do you mean by 'get'?" Earl asked.

"Not killing, not unless you have to. But immobilize them, certainly, lock them up."

"They have magic. How can we bind them so they can't just free themselves?" Earl asked. "We don't have your fancy silver chains here— unless they left them with you when they brought you here."

"Don't you have any binding or memory spells?" Mac asked. "Do to them what they've done to us."

"Have you considered any alternatives?" Brad asked.

I thought Owen would explode. I was pretty sure he was actually twitching. But if he couldn't talk, I sure could. "We think we've discovered the portal they're using to bring people here. At the very least, we've found a way out of the neighborhood that doesn't loop back on itself."

All of Brad's attention turned to me, and I felt I might swoon. "Where is this?" he asked. He knelt and drew on the floor. A map of the prison neighborhood appeared, made of softly glowing lines. It looked like we hadn't been the only ones surveying our surroundings.

I circled the map, orienting myself, then pointed to the far end. "There. It's the park on what should be the boundary. If you go up the sidewalk or the street, you'll loop back, but if you go through that gate, you wind up in a big, park-like space. We couldn't go too far because a lot of the guards were there, having some kind of meeting."

"Do you mean the elves wearing gray?" Brad asked.

I glanced at Owen to see if he would speak up, but he remained resolutely silent, even as his jaw clenched so tightly that I thought I could hear his teeth grinding. "Yes, those guards," I said. "They come and go through that gate at around eight thirty at night, about eighteen to twenty at a time." I gave Owen another glance and then plunged forward. "We thought maybe we could infiltrate that group and find out what's on the other side."

"Unfortunately, it would require illusion for us to look like elves," Brad said.

"But you *are* elves," I protested.

"We've tried, but we can't seem to shed this disguise they've given us, perhaps because the spell works on everyone's perception and is therefore beyond our control. Our elf illusion, were we to don one, would likely be more effective than that of a human's, but it would be just as much an illusion."

"What would be the purpose of this little charade?" McClusky asked dismissively.

"We might learn where the portal is, how it's guarded, perhaps even something of how they're maintaining this prison," Brad said with a smile that didn't seem to have much of a charming effect on the Council wizards. "After all, that information would be necessary for us to take any advantage of the uprising you propose."

"But this infiltration exposes us to risk," Mac argued. "We don't know how they're identifying each other, but if they spot a plant, then they'll know we're on to them. We have to act quickly and decisively to have the advantage. What we need to do is revive every prisoner we can find, set a day and time, and then everyone takes over their guards at once. Then we take a few hostages and head straight for that gateway."

Brad turned to me. "What do you think of this plan, Katie?"

I gulped. "Me? What does my opinion matter?"

Brad gave me a smile that I was certain had to be magically enhanced. "I nominate you as our leader."

"I'm in charge here," Mac insisted.

"We never agreed upon that," Brad said, his voice silky smooth, the aural equivalent of melted chocolate. "I know you would never agree upon an elf as the leader, so we will compromise. A wizard may lead us, as long as Katie is that wizard."

I opened my mouth to say that I wasn't really a wizard, but Owen elbowed me in the side. When I turned to look at him, he shook his head almost imperceptively, and I could have sworn he was fighting back a smile.

Mac sputtered, too irate for words, and glared at Owen and me. Owen maintained an expression of pure innocence. Brad's smile was even more innocent than that. "Shall we put it to a vote?" he asked with a glance over his shoulder to his people, as if to remind us that the elves had the wizards outnumbered, even if the vote split along those lines.

"Very well," Mac grumbled. "But you're making a mistake."

"Katie's been MSI's secret weapon for a while now, so you may be surprised," Owen said, speaking for the first time in the meeting.

"So, Katie, our fearless leader, what do you think about the prison break plan?" Brad asked.

I gulped and took a couple of deep breaths. I'd never led much of anything in my life, despite Owen's vote of confidence. I'd never even been an officer in a club when I was in school. I was more likely to be the person who got things done behind the scenes. "I think the uprising should be a last resort," I said when I trusted myself to speak and sound authoritative instead of like a scared little girl. "There haven't been that many uprisings that were actually successful. They've been more symbolic than anything, something to rally around without doing any practical good. Has any inmate prison uprising ever resulted in the inmates going free for good?" I directed that question at Mac. To be honest, I wasn't sure of the answer, but it didn't seem like the kind of thing that was likely to happen.

Mac shrugged grudgingly, but he didn't speak, so I continued, gaining confidence as I went on. "We're at even more of a disadvantage because we don't yet know how to get back home. Information gathering should be our first priority, and we need to know about both sides of the portal. We need to find any fellow prisoners who were taken after we were and see if they know anything more about what Sylvester's doing. Since people are being sent here for knowing too much, someone's bound to know something important. For instance, I know there's an MSI security operative here who was taken after we were, and if I find him again, he may have information."

"I will spread the word through my people," Brad said with a nod.

"But be careful about that. Mac was right that we should keep this in separate cells. If they're smart, they'll have had at least one plant in among the prisoners, someone we're likely to trust. If we don't all know each other, they won't be able to track all of us down, no matter who they catch. You have warned everyone you've awakened about writing down possible memory triggers, right?"

Everyone in the room pulled pieces of paper out of their pockets. "Good," I said with a nod, suddenly feeling very official. "Then we'll need to learn about this side of the portal. If you've got someone who could infiltrate the gray guards, that would be good. You may need to observe them a while to fit in. Check for magic use to make sure your illusions don't give you away. We shouldn't meet too frequently. Earl at the bookstore makes a good information drop point. Do any of you know an elf named Perdita?"

"Everyone knows or knows of Perdita," Brad said with a fond smile.

"She works at a café near here. I'll talk to her; she may be able to pass on messages, since she does know everyone, and her position is pretty public. Don't try to talk to me at the store, though. I suspect the other person working at the coffee shop with me is a guard." I looked around at the others and said, "So, does it sound like we've got a plan to start with?"

Mac was still scowling, but he nodded, and the others all nodded in agreement. Before everyone started to disperse, Owen glanced out the window to check for guards. He returned to us, his expression tense. "No one can leave yet," he said. "There are gray guards outside, watching the building."

CHAPTER FIFTEEN

Of course, all the others had to verify for themselves that the building was being watched. Once that was certain, the accusations started flying. "Who let them follow you?" Mac asked.

"We were here before you were and you didn't even notice us," Brad said. "Do you think they'd have been able to follow us?"

"You're a bigger group," McClusky said. "In here, you were being still, but you'd attract attention traveling together."

"Do you think we're that stupid?" Earl said. He hesitated and glanced around like he was waiting for someone to tell him to shut up. I wondered if he'd ever get over that.

Doris said, "You two were probably easiest to follow, and you were the last ones to arrive."

"We know they've already been tracking Katie and Owen," McClusky argued.

"How do we know someone in your group didn't tip them off?" Mac asked the elves. "After all, these are your people."

Listening to all the arguing was frustrating, but then I remembered that I was theoretically in charge. I clapped my hands together once, then hissed, "Hey!" When they all turned to look at me, I whispered, "If they don't already know we're in here, we're sure tipping them off with all this racket." They looked like contrite schoolkids. "Now, it seems we're stuck here for the time being. Does anyone want a cookie?"

I passed around the refreshment bag, and all the magical people conjured their own beverages. Owen handed me a cup of coffee, then went back to check out the window. "They're still out there," he reported.

"But they haven't come in here, which is probably a good sign," I said. "Maybe they're just trying to see if something is going on or who's here." I figured that part of my job as resistance leader was keeping up morale.

"Why should we trust her?" McClusky muttered into his coffee cup. "She's probably as bad as he is, since she's dating him."

Without thinking, I snapped, "Maybe I'm smart enough to rate people based on the way I've seen them act rather than on the deeds of parents they never even knew. How would you like to be judged strictly by your parents?" I hoped his parents weren't saints who were pillars of the community, or that would kill my argument. He winced ever so slightly, so I must have hit close to home.

"I trust Katie," Earl said. "She listened to me when no one else would, and she destroyed the Eye of the Moon when she could have used it to gain great power."

"She did gain power from it," Mac pointed out.

"Yeah, and it's already fizzling," I said. I turned to the elves and added, "I probably should have told you that before you elected me leader. I don't really count as a wizard. I have a finite amount of power that's almost gone."

"Even better," Brad said. "If you're neither wizard nor elf, you're neutral."

"Do *you* think I'm bad?" Owen abruptly asked Mac. "I know the Council's watching me out of caution, but you've known me since I was five. Have you ever seen any sign that I had the potential to be evil? If you've decided it's there now, maybe you should resign because you missed it all those years and your judgment is in question."

"Ah, you'll never get a wizard to trust," Doris said with a delicate snort. "It's because they know they're so untrustworthy, themselves."

"And you people are so good that we're in this mess because of your leader's power grab," McClusky shot back.

"If the wizards hadn't been interfering in our internal matters, and if you trusted your own people, you wouldn't be here," Brad said, his tone going icy.

"Um, well, actually, I called Owen for help, and that's why he and Katie are here," Earl said. "I don't consider that interfering."

"But you're working for the wizards now," Doris said to him.

"Only because my cover got blown."

"Because you were helping the wizards."

Things were getting out of control, and a second round of cookies wasn't going to stop it. I reached over and grabbed Earl's arm before he and his friend could escalate their argument, and then I hissed a "Ssshhhhh!" in the tiny moment of quiet that came before anyone else could jump in. When I had their attention, I whispered, "In case you've forgotten, the bad guys are right outside, and while these buildings look like sturdy brownstones, I have a feeling they're a lot flimsier than that. This is a time for using our inside voices, and maybe not even that much. Unless you *want* to get caught plotting against them."

They all glanced at the floor and looked properly ashamed of themselves. "Okay, then," I continued. "Since you've been making such a ruckus, it's probably best if we clear out of here right away. There's plenty of blank space in this block—pretty much the whole second floor, all the way across. Scatter and wait. Look out where you step, though. The unfinished space is *really* unfinished. When the coast looks clear, leave by ones and twos through the same exit where you entered. We don't want them to know we can move around like this. Then, to play it safe, stick to your normal routine tomorrow and don't do anything even remotely unusual or suspicious. We'll start on the plan the next day. Got it?"

There were silent, if slightly sullen, nods all around, and then the group dispersed, each faction heading off in a different direction. Owen and I went upstairs to an attic room he said he'd found when he arrived early for the meeting. It seemed to be used for storing props for this elaborate stage set, so it not only had an actual floor, it also had a small sofa wedged into a corner.

I settled onto one end of the sofa with a sigh. "There are worse places to wait things out."

His grin was borderline wicked. "Yeah, and that's where the others are." He sat on the other end of the sofa and leaned his head back against the cushions.

I scooted over to lean on him. He put his arm around me and rubbed my shoulder. "That's what they get for not scoping things out ahead of time," I said.

"Preparation is key. So is information gathering."

"Does that mean you approve of my first plan as a resistance leader?"

"You're doing a great job."

I lifted my head to look up at him. "You really think so? I mean, isn't it kind of a joke that *I'm* a resistance leader? That was just the elves messing with Mac."

"Actually, I think it was a wise choice. You are more or less neutral since you don't have a particular axe to grind here. You just want to get home, and you don't care whether that makes anyone look good or bad. Since that's what I want, too, that's the leader I want. And you've always come up with plans and solved problems. Now you've been elected to do it officially."

I lay my head back again, resting it against his chest. "I hadn't thought of it that way. But I will run things by you."

He settled his arms around me. "Nope, don't do that. Do what you think is best, and then we'll all discuss it. I'm not going to be the power behind the throne."

His tone was light, like he was joking, but when I turned to look at him, his face seemed serious. The light was bad, so his face was mostly in shadow, and I thought maybe that was what made him seem so serious, but I sensed a real tension in him. "Mac could really make it rough on you back home, huh?"

"If he gives a bad report, yeah. I should have kept my mouth shut earlier. Showing signs of a temper probably wasn't the best idea."

"A saint would be losing patience by now."

"I've looked up what my parents did, and I don't blame people for being nervous."

I rested my hands on his where he had them clasped at my waist. "There is something to be said for nurture over nature. You're exactly like James, even with no biology in common. I'd have to think that the lessons you learned growing up have a bigger role in shaping the kind of person you are than a quirk or two of genetics. If anything, the Council's practically driving you to get frustrated and lose your temper by treating you this way."

"That may be their plan. My plan is to wait them out."

"Just don't go sacrificing yourself to save the world again. I'm not sure I could take it."

Instead of replying, he craned his neck to look out the window behind the sofa. "I'm not seeing any gray guys. And there go Mac and McClusky. Let's give it another half hour."

It ended up being more like two hours because both of us fell asleep snuggled together. It meant we had to creep home in the wee hours, but on the upside, anyone who'd been watching the building had long since given up by the time we left via our respective entrances.

*

Exhaustion from the late night made it a lot easier to play "normal" the next day, in spite of a higher-than-usual number of gray guys in and around the store. Mac and McClusky were in their usual spot in the park, and Earl was at work, so it looked like everyone had made it out okay.

The subsequent morning, as I passed the science fiction section on my way to the stairs, Earl stepped into the aisle and whispered, "We're starting recon tonight."

I nodded, then out of the corner of my eye I noticed a gray guy watching us, so I said, "I think the flavor of the day is snickerdoodle spice, but I'm not sure."

Earl replied, "Oh, I was hoping for pumpkin."

"That one may be tomorrow. See you!" I fought not to let my eyes focus on the gray guy as I brushed right past him.

If the elves were starting on their part of the plan, then we needed to get going on ours. We had to be on the lookout for anyone who might have been taken after us who might know more about what was going on. Unfortunately, I didn't see anyone who looked familiar come through the coffee shop. Dan was the only MSI person I was sure of, and he'd only come the once.

I went to Perdita's café for lunch to find out if she'd discovered anyone else. She leaned on the counter and ticked off her revivals on her fingers. "Let's see, there were two ex-boyfriends, but neither of them knew anything—about any plots or about anything else, if you know what I mean. My next-door neighbor here is my cousin, but I think they got him when they got me. I dated the guy who runs the grocery store on the corner. I also dated the guy at the cleaners. Not quite to boyfriend status, but the kiss still worked. Who knew that would be my superpower? Anyway, they seemed to get here just for working for MSI." She smiled and added, "And I think my future ex-boyfriend is part of your group. He stopped by to introduce himself."

"Your future ex?" I asked, raising an eyebrow.

"My relationships *never* work out, but I want this guy."

"Yeah, I guess Brad is pretty hot," I said.

"Brad? No, I meant Earl."

"*Earl?* Really?"

"What? He's cute, seems smart, and he's not at all my type, which means it might actually work."

"Well, good luck. He is nice. You don't mind playing messenger?"

"I love it! And, hey, anything that gets us out of here, right?"

After lunch, I updated Owen, and he said, with no enthusiasm, "I suppose I'd better update Mac."

Taken aback, I said, "Why? You don't report to him. I'm the leader of this little movement."

"But it's a sign of good faith if I'm not withholding information."

"Seriously? You're really going to keep updating him, even though he has no official authority over you, here or anywhere else? If he's such a good monitor, let him figure it out for himself."

Looking pained, he said, "It doesn't work that way."

"If you're going to tell him everything I tell you, then I'm going to start treating you like any other member of the group and keep things on a need-to-know basis." My words came out a little more harshly than I intended, considering my main gripe was with Mac and his bosses, not with Owen.

But Owen didn't seem to take offense. He nodded and said, "Yeah, that's probably the best policy. If I don't know anything, I can't share it. Only tell me what I need to know to do my part."

"Okay, then," I said, my anger fizzling from the lack of opposition. It was hard to fight with someone who was agreeing with me. "I was thinking of trying to find MSI people tonight—just going out and about. Maybe we'll run across Dan again. There's got to be some point behind an operation this elaborate, and if we know that, we might get somewhere."

With a tentative smile, he said, "That seems like a minor enough development that I don't have to share it."

"So, when I get off duty, are you up for going to a different part of the neighborhood for dinner?"

"Come get me when you're ready. The nice thing about owning what amounts to an imaginary bookstore is that I only have to sort of look like I'm bothering to run it."

"Now I'll go sell some more imaginary coffee and keep your imaginary bookstore in business one more day."

I really did have to wonder why they'd bothered creating a fake neighborhood to house the prisoners in. If they'd just taken us to another world reachable only by portal, we still wouldn't have been able to escape. Was it that important to keep us from even wanting to get away? I supposed it might be, now that I thought about it. If all your prisoners had magical powers, you'd want to keep them from using those powers, and it might have been more difficult to do that for so many people than to create a fake nonmagical paradise.

Besides, once they were through with it, they could always lease it to filmmakers as a setting for cheap romantic comedies.

*

It was difficult to find a place to explore that we hadn't visited already, and it was like looking for a needle in a haystack to find one person in this entire neighborhood, no matter how confined it seemed. Still, it was a finite place, and there couldn't have been that many real people there.

"I know the best way to find him," I quipped to Owen. "I just need to develop a raging crush on him and then dash out to the corner store with no makeup on, my hair under a ball cap, and wearing a stained old T-shirt. Then I could *guarantee* I'd run into him."

"You think that would work?" he asked, raising an eyebrow.

"It worked often enough in the real New York, which is much bigger. In fact, it never fails."

"Do you think you can stir up a crush that easily?"

"That would be the difficult part, considering I've only met him twice, other than the one time here. He hasn't given me much to work with, alas."

Then I thought I saw a familiar figure ahead of us and clutched Owen's upper arm hard enough to cut off circulation. "Speak of the devil!" I breathed.

"I think you're right," Owen said, and we followed him. There were enough people on the sidewalks that we were able to blend into the crowd, and Dan didn't seem to notice he had a tail. I wasn't sure how long that would last, though. If Dan's persona in this world retained even a tiny bit of his security staff instincts, he'd be on to us in a heartbeat.

"How can we approach him?" I asked Owen. "We don't know him here. Everyone else, we've had a reason to talk to them, and Mac at least had regular habits. This may be our one chance."

"You said he was a customer."

"I made him one latte. If I recognize him in public and try to talk to him, I'll look like a scary stalker."

We followed him to a coffee shop, where he entered and took a seat at the counter. I started to head inside, but Owen held me back. "Maybe what we need to do is find a stranger he'll want to talk to."

"Should we go get Perdita?"

"I was thinking more about you."

"Me? But if he saw me, he'd think I was a crazy stalker, remember?"

"Do you think you've got enough magic left to pull off that illusion again? Your bombshell may not be quite my type, but I'm guessing it's his."

"It's worth a try. But we'd better find a phone booth for me to change in because it might attract notice if I changed here."

We hurried around the corner and found a niche under a building's front steps. There, I closed my eyes and concentrated on the spell, dredging up every last bit of power I had. I opened my eyes when I felt an additional surge and saw Owen holding my hand. "I thought I'd see if that would help," he said. "It seems to have worked."

"But, let me guess, it wouldn't work like that to maintain my power all the time."

"No, sorry. You'll lose the power as soon as I drop the connection. It's more like a power cord than a battery."

"Will I be able to maintain the illusion?"

"Creating it takes more power, but you will have to stay focused on it."

"How do I look?"

"Like someone he'd want to talk to."

I remembered Rod's lesson about maintaining the persona and the attitude as I walked down the street with Owen a few paces behind me. I wasn't the sort of woman who got a lot of looks, even when I passed construction sites, but now I was turning heads. The fact that a lot of those heads were probably mere illusion didn't make it less thrilling. The more people looked at me, the easier it was to keep my head held high and my hips swiveling.

I entered the coffee shop and placed myself on the stool next to Dan at the counter, then arranged my legs before purring, "Oh, is this seat taken?"

He turned to look at me, raised his eyebrows, then grinned. "Now it is."

So far, this was going according to plan. Too bad I didn't have a plan for after I caught his attention. I couldn't break the spell in public, and I couldn't think of a non-suspicious way to get him in private without him assuming I was some kind of hooker.

I ordered a cup of coffee, then said, "You look familiar. Have I seen you around?"

"I think I'd have remembered that," he said, giving me an appreciative glance up and down my illusion's body. I wondered if the illusion was blushing as much as I felt I was. "But I wouldn't mind getting to know you." He held his hand out to me. "I'm Dan."

I took his hand and shook it. "Victoria," I said, using the first name that came to mind to go with this illusion. "I still think you look familiar. You don't have a bicycle, do you?" I asked. "For some reason, I'm picturing you as a bicycle messenger."

He laughed. "No, I don't think so." Then he frowned, like he might have been trying to remember whether he had a bike.

"Or how about a security guard?" I asked, emphasizing the word "security."

He was still frowning, and his eyes had gone unfocused, so I felt like I was close, but I didn't know much else about him. He shook his head. "Nope, not that, either. What about you? What do you do?"

"Oh, I just work in an office, and my boss is a real gargoyle." That didn't seem to have any impact at all. Subtle might not work. The spell wouldn't be very effective if it could be broken just by words related to a person's real life coming up in conversation. I needed to find a way to put it all together in the right context, but that was going to be hard to do in public. It would probably also work better coming from someone he'd seen in the real world. He might be willing to chat with "Victoria" as a total stranger, but it would probably take Katie to break the spell. Unfortunately, I didn't dare drop an illusion in front of everyone, and I didn't have the technique or control to specify who did or didn't see an illusion, so I couldn't reveal myself to just Dan.

I resorted to chatting as flirtatiously as I could manage, and then asked, "Have you had dinner yet? I was going to go to this wonderful Italian place in my building. I usually get takeout, but I hate to eat alone. Wanna join me?" Katie wasn't the sort of girl who'd ask a total stranger out to dinner, but necessity meant Victoria was. I hoped Dan might be the kind of guy who'd at least be intrigued.

He raised his eyebrows and studied me for a moment, then grinned and said, "Wow, I don't think I've ever been picked up like that before. Do you promise that the food's good? I'm really picky about Italian."

"It's the best, I swear." I sensed a vibe of mild discomfort, so I hurried to add, "And we can go dutch. It doesn't have to be a date. Just having dinner at the same table."

Smiling, he nodded and said, "Okay, you're on."

We paid for our coffee, and I took his arm to lead him out of the café. I caught Owen's eye as we passed and shook my head slightly, warning him to keep his distance. We turned onto a side street and walked by the building where I'd put on my illusion. When we reached that spot, I pulled Dan into the niche and instantly dropped the illusion.

"What is this? What's going on?" Dan protested, trying to back away from me. "Are you mugging me? And who are you? Where did Victoria go?"

Figuring I had nothing to lose and very little time before he started shouting loudly enough to draw attention, I snapped, "Your undercover identity is as a bicycle messenger and you worked with the gargoyles to foil an elf attack." It might not have been a particularly vivid memory for him, but at the very least I thought it should provide a significant level of cognitive dissonance. With any luck, when combined with my presence, it would do the trick.

He swayed for a moment. He blinked, then his eyes widened as he took in his surroundings. A moment later, as it apparently all caught up to him, he went deathly pale. He lurched forward, grabbed the lapels of my jacket and blurted, "We have to stop him! He's bringing through an army!"

CHAPTER SIXTEEN

I grabbed his arms and said, "Are you kidding?" It probably wasn't the best way to treat a guy who'd just snapped out of a spell, but I couldn't help myself. A little more calmly, I asked, "Is that what he's using the portal for, to bring an army from the elven realms to our world?"

Dan seemed to notice that he still had a death grip on my coat. He quickly released it and took a step back. "Sorry about that. Yes, that's what seemed to be going on. I tracked a lot of the disappearances—including yours—back to a warehouse in Chelsea, and I saw the army coming through. And then somehow I was here"—he glanced around, frowning at his surroundings— "wherever here is."

"We seem to be in some kind of construct in the elven realms, meant to make us think we're other people in an idealized, nonmagical version of New York," I explained, wishing I could remember how Owen usually phrased it.

"How many captives are here?"

"I don't know. A lot, mostly elves." I tried to think of the questions Owen would ask. "How many soldiers do you think you saw?"

"It's hard to say. It seemed like a pretty steady stream, but I don't know if that was a one-time transfer or if that's going on all the time. If it is ..." He shuddered as his voice trailed off. "But I don't think they're leaving the warehouse yet. I didn't see any signs of that."

"Maybe that's why they're using a warehouse," I suggested. "You wouldn't think you'd need a building that large just for a portal, but if you need barracks for your otherworldly army, it would be just the thing." I rubbed my forehead wearily. "We've got to get back and warn someone that Sylvester's gearing up for war."

"Do you have any ideas for how to do that?"

"We found what we think is a gateway to a portal, and we have people working on finding a way to get through."

"What do you need me to do?"

"For now, the information you gave me is what's important. We'll let you know when there's something else we need. I hope it's soon if we have to stop an interdimensional war."

"How should we stay in touch?"

"You know Earl, right?"

"Yeah."

"He works in the bookstore a few blocks from here. You were there the other day for coffee."

The light dawned in his eyes. "Oh yeah, I remember seeing you there."

"But I think my coworker is one of their spies or guards, or whatever, so don't come talk to me. Talk to Earl in the science fiction section, if you can find him alone. If you run into anyone here you recognize from our world and you're sure they're on our side, you can break the spell by bringing up some vivid memory from our world that doesn't fit with this place." I tried to think of anything else he'd need to know. "Oh, and you may start seeing some elves in bland gray outfits wandering around. You shouldn't see them if you're still under the spell, so ignore them. Otherwise, just keep acting like nothing has changed. We don't want them knowing we know the truth."

He nodded grimly. "Okay, got it. How often should I check in?"

"Try the day after tomorrow. By then, we should know something more." I stuck my head out of our little shelter, saw that the coast was clear, and hurried away. I didn't look back to see how long he waited to leave.

Owen met me at the corner. "How'd it go?" he asked.

"It worked."

"Did he know anything?"

"Yeah, and I hope the elves make some progress tonight because it's a little more urgent than we thought."

"What did he say?"

I bit my lip, feeling the full weight of my position as resistance leader. It had been something of a joke, but now it felt a lot more real. "I can't tell you."

He grinned for a second, like he thought I was teasing, but the grin faded when he realized I was serious. "You're not going to tell me, *really*?"

"Hey, you said it was probably the best idea. I know you feel obligated to share information with Mac so he doesn't think you're hiding things from him out of evil intentions, and I don't trust him not to do something crazy because of this information. If I don't tell you, you don't have any dilemma about what to say to him."

"So, you're protecting me?"

I hooked my arm through his elbow. "Yeah, and you'd better get used to it."

"The power is obviously going to your head," his tone was lighter, so I felt like he really was teasing me, not just masking hurt feelings.

"You should have thought about that before you elected me the resistance leader. You know, it would be well within my rights to have you shot for unauthorized sharing of information."

"Oh, so you're the ruthless kind of leader."

"You'd better believe it."

*

When I got to work the next morning, he was chatting with Mac and McClusky in the park, so I knew I'd done the right thing, even if I felt lousy about it. If Mac knew about the army, he'd insist on carrying out his prison uprising plan, and I agreed with the elves that it would be disastrous.

I found Earl in his section and quickly told him what I'd learned from Dan. "How did your end of the operation go?"

"We'll attempt to infiltrate them tonight. If our person can get through the portal, he can pass the message on. This does make things pretty dire, doesn't it?"

"An enemy army usually isn't a good thing. We need to act quickly, before Sylvester can pull off whatever he has planned." Though it pained me to do so, I added, "And Owen doesn't know about the army, so don't say anything. I'd rather Mac not find out."

Earl winced and nodded. "I don't envy Owen."

"Yeah. I just wish I could find a way to make him look like a self-sacrificing hero—without any actual sacrifice, of course—so we could put an end to all this. It's just ridiculous."

Earl looked uncharacteristically somber when he said, "I'm afraid we might all get a chance to sacrifice before this is over."

*

I got to the store early the next morning because I couldn't wait to learn what the elves had discovered. It had taken all my self-control the night before not to return to the building across from the gateway park and spy on the operation. Instead, I'd dragged Owen to a movie—*Casablanca*, since they only ever screened classics in romantic movies and it was Owen's favorite—and then tried not to let on that I knew anything was happening so he wouldn't have anything he felt obligated to tell Mac.

Owen was with Mac in the park, although I couldn't think of what he might have to share with the Council guys, since I'd been keeping him out of the loop. I waved a greeting and then went into the store. Earl wasn't around when I went through his section, so I went upstairs to the coffee shop.

Florence was already there, and she seemed unusually jittery. "Don't tell me you've gone back on caffeine," I joked.

She didn't seem to find it funny. "Don't you have a meeting with the boss?" she snapped.

"We do meet most mornings. Has that been a problem for you? I know we get busy up here, but that's when I can catch him."

"You should probably get back downstairs and talk with him."

"He's not in yet. He's still talking to some friends across the street." I gestured toward the windows that faced the park.

She followed my gesture with her eyes, and then she took what appeared to be an involuntary step forward. I turned to look and saw that gray guys were massing in the park and heading for the store. "You're right, I probably ought to go meet with him," I managed to choke out before fleeing down the stairs.

I saw Earl first. "Hey, I was just going to talk to you," he said.

I grabbed his arm. "Not now. I think something's up. Did anything happen last night?"

Suddenly alarmed, he asked, "Why?"

I didn't have to answer, since there were now gray guys in the store. Without a word, we both ducked behind the nearest bookshelf. Instead of lurking, the gray guys were approaching people and facing them directly for a few seconds before moving on. "They're not just watching," Earl said. "It looks like they're enchanting everyone. We have to go, now." Without waiting for me to respond, he took off toward the back stockroom. I ran after him.

He magically unlocked the stock room, and when we were both inside, I locked the door from the inside and he added a magical ward. "Owen's out there," I said softly when that realization struck me, but I suspected it was already too late for him. I knew how to revive him, though. All we had to do was wait it out, then when the gray guys were gone, we could find Owen and set everything right.

That was, if he hadn't already done it himself. We were all carrying memories with us, so he was sure to find one of those pieces of paper he had stashed. He'd probably be worried and looking for me before I got to him.

"What happened last night?" I asked Earl.

"Our spy reported back and didn't seem to be discovered. Like you thought, it was a shift change. He didn't get anywhere near a portal."

"You know, the operative word there is 'seem.' How do we know they didn't turn him—or that he wasn't a mole all along?"

"Have you always been this suspicious?"

"They're sending guards around to redo the spell on everyone. I don't think I'm overreacting."

"No, I trust him."

"What about someone who might have heard the information?"

"There weren't many of us."

"Or maybe they let him go, since it doesn't sound like he learned anything we can use."

Both of us were quiet for a while, and then I said, "I think we should go back out there."

"Are you crazy?" His first word came out as something of a shriek before he remembered where he was and modulated his voice.

"If they're re-enchanting everyone, they're probably working off a list, and they'll track us down. But the spell will probably be weak on me because my magic levels are really low, and I know a shield spell that might deflect enough to keep me sane without it being obvious to them that their spell hasn't worked. I can revive you again once they're gone, and then we can go back to the way things were, with them thinking we're enchanted and us being free. We'll have to start over with waking people up, but as long as one of us stays free, that's a minor setback."

It took him a while to answer, and I could practically hear the gears moving as he thought about it. At last, he said, "Well, I guess it beats hiding in here forever."

Hoping I knew what I was doing, I collected an armful of books, secured my shield spell that would work like magical immunity, then headed into the store. Earl came behind me with his own load of books. "Now, we'd better get these shelved," I said loud enough to be overheard. Not that there was anyone to overhear. There weren't any gray guys lurking around the stockroom, so they must not have noticed our escape.

As we rounded the corner into the science fiction section, we nearly ran into a gray guy. It took me a split second to remember that I wasn't supposed to see him, and I forced myself to keep going without wincing at the imminent collision. Out of the corner of my eye, I saw Earl go still, and I felt my shields being surrounded by magic, so I, too, froze. A little of the magic made it through to tingle my skin, since my shields were awfully flimsy, but I didn't feel the magic working on me.

While I kept my eyes unfocused, I focused my mind on who I was and where I was. The tingle stopped a moment later, and the gray guy moved on. When I saw Earl resume walking, I joined him.

I still knew exactly who I was, much to my relief. I wasn't so sure about Earl, but there were people around, so I didn't dare ask him any questions. Besides, I thought it would be safer to wait until the gray guys were sure their mission had been accomplished. As long as I knew who I was, I could start the ball rolling again.

Earl and I went to work on shelving those books we'd brought from the stockroom. He didn't say much to me, but I couldn't tell if he was being discreet or if he was back to thinking he was just another bookstore employee. It seemed like forever before the gray guys left the store.

"Okay, I think I've got it under control," Earl said. "You can get back to the coffee shop. Thanks for the help."

I studied him, looking for clues of self-awareness. There certainly wasn't any "wink-wink, know what I mean?" on his face. They had him, I was pretty sure. "Just one more thing," I said. "Do you have that receipt I gave you? I thought I saw you put it in your pocket." I hoped Earl had followed directions and stashed potentially triggering memories where he was sure to find them.

"Receipt? I don't remember a receipt."

"Could you please check, just in case? I could swear I gave it to you." When he just frowned at me suspiciously, I took another approach and gave a nervous laugh. "At least, I hope I gave it to you. You're my last chance of finding it. Could you just check your pockets, please?" I gave him my best pleading look, the one that usually got my dad to cave and give me what I wanted.

With a sigh of exaggerated put-upon patience, he stuck his hands in his pockets, then his eyebrows rose when he apparently found something. He pulled his right hand out of his pocket with a piece of paper in it. "Huh, I guess this might be it," he said. He unfolded it to check, then said, "No, I don't think so. This is my handwriting." A moment later, he swayed, and I jumped to steady him. He looked at me, blinking, then said, "Whoa, they really got me, huh?"

"But you're back now?"

"Yeah. They didn't get you?"

"No. I must be running out of magic for them to work with, so they didn't seem to notice my shield spell." Then I gasped, clutching at his arm. "Maybe that's it. No one betrayed anyone. Did your guy use an illusion to infiltrate the gray guys?"

"Yeah, he had to, since he doesn't look like an elf here."

"They might have detected that and let him get away so they'd know who he was in contact with, and then they would have gone after the people they were in contact with." And if that were the case, then they might not have Owen, since as far as I knew, no one from the elves' faction would have spoken to him since the night before.

But then where was he?

"I'd better track down Owen," I said to Earl, fighting to keep my voice from squeaking with tension. "You go see to any people you have around here."

"You don't want me to come with you?"

"Not now. I'm sure everything's fine. I'll let you know if I need anything."

Forcing down a rising tide of panic, I headed to Owen's office. He wasn't there. He also wasn't at the checkout or at any of the other places I could usually find him. I ran up the stairs to the coffee shop, in case he'd gone looking for me while Earl and I were hiding in the stockroom, but I didn't see him there. Oh no, what if they'd taken him prisoner? They might have assumed he was the resistance leader, based on his notoriety in the real world.

Florence was at the counter, and she still looked a little tense, though not as jittery as before. "How'd the meeting go?" she asked.

"I didn't find him. He hasn't come up here looking for me, has he?"

"Nope. Are you sure he's in yet?"

I went over to the windows and saw him playing chess with Mac. My sigh of relief was probably audible on the store's lower level. "I bet he lost the last game and couldn't leave before a rematch," I said. Forcing a smile, I added, "One of the benefits of being the boss is that no one can yell at you for being late to work."

"Maybe you'd better go remind him that he has a store to run," Florence said. Although she seemed to be trying to smile, her voice sounded quite stern. I felt certain now that even if she was working for Sylvester, she was secretly on my side. Otherwise, she wouldn't have all but suggested that I go break the spell on Owen.

Forcing myself to sound like I didn't have anything bigger to deal with than an errant boss, I said, "If you're okay up here, I'll go drag him back to the store and see what he wants us to do to get started for the day."

"I'm fine," she said with a careless flap of her hand. "Business is really slow today. Makes you wonder what's going on, huh?"

I was afraid I knew all too well what was going on—and she did, too. But all I said was, "Be back in a sec."

I collected Earl on my way out, in case I needed backup. I checked my pockets for my written memories, then, in a moment of paranoia, before I left the store I got out a ballpoint pen and wrote on my palm, "Check your pockets."

"You're worried," Earl noted.

"I'm not taking any chances."

When we reached the park, I paused to observe for a moment. There was none of the understated tension I was used to seeing between Owen and the Council men. Even though Mac was generally more reasonable, he had a way of keeping a constant eye on Owen. All of that was gone now. They just seemed like a group of men hanging out together in the park on a nice fall day. Owen looked more relaxed than I'd seen him in months. I almost hated to ruin it, but I knew that if he looked that relaxed, something was very wrong. I couldn't imagine what spell would make Owen want to sit in a park and play chess all day. What if they'd wiped him completely and given him a different identity for this world, not just reset him to the guy who'd bought a bookstore to make bookstores cool again? I might not be able to break that spell with a memory or a kiss.

Gesturing for Earl to stay back, I approached their table. "Oh, there you are!" I said. I was aiming for casual, but my voice sounded high and strained. "I know they say that when the cat's away, the mice will play, but what happens when the cat is the one away playing?"

Owen looked up at me, and for a moment I could barely breathe when his face seemed strangely blank, like he didn't even know me. Then he smiled and blushed guiltily as his eyes focused on me. "Oh, I guess it is late. The store's not burning down, or anything like that?"

"No, but people are wondering where you are."

"I somehow doubt you're running rudderless without me."

"We might survive for a few more minutes, but after that, anarchy is a real possibility."

He grinned. "Okay, I'll finish this game if you'll keep the masses from rioting in my absence." He sounded like Owen, but then he'd sounded like Owen when he was under the spell before, only I didn't know it then because I didn't know who I really was. Now, though, I couldn't be sure. He seemed to recognize me, and there'd been enough familiarity in his tone to indicate that there was some personal relationship there. But was he putting on an act for anyone who might be watching, or had he forgotten who he really was?

Whatever his status was, I wasn't about to leave him alone. "Mind if I watch?" I asked, not waiting for his response to sit next to him on the bench.

"You might be terribly distracting," he teased. That was a good sign. If they'd reset him, they'd kept his relationship with me.

"Then maybe I should flutter my eyelashes at Mac," I said. Mac gave a slight smile but kept his attention focused on the game. I thought Owen might have pulled off the acting job, since we'd been pretending we were under the spell whenever we were in public, but this Mac was way too different from the way he was with self-awareness. They'd definitely zapped him.

It may have been the longest chess game ever played—at least, it felt like it. All the while, I searched for signs of who Owen might be right now. Was he my Owen, doing an excellent job of playing along, or was he the romantic comedy world's Owen, who had no idea he was a wizard trapped in an elven prison?

Finally, Owen won, and the easy laughter from McClusky and Mac at his victory proved to me that they weren't themselves. I wondered if I should try to revive them, too, but decided to save it for later. We were probably safest if the elves thought their reset had worked, and undoing it immediately would be a dead giveaway.

Owen said his good-byes to his chess buddies and cheerfully came with me toward the store. Earl stayed just out of sight, so it wasn't obvious that he was with me. We were just about to cross the street when I looked both ways, as I'd been taught in kindergarten, and I found myself looking one of the gray guys right in the eye.

There was no doubt that he knew I'd seen him. He reacted, then he moved toward me. I grabbed Owen's hand and dashed across the street, dodging traffic. When Earl turned to see what was wrong, he, too, couldn't help but react to the gray guy chasing us.

They knew we knew, and they weren't going to stop until they'd made sure we were back under their thrall. I wasn't about to stand for that. "Run!" I shouted to Earl as I took off, dragging a protesting Owen behind me.

CHAPTER SEVENTEEN

My only plan was to not get caught. That wasn't a great plan, but I figured I had nothing to lose. The results were likely to be the same, either way, but if I ran, I had a slightly better chance of not being caught and reset. If I didn't run, it was inevitable.

"What's going on? Why are we running?" Owen asked, but to his credit, he didn't stop running. My urgency must have been contagious.

"I'll explain later," I said, panting.

With his much longer legs, Earl loped easily ahead of us, clearing a path down the sidewalk. We needed enough distance from our pursuers for us to duck inside a building and hide before they noticed where we'd gone.

A glance over my shoulder told me that I didn't have nearly enough room to maneuver. They were closing fast, and I was sure others would arrive soon. I needed to act now.

We reached a greengrocer's, and I got an idea. This was a foot chase in a world out of a movie. So, like in the movies, I should tip things over in my pursuer's path. The way ahead of me seemed to have been *designed* for such a move.

I kicked the front legs out from under a bin of oranges, sending them crashing to the sidewalk, then knocked over the adjacent bin of apples. For a moment, I felt bad about messing up the shop like that, but then I remembered that this place wasn't real. The fruit was probably an illusion. I just hoped it was real enough to slow down the gray guys.

I didn't take the time to look, though. After knocking over a rack to block the sidewalk entirely, I dragged Owen toward a nearby sidewalk café and turned a table onto its side so that its umbrella not only blocked the sidewalk but also obscured the view of what happened beyond it. Then we darted around the next corner.

The gray guys came around the corner, and now they weren't just chasing us. They sent magic at us. I felt its approach but wasn't sure what the spell was supposed to do. I instinctively used the protection spell Rod and Owen had taught me to block it.

When their spell didn't work, our pursuers kept up the chase. "Earl!" I warned, but he didn't seem too worried. He merely turned back, waved his free hand, and there was a huge burst of light. He then shouted, "This way!" and pulled us into a narrow passage between buildings. We ran down a set of stairs leading to a basement door and huddled at the foot of the stairwell.

"What's going on here?" Owen asked, looking truly alarmed.

"I'll explain in a moment, when we're safe," I said.

He reached for the handle of the basement door. "Wouldn't it be better to hide inside?"

Earl slapped his hand away. "Not now."

I hardly dared breathe while we waited for discovery. I thought I heard footsteps. Had they followed us into the passage? Finally, Earl cautiously raised himself enough to peer out of the stairwell. When he was satisfied that the gray guys were gone, he opened the basement door and gestured for us to enter.

Earl had formed a magical light after the door closed behind us. Owen jumped back from the light, startled, then asked, "What is that? And why didn't we open the door earlier?"

"I didn't know how long my blast would obscure their vision. They wouldn't see us in the stairwell from the street, but they might have noticed the door opening."

"There was no one there," Owen protested. Then he looked around the empty shell of the basement. "What is this place? And what's going on?" He sounded less alarmed than most people might under the circumstances, but more alarmed than I was used to hearing from Owen.

It would have been pleasant if I could have snapped him out of it with a kiss, but that hadn't worked on me the last time, and I doubted either of us were really in a kissing mood at the moment. I also wasn't in the mood for trying to explain anything. "Check your pockets," I said. I suspected that under the circumstances, he'd be more willing to believe himself than me.

"What do my pockets have to do with this?"

"Just check. Please."

He reached into his pocket and pulled out a folded square of paper. I held my breath while he unfolded it and read it. If it didn't work, I wasn't sure what to do. I had a lot of memories of him, but picking the one that was a surefire hit would be a challenge. As he read, he blinked, and I couldn't tell what had happened.

Because I couldn't bear to wait for the outcome and I couldn't risk not restoring him, I said shakily, "On our first real date, the restaurant caught fire. Then there was the time I fell through the ice in the Central Park rink. Oh, and you had pet dragons." That had to either jolt him back to himself or convince him I was insane.

He gave me a funny look, then his eyes focused and I could tell he was my Owen again. He swayed, and I rushed forward to catch him.

He fell into my arms, but more out of relief than because he was fainting from shock. "Oh, thank you," he breathed in my ear as he held me.

"You're you again?" I asked, just to be sure.

"Yeah, wizard and all. What happened?"

"Something must have gone wrong with last night's operation," Earl said. "Maybe they sensed the illusion our spy used. It seems like they've gone around resetting all the prisoners."

"We're now fugitives. We've entered the lurking in basements and attics phase of the resistance movement," I added. "I was afraid they might do something more drastic than just resetting me again if they caught me, since they thought they'd already got me once."

"How did you avoid it?" Owen asked.

"I think it was a mix of my magic being weak and me shielding it slightly."

"Good work! So, now what, boss?"

My legs were shaking from our desperate escape, so I sank to sit on the floor, and the two guys joined me. "I guess we'll have to start all over again, waking people up, and we'll need a new plan," I said. "That will be more complicated while we're fugitives."

"I'm not sure we should wake everyone," Owen said.

"I take it you're not going to revive Mac right away?"

"I'm not going to revive *anyone* right away. We need to lie low."

"I just wish we could find a way to get word back home. We don't seem to be able to get to their portal. It's too bad we can't make one of our own."

"Maybe we could," Owen said.

"Between worlds?" Earl asked, his eyebrows rising.

"Not big enough to send us, but a message, maybe. If I can aim it properly, we could send it where we're sure our people would find it. It'll take a lot of power, so we'll need to revive enough people."

"You know how to do that?" Earl asked.

"I've never tried it, but I know the theory." Owen didn't sound confident enough to reassure me.

"If the illusion was enough to get their attention, wouldn't that kind of power be noticeable?" I asked.

"It depends," Earl said. "There's a lot of magic going on here all the time, just keeping this place running. What they noticed was magic they didn't expect to be there. If we can hide among their magic, we might get away with it."

The two of them looked at me, and I realized they were waiting for a decision from their leader. "Do you have any other ideas?" I asked.

"I don't think Mac's prison riot would help much," Owen said.

"And it doesn't look like we can get through a portal, ourselves. Sending out a message may be our only hope, and we don't have a lot of time to waste." I took a deep breath, then said as forcefully as I could manage, "Let's do it. How many people do you think you'll need?"

"At least five. More if we can swing it."

I turned to Earl. "Do you think you can get that many without being noticed?"

"I should be able to. With any luck, the memories we've all got hidden will have already done the trick, but I'll go round people up."

"Be careful," I warned. "You're a known fugitive."

"I'll get one person and then that should have a ripple effect."

"We could try working it some from our end," I said.

Earl shook his head. "No, you're the one who's public enemy number one, the one person the whammy didn't affect. They'll be out to get you. It's probably safest if you stay put for a while." He checked his watch and said, "I'll meet you back here in two hours."

When Earl was gone, Owen put his arm around my shoulders and said, "I did thank you for rescuing me, didn't I?"

"It might have come up," I replied, unable to hide my smile.

"Well, you were incredible. Thank you." He bent and kissed me, and I sighed with relief to have my Owen back.

When we ended the kiss, I leaned against him and asked, "Do you think you can really do it?"

"I've got to."

"You do know that needing to do it doesn't necessarily mean you can, right?"

"I've read some books about it, and I've even done some study of elven magic. The trick will be getting enough power. It'll take as many elves as Earl can round up, and possibly you, too." He paused before adding, "It'll probably drain you entirely."

Forcing bravery I wasn't sure I felt into my voice, I said, "We knew it was going to happen eventually, anyway. It might as well be for a good cause, and I'd rather get back to the real world than be able to make glowy balls of light. Even if that is kind of cool," I added wistfully.

He turned and kissed me lightly on the temple. "I'm sorry."

"To be honest, I'm not sure if I'm cut out to be magical. I think I'm a pretty great immune, but let's face it, I was a mediocre wizard."

"That's not true at all. You caught on very quickly. You only started having problems when your power ran below a certain level. If you had full power like a real wizard, you'd be formidable. Your technique was excellent—even if it was a mix of traditional magic and whatever it was your grandmother was teaching you."

With a soft sigh, I settled my head against his shoulder. "I never thought I'd ever say this, but I wish she was here now."

He chuckled and said, "Yeah, it would be interesting to see what she'd do in this situation."

"She'd probably take one of the gray guys hostage and work her way up the chain of command." I hesitated, then said, "You know …"

"If the portal idea doesn't work, we may consider that."

As confident as he sounded about being able to open a small, perfectly aimed portal, I started thinking about every movie or TV show I'd ever seen involving a kidnapping so I could get ideas for the best way to take one of the guards hostage. We'd have to find a way to neutralize their powers, or else our hostage could put the whammy on us even as we took him prisoner—maybe even while he was a prisoner. I supposed I could always burn through my remaining magic supply so at least one of us wouldn't be affected, but it would be hard to convince Owen of that. His stance made sense in that, to him, being immune to magic had been like a punishment, and getting his powers back had come as a great relief. He couldn't imagine that I might prefer to go back to what was normal for me.

*

I tried not to look at my watch too often, since that made time pass more slowly, but we were getting awfully close to that two-hour mark, and there was no sign of Earl. I didn't say anything about it until it was five minutes past the time he was supposed to have returned. "Earl's late," I remarked, trying to sound matter-of-fact.

"He may have run into something."

"That's what I'm worried about."

"It may not be something bad. He may just be taking extra precautions."

"You're probably right. Two hours wasn't long enough. I'd rather him be late and stay safe. Let's wait longer."

Owen conjured lunch for us, and that passed some time. When another hour had passed, I said, "Okay, I'm officially worried. What should we do?"

"You're the one in charge."

I let out an exasperated sigh. "We don't have to maintain that pretense now. The Council guys are still enchanted and the elves aren't here, so you don't have to act like the good little soldier."

"I'm not acting. You're legitimately in charge. They agreed, and you've done a good job. What do *you* think we should do?"

I clenched and unclenched my hands, thinking. This was more

responsibility than I was used to having. Sure, I theoretically ran a department, but Perdita was the only person who reported to me. I was generally more of an assistant type who was surrounded by experts.

Thinking of Perdita gave me an idea, though. "It's probably safest to assume that something happened to Earl," I said. "Fortunately, we didn't put all our eggs in one basket. We'll carry out the plan ourselves. If they got to Perdita, she should be easy to revive, since we didn't even have to try the first time. She's got a good network and should be able to round up enough people to make your portal. If Earl is okay and was just delayed, he'll know we had to act, and he knows to check in with Perdita."

"So, to Perdita it is," he said, standing and offering me a hand to help me up. "Maybe we can find a path through the building that will take us out far from where we entered."

"And let's hope that they've given up on finding us around here," I added.

There was a door on the other side of the empty room, so we started there. The door led to an interior stairway. The door at the top of the stairs opened without a key into another nearly featureless space. We made our way down the block, treading carefully on the incomplete floors. When we reached the end, Owen looked out the windows on the side of the building. "I don't see any of the gray guys, but that doesn't mean some of the other people out there aren't guards who might be looking for us."

"So how do we get out of this building?"

"I don't think they'll notice a little illusion, since most of the people here aren't real. We should be able to get away with that much magic."

We went back to the last stairwell door. Before he opened it, Owen took my hand, and I felt the magic surrounding me. Safely disguised, we stepped into the stairwell and went down the stairs. There was a mirror at one landing, and I paused and did a double take when I saw an elderly couple looking back at me. "That's us?" I asked.

"A little preview of our future, perhaps," he said with a slight smile. "Now, remember what Rod told you about carrying off an illusion. Try to move like the woman you saw in the mirror."

We paused just inside the front door to get into character. Both of us bent over slightly, and I took his arm at the crook of the elbow. As we left the building, we moved slowly and carefully, then went down the front steps with painstaking care.

Knowing we were fugitives made me want to hurry from one safe place to another. I resisted the impulse and stayed in character. They were looking for young people, not a couple of old-timers. Unless they detected Owen's magic, they shouldn't notice us at all.

We crossed the street and went up a block, then paused at a corner grocery to act like we were shopping. I didn't see anyone giving us suspicious looks, but when we stepped out of the store, one of the gray guys was on the sidewalk outside. I fought not to hold my breath or do anything else that would make me look more nervous than someone in my position should be. Maybe he was there watching someone else, not staking out the place for us. Why would they even think to stake out that place? It wasn't as though the grocery store was an obvious destination for fugitives.

We moved past him in our elderly shuffle, but since I didn't dare turn to look at him, I couldn't tell if he even noticed us. It was sheer agony to keep moving slowly instead of hurrying away. "Easy, easy," Owen breathed, apparently picking up on my tension.

But then I saw another gray guy ahead of us, not quite at the end of the block. "Owen," I moaned under my breath.

"I see him. Don't change the way you're walking. Act normal—the old version. We'll go up that next set of stairs."

"Is it an empty building?"

"I have no idea. I didn't case this street."

The gray guy was moving toward us, but I couldn't tell if he was heading for us or just walking down the street. I had to fight not to allow my eyes to focus on him. It seemed like the longest twenty feet I'd ever walked before we reached the next set of steps. To maintain our illusion, we had to go up them slowly, one step at a time. All the while, I felt the guard drawing nearer.

I stood so that passers-by couldn't see that Owen was unlocking the front door without a key, and just as he opened the door, the gray guy reached the steps. He started to walk past as we entered the building, but as the door closed behind us, I heard his footsteps stop.

The inside of this stairwell was blank, just a structural shell, so apparently no prisoners lived here. That must have given us away. We didn't have time to worry about that, though. Forgetting about looking old, we ran through the featureless space as quickly as possible while still hitting the floor beams. The gray guy hadn't come inside yet, but I feared it was only a matter of time. I estimated we'd run to the next building when we reached a doorway. Owen flung it open and we ran out into a finished stairwell.

"Out?" I panted.

"Up," he replied.

Owen tried the door on the next landing, but it was locked—probably the home of a prisoner. We ran up to the next level, where the door opened and we were able to enter another empty space. We put at least two more buildings behind us before we slowed down and took refuge against an exterior wall, between two windows.

"He didn't follow us, did he?" I asked when I caught my breath.

"I don't think so."

"Did he see past our illusion?"

"It's hard to tell. Maybe he detected the difference between wizard magic and elf magic. Or maybe he knows the illusions that are supposed to be in that area and we didn't fit."

"If he can see us, how do we get out of here?"

"Let's wait a while. Maybe he'll go away."

We waited half an hour before we dared peek out the window. There were two of the gray guys on the street below. They seemed to be looking for something, and it was easy—and probably safest—to assume it was us.

We kept going until we reached the end of the block, where we could see out of two sides of the building. The corner building wasn't a brownstone. It was a regular apartment building with shops on the ground level. "I think we might be over Perdita's café," I said when I had my bearings from the view. "All we need to do is find a way out of here without getting caught."

There was a door that opened onto an interior hallway. The nearest "exit" sign indicated a stairwell that went all the way down. The bottom level was empty, and Owen had to use magic to light our way. We found a door that came out into the basement supply room of a restaurant. "Is this the right place?" Owen whispered.

"How am I supposed to know?" I replied. "I eat here. I don't lurk in the basement." I was about to say something else, but then I thought I heard a sound from the other side of the room. I gestured to Owen, and both of us ducked behind shelves as Owen doused his magical light.

There was definitely someone else in the basement, but he seemed to be trying to stay as hidden as we were. A restaurant employee would have called out to ask who was there. Instead, it was as though the other person was holding his breath and staying as still as possible.

I glanced back at the door where we'd entered and was just about to tug Owen toward it when a voice from the darkness on the other side of the basement said, "Katie, Owen, is that you?"

"Earl?" I whispered.

"Yeah," came the response. "So it *is* you?"

We met in the middle of the room. "What are you doing here?" I asked. "We were worried when you didn't show up." I didn't ask the obvious question. If he was under the spell, he wouldn't be hiding in a basement.

"I was pretty sure I had a tail, and I didn't want to lead them anywhere near you. I decided it would be safer to lose them and hide out for a while, and I was close enough for Perdita to help me."

"Is she okay?" I asked.

"They didn't come anywhere near her."

I turned to Owen. "That's weird. If they managed to get to us through the spy, surely they'd have eventually tracked back to Perdita."

"Maybe their precautions weren't about what we've done here, but about what we do back home," Owen suggested. "The Council guys are essentially magical cops, we foiled Sylvester's last scheme, and Earl is a known rebel. Perdita may have been under their radar."

"What happened to you two?" Earl asked.

"When you didn't come back, we figured Perdita would be a contact point," I said. "How did things go for you?"

"They got to Brad, and I was able to snap him out of it," Earl said. "We're on for tonight. We figured sundown in what passes for Central Park, at the spot just before it loops back to Riverside—it's a lot like Cherry Hill, but not quite. There has to be a lot of magic in that area to form that kind of boundary loop, so maybe our portal won't be quite so obvious."

Owen checked his watch. "We've got a few more hours to kill, and if the vultures aren't circling us, we may as well wait here until then."

We made ourselves as comfortable as we could on the floor behind some shelves, where we weren't visible from the stairs. I wasn't aware of drifting off to sleep, but the next thing I was conscious of was feeling a little stiff from sleeping on Owen's shoulder. I kept my eyes shut, hoping desperately that this whole thing about living in an alternate reality straight out of a bad romantic comedy was nothing more than a dream.

Even Owen nudging me gently didn't have to ruin things. That could happen if I'd fallen asleep during a movie. "Katie, wake up," he whispered. "We need to go."

Reluctantly, I opened my eyes and had to accept that my predicament was very real. Nearby noises told me that Earl was also stirring. In the very faint light, I saw Owen crawl to the hatch that led to the sidewalk. He peered out, then said, "I don't see any gray guys."

"We should probably split up, so if they catch one group of us, they won't catch all of us," I suggested. "Earl, you go with Perdita. We'll meet you there."

We climbed the steps and emerged on the sidewalk. It was the evening rush hour, so the sidewalk was busy and crowded, and we didn't stand out too badly. We melted into the crowd and made our way toward the park.

We'd gone a few blocks when I noticed one of the gray guys on the opposite side of the street. I nudged Owen, but he didn't seem to respond at all—until we reached the next intersection and he casually turned us down the side street heading toward the park, as though that was where we'd been going all along. I couldn't tell if the gray guy had seen us, and looking back over my shoulder to see if he'd followed us would be a dead giveaway.

"What do we do?" I whispered to Owen.

"Just keep going." In the middle of the block, he stopped and knelt to tie his shoe, then stood and reported, "He didn't follow us."

"Then let's go before another one shows up," I urged.

We didn't encounter any more of the gray guys. I felt a lot better once we were inside the park even though I knew that we weren't necessarily safer there. I just felt a lot less exposed surrounded by trees. The others soon joined us at the designated meeting place.

When we were all gathered, Owen said, "This should work better on natural ground, say, over there under those trees." We trooped over to the place he'd pointed out, then he closed his eyes for a moment. Nodding with satisfaction, he said, "Yeah, this place should work."

He found a stick and knelt to scratch something in the dirt. As he did so, he directed, "I need you guys to find me some small stones, preferably smooth and round." The elves and I scrounged around on the ground, picking up rocks. Owen arranged the rocks in a circle around the symbols he'd been drawing in the dirt. "I should probably set up wards to keep this magic from being detected," he said as he worked, "but I'm afraid we can't spare the power. We'll just have to make it quick, get our message out, then dash—and hope it works so they'll send help in case we get caught." He gestured for the others to join him and said, "In the absence of wards, Katie, you stand guard. I'd rather not draw on your power unless we have to. Yell if you see anyone coming."

I wanted to see what they were doing, but I had to admit that keeping watch was more important than observing magic I'd never be able to do. Before I turned away, I saw Owen writing a note. Soon afterward, he started an incantation in a language I didn't know. It might have been elvish, since the elves soon joined in.

I forced myself to focus on the surrounding park, looking for any sign that we were being watched. I was only one pair of eyes, though. Anyone could sneak up on us from behind wherever I was at the time. I settled for walking in rapid circles around the spellcasters, hoping that anyone who did approach us wouldn't move quickly enough to reach us in the time it took me to get around the circle.

A slight glow was just starting to form in the circle when someone stepped out of the shadows right next to me, making me jump and yelp.

It was Florence, my colleague from the coffee shop. "Owen!" I called out. "We've got company!"

But she made no move to stop us, to hit us with the whammy, or to call the authorities. She just put her hands on her hips and snapped, "What do you fools think you're doing?"

CHAPTER EIGHTEEN

Behind me, the incantation stopped, and the park grew dimmer as whatever they'd generated faded away. "Um, nothing, really," I said, trying to play innocent, in spite of the evidence around me.

"You weren't trying to open a portal, were you?" Florence asked. "Did you really think you could escape that way? Do you know the kind of power it would take to punch a hole like that between realms?"

"Yes, which is why it was going to be a very small portal," Owen said, sounding surprisingly calm as he came over to stand at my side.

"And did you think you could use that much power without anyone noticing?" Florence scolded.

"No. I just hoped we'd get our message through before we got caught."

She shook her head and made motherly "tsk, tsk" noises. "It would never have worked. Now, come on, I need you to get away from here before anyone else shows up."

The others all looked at me, and I said, "She's one of the guards, but she's always had my back, and tried to clue me in about what was going on, even before the spell broke. We may as well trust her."

"It's not like we have a lot of other options," Earl grumbled, but they all followed as Florence bustled us away from that part of the park.

When we were in an area sheltered by hedges, she gestured for us to sit down, and then her appearance shimmered for a second before solidifying into something that was very different, if still recognizable as Florence. Her face was thin and angular, her body was willowy, her eyebrows slanted, and her ears pointed. She turned to Earl and Brad and said, "You're with the underground, aren't you?" Then she did something with her hands that looked like a graceful and elegant gang sign. Earl and Brad returned the sign.

"She's okay," Earl said. "She's one of us."

"She's a double agent," I said.

She sank to sit among us. "You figured me out? Yeah, I got in really deep with Sylvester's organization and next thing I know, I've been shipped off to the Homelands and put to work as a cast member in the world's creepiest theme park."

"You knew what Sylvester was doing all along, and yet you did nothing? You told no one?" Earl accused.

"Don't you think I've been trying to find a way to send messages back? That's how I know you can't make your own portal. Once you're here, you're here, even if you're staff. There's one portal, and it's warded so heavily that no one can get through, not even those of us who are in on the scheme. I guess they figure there's a chance some of us could be double agents, so they're not letting us communicate with anyone back home. All I could do was sabotage their efforts."

She turned to me. "You were right that I was trying to nudge you toward breaking the spell without breaking my cover. And man, but you were dense. I thought you'd never get it. To be honest, I'm not sure how you did eventually break through."

"It wasn't that I had a brilliant breakthrough," I admitted. "It's just that normally I'm immune to magic. My current magic supply is extremely limited, and as it wore away, it seems that the spell lost its grip on me." Then I had a sudden burst of inspiration. "You said the portal is warded. Could a magical immune get through?"

She frowned in thought, but before she could answer, Owen protested, "Katie!"

"Actually, she may be on to something," Florence said, nodding slowly. "Can you normally get through wards?"

"All the time," I said.

"How hard would it be for you to get back to your immune state? You said your power was wearing off."

Owen didn't give me a chance to answer. He grabbed my hand and said, "This isn't a good idea."

I squeezed his hand as I turned to face him. "You said I was running low on magic and would eventually run out. Why don't I just burn myself out and then make a break for it?"

"You'd give up your magic?"

"It's not like I have a choice. It's eventually going to be gone anyway."

"But draining your power should be a last resort."

"This *is* a last resort," I snapped. More gently, I added, "I'm okay with it, really. I like being immune. I think I'm more useful that way." I curled my fingers around his. "I know you hated being without magic, but that's who you are. Being immune is what I am, and going back to that would mean being myself again."

"I'm not sure what this place would be like to someone who can't be affected by the illusions. You probably wouldn't be able to hide the fact that you're not affected for long. It could even be dangerous."

"Have you got any better ideas?" Florence asked. "Because I'm all ears if you do. But I'm thinking that having an immune is our ace in the hole, and this is time to use it."

"This is even better than sending a note," I argued. "I can tell Merlin directly what's going on."

"You'd be coming through the portal into their headquarters," Owen pointed out.

"Yeah, and they'll use magic to fight me. Which won't work because of the immunity thing." I was feeling more and more confident about this plan.

"If you're going to burn off magic, I suggest you do it here," Florence said. "It won't be as noticeable in the park, but then that means you'll have to get across town without magic, and I honestly don't know what that would be like for you. Magical immunity is incompatible with this construct."

"I can only burn off so much power on my own," I said. "I can get down to normal human levels of magic—enough to be affected by it—here, and then one of you can draw on me to drain me the rest of the way once we get to the portal. Something tells me I won't be able to just walk up to it and waltz through it."

"We'll have to fight our way to it," Florence confirmed.

"Then a little extra juice might come in handy for one of you," I said. "We probably also need a better plan than just me walking through the portal." I checked my watch. "It would be best if we could time it for right after the shift change—the fewer guards, the better. And maybe we should create a diversion elsewhere in the neighborhood to draw more guards away."

"We could give Mac his uprising," Owen suggested. "That would make him happy."

"We'll have to find Mac to revive him and loop him in," I said. "Do we even know where he goes after dark?"

"You mean the two guys who play chess in the park all day, the Council men?" Florence asked. "I know where to find them."

"You'll have to go revive them," I said to Owen. "You're the one with memories that might trigger Mac."

"I'm not leaving you alone while you drain your magic," Owen insisted stubbornly.

"Maybe any memories from when he was himself will work, even if they're from here," Brad suggested. "Some of us could go to him and try that. If he followed directions, he has some written memories, too. We just have to make him look at them."

"Let's go with that approach," I said with a nod. "You go get Mac and anyone else you can find, and then cause as much trouble and noise as you can, starting at eight thirty. Anyone who's still standing and themselves an hour later should head toward the portal. If I'm able to send help, it'll be easier if we have most of our people nearby."

They all nodded in agreement. I stood and brushed grass off my skirt. "We may as well get started." Florence gave Mac's address to Brad, and the riot team headed off. I turned to Owen and said, "Now, how do I want to use my very last magic? Maybe a few more minutes as a blond bombshell."

Owen winced as he stood to join me. "Please, not that one."

"Okay, how about this?" I sent up a shower of sparks that danced down around us. It was like that night in the bookstore when we'd discovered our powers, and Owen smiled, at last.

Watching the sparks fall, I found myself growing wistful. As much as I believed every argument I'd made in favor of this plan, I couldn't help but feel a little regret at losing magic for good, if only because I wouldn't be able to do fun little things like this.

I twirled around, surrounding myself with magical sparks and laughing with the joy of it. Belatedly, I realized that putting on a light show wasn't the stealthiest thing to do under these circumstances. I killed the sparks, then conjured up a bottle of champagne and enough glasses for all of us. Owen opened the bottle and poured the champagne, and I passed out the glasses.

"A toast to the last moments of magical Katie," I said. "It was fun while it lasted, but I think I'm ready to be my normal self again. After all, if I'd been my normal self, I'd never have ended up here."

"To magical Katie," Owen toasted. I noticed that he left out the "end" part.

I'd never made the telepathy spell work the right way, but I tried it now, pouring every bit of power I had into it to direct a thought to Owen's mind. *I really am okay. It's not the same as for you,* I sent.

I barely detected the slightest whisper in my mind, so faint I had to think to decipher it. *You're braver than I would be.*

I didn't have the energy to send another mental message, so I whispered to him, "I thought you'd already been that brave. Why shouldn't I be?"

Instead of answering me directly, he said, "Try some more magic."

I tried for the sparks, since they were the most obvious indicator of how much power I was putting out. Instead of the big showers I'd had earlier, I barely managed a few sputters at the ends of my fingers. Since that was barely visible a few feet away, I kept going until I couldn't even generate a faint glow. "Okay, looks like I'm done," I said.

I forced myself not to shudder. I was fine with being a magical immune, but I wasn't looking forward to the in-between stage when I'd be like most humans—susceptible to magic, but unable to use it. I'd lost my immunity a time or two from a potion, and it had been a nightmare. I wasn't sure how normal people survived. Being "normal" to me was as bad as the way Owen saw being immune.

"Then we should go, now," Florence said, standing from where she'd been watching the magic-draining process. Her human appearance returned as she stood. "I think I can get you through the streets without any major guard encounters. If someone does stop us, try to act like you're under the spell, and I'll pretend I caught you. I'd rather not blow my cover if I can help it."

Despite her assurance, I wasn't happy about leaving the relatively safe harbor of the park. I associated the cityscape with being hunted and on the run. Once we were back in the city, it didn't look any different to me, but I supposed it wouldn't yet.

Owen took my hand in his as we walked. "I don't know how long it will take to drain the last of the magic, so maybe I should start now," he murmured.

"Good idea," I replied, keeping my voice too low for the others to hear. "We won't exactly be able to tell the portal guards to hold on a sec while we restore my magical immunity so I can get past their wards." I shivered as I felt the tingle between our clasped hands.

Florence must have known the pattern of any patrols because we didn't run into anyone on our way to that small park. By the time we got there, my magic levels must have been hovering around the "E" on the gauge because the buildings flickered when I looked at them out of the corner of my eye. There was still something there, but it was just a big, blank box instead of a block of picturesque brownstones.

"This place isn't nearly as nice without the illusion," I whispered to Owen. "It really does look like a prison."

Then I did a double take. On top of the building across the street from the park was a row of gargoyles. I didn't see them if I looked directly at them, but they flickered in and out of sight if I didn't try to focus on them. I reached around and grabbed Owen's jacket with my free hand. "Owen, they've got gargoyles here! Instead of trying to make them look normal and enchanting them to think they belonged here, they must have just brought them through the portal, stuck them on the nearest building, and veiled them." I paused to think about it, then added, "Though I suppose they could have enchanted them to think they really were regular gargoyles who can't talk or move. I know I didn't see them when we were here before."

He turned to look, even though he couldn't see them. "Do you recognize any of them?"

"They're pretty far away, and I still don't see them if I look directly. But if we could snap them out of it, they'd be helpful in getting to that portal."

"Florence!" Owen called out. She stopped and turned around. "Can you see the gargoyles on the roof?"

"Nope. My security clearance is pretty low. I had a limited assignment. You're saying some of your gargoyles are up there?"

"Maybe."

"We have to try," I urged Owen. "We still have some time before our diversion starts."

"Give us a few minutes," Owen said. Still holding my hand, he led me to the nearest set of steps, and then we went into the building and up until we reached the stairs that led to the roof.

The higher we climbed, the less substantial the staircase looked. The upper landing was as blank as those unformed rooms had been, without all the touches that had made these buildings seem real. It was disconcerting. To cover my dismay, I said, "You know, I feel ripped-off. If they were going to give me the ideal New York movie life, I should have had access to a romantic rooftop oasis, where we should have had at least one good scene. There'd be twinkling lights, some potted plants, and space to have dinner for two before dancing in the rain."

"Really? That's something you want? Dancing in the rain?"

"It's what's in all those movies. I don't know if it's actually any fun, though. I've never tried it."

This rooftop wasn't at all romantic, probably because I was back to my usual state in which illusion no longer worked on me. Part of me wanted to cry out in relief, but this wasn't the best place to be a magical immune. The most realistic thing I saw was a row of frozen gargoyles.

I moved closer to them, still holding Owen's hand, so that now I was leading him instead of the other way around. Sam wasn't among the group, much to my relief, since I wanted him to be around on the other side to help take care of Sylvester, but I knew two of the gargoyles, Rocky and Rollo, who made the most unusual chauffeur team I'd ever met.

I faced Rollo and said, "Hey, Rollo, BRAAAAAAKE!" It was all I could think of, and I figured that tag-team driving, with one looking out the windshield and steering and the other working the pedals, was something truly unique to their existence in the real world.

The gargoyle shuddered, then slowly turned around to face me. "Oh, hi, Katie." Then awareness of his surroundings seemed to hit, and he asked, "Where are we?"

"Not in Kansas," I quipped. When he obviously didn't get the reference, I said, "We're prisoners in the elven realm, and you've been enchanted. But we're about to try to get to the portal that will let us go warn Merlin about what's happening."

"Oh, okay," he said, nodding as though that was a perfectly reasonable explanation. "Do you need some help with that?"

"Yeah, as a matter of fact. Do you know all these other gargoyles well?"

He looked up and down the row, then said, "Sure do."

"Then talk to them. Call them by name and say something that should remind them of the real world. And then join us across the street."

"Got it," he said. He wasn't the sharpest tool in the shed at the best of times, but I figured I could count on him for that much, so Owen and I left the rooftop. I avoided looking beyond the immediate vicinity because I didn't want to see what the idealized New York romantic comedy neighborhood looked like now. From the bits I'd seen, I had a feeling I'd have enough nightmares about being trapped in a featureless world, as it was. Without the illusions, it was like something out of a dystopian science fiction movie.

"Were they ours?" Earl asked, his voice tight with concern.

"I recognized Rocky and Rollo," I said. "I was able to wake up Rollo, and he's taking care of the rest." Sure enough, dark shapes were already swooping down from the rooftop to join us.

At the same time, there were loud booms in the distance. It sounded like our diversion had begun. We hurried to hide behind a set of front steps and watched as gray guys ran from the park and into the neighborhood.

"Looks like we're ready to go," Florence said with a smile of grim satisfaction. "Are you fully immune now? Because hitting the wards would be a bad time to find out you aren't."

"I was able to see the gargoyles," I said. "And this place no longer looks anything like the Upper West Side."

"I'll make sure she's okay," Owen said.

The gargoyles flew in first, doing some aerial reconnaissance, then returned to report that there were four guards, two at the gateway and maybe two more at the portal. I started to feel like that was more than manageable, but then I realized that if they were at the portal, they were *inside* the wards, and I'd have to deal with them on my own.

"Um, how am I supposed to take out two guards?" I asked nervously.

"You don't have to take them out. You just have to get past them," Florence said.

"They'll probably use magic to fight you, and by the time they notice that it doesn't work on you, you should be through the portal," Owen added.

"Maybe we can do something out here that will draw their attention so you can sneak past," Earl suggested. "I'm sure we can pull off another diversion."

"Oh, that's a great plan! I like that idea!" I said, perhaps a wee bit too enthusiastically.

"We'll make the guards at the gateway scream for help," Earl said, and the tone of his voice implied that he'd greatly enjoy doing something to make them scream.

"First, let's make sure you're immune," Owen said. He squeezed my hand tighter for a few seconds, then released me and stepped back. I felt the tingle of magic surrounding me, but didn't notice anything else happening. "Okay, you're immune," he said, perhaps a bit mournfully.

"Then let's do this," I said. I wanted to get it over with before I lost my nerve—and before I had to spend another minute in this crazy place.

We entered the park, the gargoyles flying ahead. It didn't look like a park to me now. It was just a blank space with a couple of plain benches and a few shapes that might have been trees and bushes. Instead of having the wall of a building at the far end, the space stretched on, the way it had the first time we'd found it. Just beyond where the wall should have been stood the first two guards.

By the time we reached the guards, the gargoyles were already upon them, dive-bombing them and grabbing at them with their talons. I'd experienced a gargoyle attack like that, and I didn't envy the guards.

According to plan, the guards started shouting for help. I hoped the portal guards were the ones to respond because things would get a lot more complicated if other guards appeared and we ended up with more people to fight.

And, of course, as luck would have it, reinforcements appeared from elsewhere in the park. Earl and his friends turned just in time to fight them off. "There goes my cover," Florence muttered as she joined the fight. Owen held me off to the side so I'd be ready to run as soon as the way was clear.

Our luck improved when one guard arrived from beyond the gateway. "This may be the best we can hope for," Owen said.

I didn't trust myself to speak, so I gave him what I hoped was a firm nod. There wasn't really anything firm about me at the moment, as my legs seemed to have turned to jelly and my insides felt all watery. But I still managed to run as Owen and I dashed past the first set of guards and through the gateway out of the containment area and into the elven realm.

Without the illusion of dense park vegetation or whatever else they'd used to hide it, I could see the portal just ahead, a shimmering oval casting a greenish glow on the surrounding area. We stopped at a safe distance, and he waved a hand in what I recognized as a veiling spell. "So, I just go through it?" I asked, even as I winced at how badly my voice shook. "No spell, incantation, or anything?"

"I think it should be as simple as just going through it. With the kind of energy required to create a portal between realities, they'd have to keep it open."

"What'll I find when I get through to the other side?"

"That would be the tricky part," he said with an audible gulp. "It should be that same warehouse where we first found the other end of the portal, but what's there now, we don't know."

"And I should be able to go through, in spite of being immune to magic?"

"It shouldn't make much of a difference."

"Then what stops them from sending me right back here?"

"They can't mess with your head the way they did before, and they'd have to use physical force to make you go through the portal."

"That's not very reassuring."

"This was your plan," he reminded me.

"Yeah, I know, and I still can't think of a better option."

"Me, either," he admitted. "You're on your own after this. I can't go any farther."

"What'll happen to you on this side?"

He gave me a smile that strained at being cocky but didn't quite make it. "Remember, you're going to come rescue me." More seriously, he added, "If we can hold off the guards long enough, I may be able to do something about these wards. It'll take time, but now that we're here and have the guards busy, we'll see what I can do. I may join you before you know it."

I was about to give him a jaunty salute and then head boldly through the wards, but he abruptly reached for my hands and held them clasped tightly in his own. His palms were clammy with what I suspected was fear, and my suspicion was borne out by the tremor in his voice as he said, "Take care of yourself. Above all, stay safe. Put that above sending messages, getting help, or getting us back."

"That sort of defeats the purpose of me doing this," I said, but the tremor in my own voice diminished my attempt at a snarky tone.

"I just don't want to lose you."

"I don't want to lose you, either. And that's why I'm going to go through that portal and do whatever it takes to get everyone back home and stop Sylvester's scheme." I managed to crack a smile. "I think you just don't like the idea of being the one to be rescued. You make a lousy damsel in distress."

"I do, I really do," he agreed, sounding a little more like himself. He released my hands, but before I could move away from him, he grabbed me and held me in a tight hug.

"I'm only going to another reality," I gasped, struggling for breath with my chest constricted. "It's not like you'll never see me again."

He eased his hold just enough to kiss me. If I hadn't already been breathless, that would have done the trick. "I'll find you again, no matter what," he whispered hoarsely, his lips still lightly brushing mine.

"Right back at you, handsome," I said. "See you on the other side." I reluctantly slipped out of his embrace, and he let me go.

I felt the wards before I reached them. I was used to the wards Owen put around his office and his home, and I thought they were powerful, but these were industrial-strength. My hair felt like it was standing on end, like I was touching one of those things my physics teacher used to demonstrate electricity. I steeled myself, took a deep breath, and stepped through the wards, hoping Owen was right about having removed every last trace of magic from me. If he hadn't, I had a feeling things were about to get really unpleasant.

The sense of passing through powerful magic walls took my breath away, but nothing stopped my progress, and soon I was safely on the other side.

Unfortunately, that brought me to the attention of the remaining guard. He seemed more than a little taken aback to see someone on the other side of the wards. I got the feeling that up until now, he'd thought he had the most boring job around, guarding something that no one could reach. Now he didn't know what to make of someone who could reach it.

"Hi there!" I said with a friendly wave. "Whatcha got there? It's very shiny."

He hit me with some magic, but it had its usual lack of effect on me. I laughed out loud with the joy of being back to my usual self. Being able to do magic was cool, but this was who I really was, and I knew how to work it in a way I'd never understood magic.

My sense of triumph died when I saw that Owen was no longer alone on the other side of the wards. More guards approached him from behind. I shouted a warning, though I wasn't sure the sound would carry through the wards. At the same time, the guard on my side of the wards hit me with another bit of magic that I ignored while I watched Owen. He turned just in the nick of time, but he was badly outnumbered. They would overwhelm him in a moment.

I started to rush toward him, but stopped myself. More of our people were on the other side of the wards, and I was the only one who could get through the portal. I was our only hope. As much as I hated leaving Owen behind, I forced myself to focus on my mission.

The guard kept attacking me magically, astonished that his magic had no effect on this impossible interloper. I took advantage of that by rushing straight at him. He ran toward me, and at the last second, I veered aside to aim for the portal. It was an old fake-out I'd learned when playing touch football with my brothers, and since this guy obviously hadn't experienced the joys of football, it took him a while to react.

About two seconds too long, in fact. I was almost to the portal when I felt a breeze against the back of my neck as he reached out to grab me, but I ducked and rolled in the nick of time. I went through the portal in a somersault.

And then I emerged in the middle of the biggest party I'd ever seen.

CHAPTER NINETEEN

At first, I thought I'd wound up in the wrong place, despite Owen's assurances. This wasn't some old warehouse where an alien army was being assembled. It was a New York City rave.

No, make that a disco, I mentally corrected myself, since the song currently blasting through the cavernous space was the extended dance mix of "I Will Survive." A disco ball overhead sent shards of greenish light reflected from the portal around the room, and beams of colored light played around the dance floor as a mass of people—make that elves—partied like it was 1979.

In the middle of the elven version of *Saturday Night Fever*, nobody even noticed that someone had come through the portal. In fact, I stood out more by sitting still on the floor than I had from somersaulting out of the portal. I jumped to my feet and attempted to move like the dancers. Immediately, I had two elven soldiers move to dance with me. They glared daggers at each other, then the one who'd arrived a split second later sighed and backed away.

While I danced awkwardly in front of the gyrating elf, I glanced around the room. I wasn't the only female present, but we were definitely in the minority, and we were very popular. Being an in-demand dance partner might make it harder to escape than any guards would.

Although I hadn't anticipated landing in a party, I supposed it made sense. If you kept a bunch of elves cooped up in a big space like this, and if they were from another world and they were just discovering disco, this was what was likely to happen. I said a mental prayer of thanks to Saint Gloria of Gaynor because as weird as this situation was, it sure beat landing in the middle of drilling soldiers.

When the song shifted to a Bee Gees tune, I moved on to dance in front of another elf, aiming for the exit on the other side of the room. So far, no one had noticed that I was human or an outsider. It took four songs for me to get within clear view of the exit, and then my hopes fell. The party ended at the doorway. Beyond that, in the hall that led to the street entrance, there were several armed guards who didn't look like they were having any fun. They were facing out, like they were keeping people away rather than keeping people in, but I didn't think they were likely to just let me leave. I needed to find another way out.

During a group participation rendition of "YMCA," during which I was unable to make any progress, I noticed a staircase leading to a balcony surrounding the portal room/disco. That gave me an idea. If some gargoyles had disappeared from here, that meant MSI security knew something about this place, and if I knew Sam, he'd be staking it out.

As soon as the song ended and a Donna Summer tune started, I danced my way toward the stairs. I might not be able to escape via the roof, but I might be able to get a message out that way. There were a number of elves hanging out on the balcony, watching the dance floor below, and I paused to do the same before moving on to look for a roof-access stairwell.

Although my mission was urgent, I forced myself to look casual. This was a clear case of nobody questioning you if you acted like you belonged. So far, I was getting along just fine in enemy territory, and I didn't want to do anything to jeopardize that.

This building might have been Elf Central, but it was still in New York and subject to the building code, so there was an exit sign over a doorway, indicating a stairwell. Unsure if the elves' lack of interest in me would extend to me going through an exit door, I leaned against the balcony railing for a while, watching the dance floor. It was hard to think of all these dancers as a potential threat to my world. Did they even know what they were being used for? And were they on board with this mission? Maybe all we needed to do to stop the elven invasion was introduce the would-be army to the New York club scene. Then Sylvester would have to turn to Plan B for taking over the world. These guys didn't seem like they'd want to change or destroy a world with nightclubs in it.

When "Dancing Queen" came on, the partiers whooped with joy and enthusiastically threw themselves into dancing along. Even the elves on the balcony joined in the dancing. They were all so caught up in the music that they didn't notice me easing open the stairwell door and slipping through it.

There were no guards in the stairwell, so I was able to run up to the roof level. I cautiously opened the roof door, made sure the coast was clear, then wedged a piece of wood I found nearby between the door and the frame so it wouldn't close all the way, in case the door automatically locked from the inside.

At first glance, the rooftop seemed empty. The good news was that there were no elves up there, whether guards or partiers escaping the crowd. The bad news was that I didn't see any gargoyles, either. Now would have been a good time to have magical powers, I thought. I could have sent up some kind of signal. A cell phone might also have come in handy. I was starting to rethink my stubborn stance on refusing to have one. Then again, even if I'd had one, I wouldn't have it now, since it seemed like all our stuff had been taken away from us when we were sent into the other realm. I wondered if jumping up and down and waving my arms would do any good. The danger there was that I had no idea what I'd attract.

That made me realize how visible and vulnerable I was standing there on the rooftop. There was a waist-high wall around the edge of the roof, and I ducked so that I was beneath it. Crouching, I made my way around the roof, peering up occasionally. It would have been lovely if I'd spotted Sam perched on an adjacent rooftop, watching this place, but I didn't.

What I did find was a fire escape on the opposite side of the building from the entrance. It was a long way down, but it was a way out, and I couldn't forget that Owen was still in danger. I watched over the edge for a while, making sure there weren't any patrols, then I gathered my courage and stepped off the roof onto a fairly rickety metal ladder. These things had to be inspected regularly, right? Elves might own this building, but they'd still have to have a working fire escape, I was sure.

The ladder rattled and creaked alarmingly, but it remained firmly attached to the building. I had to stop and rest with my arm hooked around the ladder every so often because my fingers grew tired and numb from the death grip I had on each rung. When I finally stole a glance at the ground below—which I'd been avoiding doing—it was near enough to be in focus, much to my relief. I came to the end of the ladder and stepped cautiously onto the part that extended to reach the ground. It shot downward so quickly I had to bite back a squeal of fright that surely would have alerted the guards on the other side of the building. Then again, they'd have had to hear it over the pulsing sounds of disco music. In this neighborhood, I figured the guards would have their hands full persuading outsiders that this really wasn't a nightclub too hot to have a sign advertising it.

After taking a moment to catch my bearings, I ran away from the building. I quickly became acutely aware that this was the real New York, not the sanitized only-in-the-movies version where I'd been imprisoned. The city was generally safer than its public image suggested, but it still wasn't the sort of place where it was smart for a woman to walk alone at whatever after-dark time it was. It must have been very late—or, rather, early—because the streets were just about deserted.

Now I really wished I had a cell phone. Since everyone else had one, pay phones had become scarce. Not that I had any change for a pay phone. Or money or a MetroCard for the subway. Or keys to my apartment. I was pretty close to Fourteenth Street, so I supposed I could walk home across town and use the phone there to call the office. That was, assuming my roommates were home and would open the door to me—and then not call the police because I'd suddenly returned from having been missing. I wondered how long I'd been gone. The weather didn't seem too different from when I'd left, and the clothes I'd been wearing in prison were appropriate for the temperature, though I'd have been a lot more comfortable with the coat I'd left in the bookstore when we'd fled.

I reached Fourteenth and was wondering if I could convince a cabbie to take me home and then wait for me to have one of my roommates bring money for the fare when a voice called out, "Is that you, doll? I've been following you for blocks."

I screamed and jumped, terrified that some late-night lecher was taking advantage of my solitude, and then I saw the gargoyle alighting on top of a nearby sign. I'd never seen a more beautiful sight. Tears of joy sprang to my eyes. "Oh, Sam, thank goodness! I didn't know what to do or where to go and I have to warn Merlin." My voice was alarmingly wobbly, sounding like I might burst into tears at any moment.

He hopped over to a street sign closer to me and draped one leathery/stony wing around my shoulders. "There, there, sweetheart," he crooned in his gravelly voice. "It's okay. I got you. But where the hell have you been for the last week? We've been lookin' everywhere."

"A week? That's all it's been?" Then I pulled myself together and told him, "We were captured by the elves—all of us, all the ones who've gone missing. Owen was with me, and Earl and Perdita were there, too. Dan showed up recently, and I just found Rocky and Rollo. In that warehouse there's a portal to the elven realms. That's where they had us, and we were under a spell that made us think we were still in New York, but we didn't know about magic, and it's all very complicated. What I need to tell you is that Sylvester's bringing through an army from the elven realms. At the moment, they're busy dancing the night away, but I think it could still be a problem. And everyone else is still trapped in the elven lands because they can't get through the wards to the portal, and Owen's under attack. He was in trouble when I left, but I had to go." I stopped, totally out of breath and drained now that I'd accomplished my mission to warn someone.

Sam patted my shoulder and nodded. "Well, it's okay now, doll. Lemme call this one in, and then we'll get you to a safe place." He reached up a clawed hand to tap his ear, then gave a rapid-fire series of orders. I was so relieved and exhausted that I didn't even register what he said. I was too focused on what I'd managed to do and what there still was to do. I couldn't forget the last glimpse I'd had of Owen under attack.

A moment later, Sam said, "I'm gonna put you in a cab, since I don't think you're up for a magic carpet ride right now."

"Nope, I'm still not up for that," I said, shuddering as I remembered my last experience with magic carpets.

"Then I'll meet you back at the office, and we'll talk to the boss, okay?"

"Okay," I said meekly.

A cab pulled up a moment later, and it was only after I was safely ensconced in the back seat that I realized just how exhausted I was. I must have dozed off because it seemed like only seconds before a blast of chilly air woke me. I opened my eyes to see that the cab had stopped in front of MSI headquarters, and Merlin was holding the cab door open for me. He offered his hand to help me out.

I'd barely left the car when something struck me and held me in a viselike grasp around the waist. I started to squirm away, then realized it was my grandmother. Granny had never been much of a hugger, so this reaction told me how worried about me she was. Before I could return her hug, she released me and stepped away, her expression making it clear that this had never happened. "It's about time you got back," she snapped, only a slight rasp in her voice revealing her emotions. "What were you thinking, wandering off like that?"

I didn't get a chance to reply before someone else caught me in a bear hug. "It's so good to see you. We've been worried," Rod's voice said into my ear. He pulled away and frowned. "But what about Owen?"

"We should let Miss Chandler sit down before we interrogate her," Merlin said. He tucked my hand into his elbow to escort me into the building and up to his office. Once we were there, he got me settled into a chair and handed me a hot cup of tea. Granny and Rod pulled up chairs nearby, like they were afraid to let me out of their sight.

"It is good to see you safe, Miss Chandler," Merlin said, his voice gruff with a surprising amount of emotion. "We'd feared you were lost for good, along with the others. I know you need to rest after your ordeal, but I'm sure you appreciate the gravity of the situation."

I swallowed the sip of tea I'd just taken and said, "I totally get it. That's why I'm here, to spread the word and get help." I drank the rest of the tea to fortify myself before I launched into the story, far more coherently than I'd told it to Sam. I left out most of the romantic comedy details, focusing instead on what we'd seen before we were captured, what we'd learned after we broke the spell, and what I'd discovered upon returning to the warehouse. "And I've only been gone a week?" I concluded. "It's been a really, *really* busy week."

"The enchantment likely altered your sense of time, and time does move differently in other realms," Merlin said with a wryly amused smile.

"Does that mean I'm a month or so older than I should be?"

Granny snorted. "You're too young to worry about that."

Merlin's expression grew more serious. "And now we must stop Sylvester's army before he can act."

"Not to mention gettin' the rest of our people home," Sam added. I hadn't realized he was there, though now that I thought about it, he would have arrived far ahead of the cab. I must have been really out of it before that tea.

"From what I saw in that warehouse, I'm not sure the army will be too tough to deal with," I said. "They're having a big party right now. It seems they've discovered disco. I don't think they're true believers in the cause. I even wonder if they came voluntarily or if they were brought here the way we were sent into that other world and don't know the real reason. If they've been enchanted, they may think this is something they have to do." I sighed wearily. "But if that's the case, I don't know how to break the spell on them because it requires knowing something about their real lives."

"How many of 'em were there, do you think?" Sam asked.

"A few hundred."

"That would be enough to solidify Sylvester's power and eliminate anyone who might oppose him, but not enough to take on the rest of the magical establishment," Rod said.

"We could probably find a way to trap 'em in that warehouse for the time being," Sam suggested. "Then Sylvester won't be able to use 'em."

"What we need is an iPod with a really good dance music playlist," I said, half in jest, but in my exhaustion-addled brain, I had a feeling I was on to something. I babbled on while I tried to make sense of it. "Our music seems to be totally new to them, and they're really getting into it. Elves have a thing for music, right?" And then something that I should have thought of earlier dawned on me. "Maybe that's how Sylvester's controlling them. There had to be someone from our world involved in it, because they were doing all the motions to 'YMCA,' and that's not something you just know if you've never seen anyone do it before."

Now even more about what I'd seen was making sense. "I think they were all under a spell. That may be why they didn't seem to care I was there. The spell must be in the music, and it didn't affect me since I'm immune again. But if we switched the music, they might still enjoy themselves without being under Sylvester's thrall."

The trick would be finding someone to DJ for the forces of good. Perdita would have been a good choice if she hadn't still been a prisoner. My roommate Gemma used to hit the club scene, but she hadn't done so in a while and I didn't want to risk dragging her into this. She was disturbingly enthusiastic about magical missions. "Jake!" I said abruptly. Owen's assistant was more into punk, but I was pretty sure he could put together a playlist that could save the world.

"I'll get him," Sam said. "He may even still be here. He's been pulling extra hours while Palmer's been missing."

A few minutes later, Jake ran in, breathless. "You need me?" he asked.

Then he saw me. "Katie! You're back! You're safe!" His gaze moved beyond me, searching, and I shook my head.

"Sorry, he's not with me. I was the only one who could get past the wards to escape, but I know where he is." I left out the fact that when I'd last seen Owen, he was about to come under attack by elven prison guards.

"But, getting through wards?" Jake asked, his forehead wrinkling. "I thought …"

I groaned inwardly. It had completely slipped my mind. After the number of times we'd explained Owen's returning magical powers in the other world, I should have remembered that it wasn't widely known in this world, either.

Merlin came to my rescue. "It's a long story, and I'm sure Owen will explain it to you when he returns."

Jake didn't look too upset by the news. He merely nodded and said, "That would explain the books he was having me find on magical infusion. But I bet that's not why you want me."

"Actually, we want your musical knowledge," I said. "We need the ultimate playlist."

He looked even more taken aback by that than he had been about the idea that Owen had magic again. "A playlist? Why?" he asked.

I gave him a quick recap about the partying elven army. "I think their music contains a spell. If we could switch it, that might break the spell. If they really like the new tunes, then maybe they won't want to go into battle. We might not convince them to go home, I suppose, but we can worry about that later."

"So you want music fun enough to stop a war? I think I can handle that."

"They were really grooving on disco, and remember, these are elves, so melody and harmony are important. They seemed to love the Bee Gees. Come to think of it, with those unearthly voices and tight harmonies, it would explain a lot …"

Jake grinned. "I'm surprised you hadn't figured that out already." He pulled an iPod out of his lab coat pocket and started scrolling through the screen. "Fortunately, my musical tastes are really broad. I've got a lot of stuff here that should work. Just give me a few minutes. How long a playlist do you need?" His thumbs worked rapidly across the device as he spoke.

"I don't know. Say about half an hour, maybe?"

He didn't look up from the screen as he said. "Okay."

While he worked, I turned back to the others. "I think I can get back into the building and swap out the iPod in the sound system's dock. All the partiers are blocking the portal, which should help keep anyone else from being whammied and sent to the other world." I waited for someone to tell me it was too dangerous, but Owen wasn't there. As annoying as his overprotective instincts could be, I felt a little lost coming up with a potentially dangerous plan without having to overcome any objections. Some of my best ideas came from addressing his concerns, so I hoped I wasn't missing anything.

"I don't like you going in there alone," Granny said. "I'm coming with you." Her objection wasn't quite the same as Owen's, but it did force me to think.

"That would be a bad idea," I said. "Until I can switch out the music, the spell might affect you. And after having been under the elf whammy, I can tell you it's not something you want. They can make you forget who you are. I have to go in alone on this one."

"I'll need your assistance," Merlin told Granny. "You're the one who has the best elf underground contacts."

"You're with the elf underground?" I asked her. Resistance seemed to run in the family.

"I met some nice people that night in the park when the Eye of the Moon was drawing them, and Earl introduced me to some others. We meet occasionally. And I didn't tell you because secret organizations are supposed to be secret."

"I'm going with you, though," Rod said, his jaw set stubbornly. "I won't go into the building until you give me an all-clear, but I'll be on the roof in case you need me."

"My guys and I will keep anyone from getting out into our world," Sam said. "That just leaves neutralizing the real bad guys."

"Leave that to me," Merlin said.

"Do you just want dance music, or do you want some ballads?" Jake asked.

"A few ballads would be okay," I said. "They did a nice sing-along with one slow Bee Gees song."

"And do you want to replicate the songs they were already hearing or do all new stuff?"

"How about a mix? Start with the stuff they were already hearing so the switch won't be so obvious. Then mix in new stuff." I listed the songs I remembered hearing.

"Gotcha. Just a few more minutes. I'll have to save this list for the next party I have. It's nothing short of awesome, if I do say so myself."

Sam flew over to land on the arm of the chair where I was sitting. "You know, doll, you're not gonna like it, but there's one good way to get you on that rooftop," he said softly.

"Yeah, I'd already figured that out. If you can keep the antique zombie gargoyles away, I'll be okay." The last time I'd been on a magic carpet, an evil gargoyle attack had nearly killed us. It wasn't an experience I wanted to repeat.

"I won't let 'em near you, I promise."

Jake finished his playlist, then handed me his iPod. "Take good care of her," he said, his fingers momentarily clutching on the device before he gave in and released it to me. "I want to make sure I can keep that playlist for later." He reached into his lab coat pocket and pulled out a cable with plugs on either end. "Oh, and you might need this. If it's a real docking station, you can just dock it, but otherwise you can connect through an auxiliary input jack with this."

Wary of the technical stuff, I thought about bringing him with me, but the same argument I'd given Granny applied.

"While we're handing out technology," Sam said as he flew to Merlin's desk. He picked up something and flew back to drop it in my lap. It was a cell phone. "The numbers you'll need are already in there."

"I guess I couldn't hold out forever," I said, turning the phone over in my hands. When I needed a phone, I usually used Owen's, since we were always together. Needing my own phone made me miss him.

"Call us when you think the spell is breaking," Sam instructed. He looked back over his shoulder and said, "And it looks like your ride is here."

I hated stepping out of Merlin's office window onto the magic carpet, but time was of the essence. Sam hovered alongside me as I made the frightening transition, with a little help from Rod. The carpet was driven by a small pixie-like creature. These guys knew what they were doing, and my last driver had saved us in the middle of an attack, so I felt a little better. To distract myself during the trip, I focused on the mission: infiltrating the Elf Lord's lair and confronting his whole imported army, armed only with an iPod. That was even more frightening than whizzing up Manhattan several stories above the ground.

"So, I've been gone a week, huh?" I said to Rod as we flew.

"Yeah. We've been worried."

"What about my roommates?"

"I told Marcia you had to go on a last-minute business trip. I thought it would probably be best if they didn't have reason to worry."

"Thanks! I wasn't looking forward to explaining where I've been. I'm still not sure I understand it."

In no time at all, we were back at the warehouse, and the carpet was settling gently onto the rooftop. The door was still propped open the way I'd left it. Rod gave my hand a quick squeeze and said, "Good luck. Call if you need me—and then call when you think it's safe."

"Will do." I hurried down the staircase to the balcony level, then cautiously slipped out onto the balcony. The party was still in full swing on the floor below, but there was something different about the atmosphere. It was less free-and-easy, more intense. Instead of free-form dancing for the pure joy of moving to the music, the elves were moving in unison, as though they'd been choreographed and directed. They weren't smiling, either. This looked like serious work, not fun. The music hadn't changed, so I suspected it was whatever lay behind the music. And if they were making the elves dance in lockstep, I was afraid they were stirring up their army for an attack.

CHAPTER TWENTY

I had to find the source of the music before the army-creating spell could be completed. I looked around for anyone who looked like a DJ, but there was no one doing anything so obvious as spinning records while wearing headphones. I walked as casually as I could around the balcony, searching for signs of a stereo system, computer, or anything else that might be providing the music.

When I reached the far side, I noticed that behind the portal on the lower level there was a table with electronic equipment on it. Thinking that would be my best bet, I continued around the balcony to the staircase I'd used earlier and made my way to the dance floor.

I had to dance my way across the floor again, mimicking the elves' moves—step, kick, spin, clap hands. They were all so graceful, even while being controlled, that I felt horribly klutzy in comparison. It reminded me of the one high school dance I'd dared to go to, early in my freshman year. It had been such an awkward experience that I'd avoided dances ever since. This was a hundred times worse. At that high school dance, my friends' lives hadn't been at stake.

When I neared the portal, I worked my way to the edge of the room so I could get around behind it. Although this controlled dancing was ominous to watch, it was easier for me to blend with. I was slightly less awkward when I didn't have to make up my own dance moves. Fortunately, no one seemed to notice that I was always about a beat behind.

They must not have expected any threat, since there was no guard at the sound system. I reached the table and found to my great relief that the stereo had a dock with an iPod almost identical to Jake's, just in a different color. I wouldn't need help making this work. I took Jake's iPod out of my pocket and waited for the current song to end. Then, moving quickly, I removed one player from the dock, stuck the other one in, and hit "play."

The music continued with only a slightly longer-than-usual pause between songs, and no one seemed to notice the break.

Sticking the other iPod in my pocket, I hurried away from the sound system and blended back into the crowd. Jake had really outdone himself in finding songs you couldn't help but want to dance to. Even I had no choice but to move my feet. I was so relieved to have accomplished my goal that I let myself give in to it with some exuberance. Besides, I figured getting busy on the dance floor was good for my cover.

The intense air in the room eased significantly by the end of Jake's first song. The dancers went back to doing their own thing. By the second, some of the dancers had odd looks crossing their faces. They looked a lot like our people had when we'd broken the spell on them. The third song was a slower ballad, and everyone stopped dancing just to listen to it.

During the song, a murmur ran through the room, gradually rising in volume. The murmur grew more agitated, and then I heard someone near me say, "Where are we?"

Another asked, "What did they do to us?" There were other similar questions being asked all around me, and then I saw an elf darting for the stairs.

When he reached the balcony, he leaned over the railing and shouted, "All of you, listen to me!"

"Who are you?" someone called out.

"I am your commander, and you will do as I say."

The army just stared at him, not snapping to attention or doing anything that looked like a response to an order. I believed the spell was well and truly broken. I edged away from the increasingly angry elves and took out my new cell phone to call Rod. "It worked!" I said.

"Great. I'll let Sam know, and I'll join you."

The elf on the balcony cried out, "You're here to fight for your people! They've been mistreated and exploited in this world, and you're here to win their freedom!"

In a miracle of bad timing, Aretha Franklin's "Think" started playing, with its "Freedom!" chorus coming through loud and clear. The mood shifted, and the elven army turned to the would-be commander. Most of them looked like they were interested in what he had to say.

"And now I think we may need a Plan B," I said into the phone to Rod. "Propaganda seems to be working."

"What's the situation?" Rod asked.

"One elf is convincing the soldiers that they need to fight for the freedom of elves in this place. He said he's their commander."

"This situation should be right up your alley."

"What do you mean?"

"You're director of marketing. What's propaganda if it isn't marketing?"

"Well, when you put it that way," I said. "I'll see what I can do."

After ending the call, I crept back to the stereo and hit the "forward" button to move to the next song before Aretha could whip the army into a freedom-fighting frenzy. In a miracle that made me want to kiss Jake, the next song was the Bee Gees' "Jive Talking," and the combination of the harmonies, the danceable beat, and the lyrics questioning someone's veracity shifted the room's mood once again. The elves went back to dancing even as the commander shouted at them.

I slipped back into the middle of the crowd and said loudly enough to be heard by the people around me, "If it's about freedom, then why did they take us against our will? They could have *talked* to us about freeing our brethren." Then I ducked out of the way before anyone could notice who'd been talking. A ripple of conversation spread.

I moved to another part of the room and said, "It makes you wonder what's really going on here. Are these people trying to *free* this world's elves, or *keep* them from being free?" Again, I ducked out of the way and let the elves discuss that. Judging from the rise in conversation volume, I thought the seeds I'd planted must be growing.

I jumped when someone touched me on the shoulder, and I turned to see Rod. "How's it going?" he asked.

"I seem to have stirred up a little discord."

"That sounds like fun. I think I'll join you." The two of us moved through the dance floor, questioning what the commander had said or complaining about what had happened, and then moving on. Soon, the murmur of conversation was almost drowning out the music.

The commander tried to rally his troops again, but then "YMCA" came on and he lost their attention entirely. There were a few elves not joining in the dance, and I wondered if they were Sylvester's henchmen rather than imported soldiers. Even if I succeeded in keeping the newcomers from joining the fight, our people still might have to face this world's loyalists.

I called Sam. "We may have the situation more or less under control at the moment. I don't think the army's going to rally behind Sylvester's cause, but he does have some people here. Do we have any elves who can come deal with the new guys and provide another perspective?"

"Granny rounded up a few. Now, we're about to make a move, so get yourself someplace safe and out of the way."

I felt a wave of magic that made me reel even if it didn't affect me, and the dancing stopped. "Uh oh, they're trying again," I whispered into the phone as I hurried toward Rod, worried about how he might be affected.

"Now is the time for our glorious crusade!" the commander shouted, his voice ringing with a magical undertone.

Murmurs of "glorious crusade" echoed through the dance floor as the elves stared enraptured up at the balcony. Fortunately, Rod didn't seem to be affected by the elven spell, but he looked as concerned as I felt. I wasn't sure there was any disco music strong enough to counteract this magic. But then "Stayin' Alive" came on, and most of the elves shook themselves out of the spell to dance. One benefit of most of the dancers being from another world was that none of them tried to impersonate John Travolta.

Not everyone was liberated by the music, though, and the leaders were able to line a number of soldiers up in ranks, ready to head out into our world. I didn't know what our people had set up out there, but I hoped they were ready for it. Then I remembered that I could warn Sam, so I called him back and said, "They're coming out. Not all of them, but enough."

"Thanks for the heads-up, doll."

The soldiers marched out, and I held my breath, waiting to see what would happen. It wasn't long before they came flooding back into the main room, followed by MSI's forces. There were even a few people in Council black, so Merlin must have really brought in the big guns. Waiting for the warehouse to open had allowed the MSI group to get in past the guards, who were swept up in all the confusion.

I rushed over to the stereo and turned up the volume. I didn't recognize the next song that came on. It sounded like the kind of dance electronica that got played at nightclubs. I wouldn't have thought the elves would be all that into it, with its lack of discernable melody, but the novelty seemed to strike them, and they were completely distracted from the fight going on between the MSI group and Sylvester's people.

One struggle was between an MSI elf and one of the elf loyalists. Our guy must have been briefed by Sam, for he shouted, "These elves are trying to seize power over the elves of this world! They're oppressing us, and they want to use you to help them!" Soon, some of the foreign elves had rallied to his side.

The commanders were too busy to use magic on the captives, so it was idea versus idea. Some fell in with Sylvester's side, others joined the MSI side, and others just kept dancing. It was hard to tell how the fight was going, but I figured it was okay as long as no armies were leaving the building to go take over the world. I wasn't even sure where they'd have gone.

I felt triumphant until I saw someone heading for the sound system. They must have realized that the soundtrack was no longer enchanted. I barely reached the sound system first and blocked it with my body. The elf tried using magic on me, to no avail. That confused him enough to buy me a little time. I hit the redial button on my new phone and shouted, "Sam! I need backup at the sound system."

"You changed the music!" the elf accused.

"You enchanted it!" I countered. "There's gotta be a special place in hell reserved for anyone who'd use disco for mind control to force people into an army."

He lunged for the stereo, and I blocked him. I still had the iPod holding the enchanted music and he wouldn't be able to re-whammy his army, but I figured if I didn't put up a fight, he might get suspicious enough to look for the enchanted device. Besides, Jake would never forgive me if I let anything happen to his iPod.

I felt a rush of air as a small gargoyle I wasn't familiar with swooped in and landed on top of the stereo. "Your DJ days are over, elf," the gargoyle snarled. I dove out of the way as the gargoyle and elf launched into a magical battle, but everything the elf sent against the gargoyle bounced off an invisible barrier. Sure that the music was safe for now, I turned my attention to the dance floor and the portal.

I had to get our people back to this world—get Owen to safety. I hated to even think about what could have happened to him by now. One of the commanders had to have the key to the wards on the other side of the portal. The trick would be getting him to cooperate. I wondered if threatening to play Barry Manilow would work.

As the battle went on, sparks of magic flying through the air overhead, I started to realize that it wasn't going our way. Some of the foreign elves were helping our people, but more of them were staying out of it or were helping Sylvester's side, and there were more of Sylvester's people here than I'd thought. We didn't seem to be anywhere near subduing the fighters or getting anyone in a position to coerce them into bringing the captives home.

We were keeping them from leaving to try to take over our world, but how long could that last? If they overwhelmed us and got out, we didn't have too many more reinforcements outside. I wasn't even sure where they'd attack. Would they go after MSI while we were all here, or would they go after the Council? Or was it really all about controlling our world's elves, and would the army first be used to subdue Sylvester's opponents?

I'd done my part and it wasn't my responsibility to manage the big picture, but at the moment I was probably the person who knew the most about what was going on—other than the ones carrying out the plan, of course. Surely there was *something* I'd learned in the elven realms that might be of use here. We couldn't have gone through all that only to fail.

The portal shimmered, and a bunch of figures came through. I shouted to alert our people to the influx of more enemies, but then I recognized the first arrival and realized they were on our side, not more elven reinforcements. "Owen!" I shouted, running toward him and throwing my arms around him. "You're safe! I was so worried."

He held me even tighter than I was holding him. "I'm fine, I'm fine," he reassured me. "The others came to my rescue pretty quickly. Are you okay?

Have you been trapped here in the middle of this battle?" he asked.

"I'm fine. I got out, and then I came back with help. It seems the elf soldiers were enchanted and brought here the way we were brought there, and I broke that spell with Jake's iPod. You broke the wards?"

He blushed and said, "It was tricky because elven magic is a little idiosyncratic, but I figured it out eventually. By then, Mac and the others had finished their riot, so here we are."

"It was perfect timing because we need the help. Most of these soldiers don't really want to fight, but they don't want to help us, either."

More and more former captives were spilling through the portal and jumping right into the fray. It looked like a war had broken out in a discotheque. There was something incongruous about that peppy music providing the soundtrack to a battle. It was hard to tell which of the lights flashing around the warehouse were sparks of magic from the fight and which came from the disco ball spinning overhead.

I didn't want to release Owen now that I had him again, but he slipped out of my grasp and joined the fight. I didn't think he'd thought that through, since him doing magical battle probably wouldn't go over very well, but his secret was soon to be out, anyway, and I doubted that anyone was paying much attention at the moment. Quite frankly, we needed all the assistance we could get, and Owen's talent with wards was sure to help.

I was really surprised when the elf version of Florence came through the portal and approached me. "What are you doing here?" I asked her.

"My cover was blown anyway," she said with a shrug. "Take out a few guards, and they notice. If I can't be a double agent, I may as well openly join the resistance. Now, if you'll excuse me, I have freedom to win. When this is over, movie night?"

"Sure. But does it have to be a romantic comedy?"

She made a face. "Please, no!" And then she zapped an enemy elf who was coming at her.

I headed up to the balcony. Since I was magically useless, I thought I might be able to help by getting a bird's-eye view. Once I got up there, though, I saw it wouldn't do much good. Sylvester's elves hadn't obliged us by wearing uniforms that made it obvious which side was which, and that made it hard to track the progress of the fight. I could see Owen setting wards to divide the vast space into segments so people from one battle zone couldn't move into another.

There was a loud noise from nearby, and I turned to see Brad the elf standing on the balcony near me, holding his arms out in an expansive gesture. At the sound, everyone below paused to look up at him. I waited to see what he'd say, but instead of speaking, he sang.

I didn't understand the words or recognize the tune, but the elfsong was heartbreakingly lovely. I caught the eye of the little gargoyle guarding the stereo and gestured for him to shut off the music. Most of the rest of the elves joined in the song with their unearthly harmonies. I felt privileged to be allowed to hear this.

I didn't know what Brad's plan was, but it seemed to be working. The fighting had stopped entirely, and elves from the MSI team, from the foreign army, and even from Sylvester's team were singing together. They were having a real "Kum-ba-ya" moment. If it hadn't been for Owen's wards separating the warehouse into grids, I had a feeling they'd have all been holding hands and swaying. I wondered if I should signal to Owen to drop the wards so they could do so. Then again, we didn't want them to be able to fight again if the togetherness wore off.

The MSI non-elves moved out of the way and watched warily to see what would happen. I wondered where Sylvester was. Surely if he'd been building an army to help him solidify his power over the elves or even over the magical world he'd have been here to lead the attack. Or did he have something else planned?

Then I remembered the commander talking about this world's elves being oppressed. An army wouldn't be much good against an underground movement like Sylvester's enemies. But if Sylvester created an outside threat with an attack by an army of otherworldly elves, that might rally the elves to support him. And if not otherworldly elves, then wizards just might do the trick.

I scrambled for my phone and found that someone had conveniently programmed Merlin's number into the directory. "You may be walking into a trap," I blurted when he answered. "I don't think he's using the army to actually attack his enemies. The army is playing the role of enemy, and since they're not coming, you'll do."

"Interesting theory, Miss Chandler. How goes the battle?"

"One of the guys from the elf underground started a singalong, so we're good for now. And a lot of our people got free and back through the portal. But maybe you'd better get over here instead of going after Sylvester."

"We are already on our way, since Sylvester doesn't appear to be at home."

That worried me. Sylvester had proven to be rather subtle thus far—that was, when he wasn't under the influence of an evil magical gemstone. His schemes tended to involve making other people *want* him to be in power so he could take on even more power. His attempt to use magic had failed when someone else used the same gizmo for a different scheme and that got the whole magical world involved. Now I was sure his contingency plans had contingency plans. He had to be up to something, and that something would likely hit us hard.

On the former dance floor below, the elf love-in was going full-force. Even though I was immune to any magic in the song, the sound still sapped all aggression out of me. I wasn't sure I could have been mean to anyone if I'd tried. By this time, all the elves were singing, even those who'd been leading Sylvester's forces. I glanced at Earl, who was standing next to Brad, and saw that he was smiling slightly.

Brad led the group in one more song, as though to ensure that the effect would hold. When the song ended, he let the last note linger until it faded into nothingness. Then Earl took a deep breath and opened his mouth to speak.

But before any sound left Earl's throat, another voice rang throughout the warehouse. I glanced around for the source and saw Sylvester standing on the opposite side of the balcony, near the stairwell where I'd escaped and reentered.

"My fellow elves," Sylvester boomed as I glanced back to see a scowling Earl, who hadn't had a chance to get a word in edgewise. All the elves below turned their attention to the Elf Lord, who continued once he knew he had the crowd's attention. "We have all been victims of a cruel scheme. Those of you from the elven realms have been brought here against your will as an invasion force. We sealed off the barriers between worlds ages ago to prevent such a thing, but now those from the other world have broken those barriers, and it seems that anyone who discovered this portal was captured and silenced. But thanks to our friends in the wizard world, we've stopped this invasion and freed our fellow elves from their enchantment."

"We?" I muttered to myself. That was rich.

"Now that we've remembered that we are all elves, no matter where we live, I propose that our foreign friends return home and return their captives to us. Then we will seal this portal, and I vow that our forces will be extra-vigilant against this threat in the future."

There were cheers from below, and while I was glad about the cessation of hostilities, there was something terribly wrong about how this was working out. The bad guy was supposed to be stopped and punished, not hailed as a hero and savior.

I ran down the stairs and found Owen. "What do we do?" I asked, grabbing his arm. "We've got to stop him."

"Stop what?" Owen asked, giving me a perplexed look.

"He's using the failure of his plan to carry out his plan. Now the elves are going to see the elves from the other realm as a threat, and they'll feel like they have to support him against the common enemy. We can't let him do that."

"But what can we do? We didn't find any hard evidence that Sylvester was behind it."

"We know he was!" I argued.

"Yeah, but what do you think will happen if you say that? You'll just give him a reason to make MSI the enemy. At least this way he has to make nice with us and pretend we're all on the same team. That should slow him down and give us a chance to stop his next scheme before it starts."

I wasn't satisfied with that. The Elf Lord had ripped us out of our lives, messed with our memories, and made me date a real loser. He was *not* going to get away with this, not if I had anything to say about it.

"Florence!" I said suddenly.

"What about Florence?"

"Maybe she has some proof. She was one of the guards. Or she'd know someone who took direct orders from Sylvester and isn't willing to take the fall for him." He looked doubtful, so I squeezed his arm and said, "Please? I'm not ready to give up."

With a sigh, he said, "Okay. I have to admit I'd rather stop him now."

We wove our way through the rapt elves still listening to Sylvester's campaign speech and found a scowling Florence. "That isn't the truth, is it?" I asked her.

She quirked an eyebrow and smirked. "Seriously? You have to ask?"

"Do you have any proof? Or do you know anyone who does?"

"He came to give us a pep talk before we were sent over there to set up the prison—and before we found out that we were just as trapped as our prisoners were. But do you think me standing up there and saying that would do any good?"

"What if there's more than one of you?" Owen asked. "Do you think any of the other guards would be willing to talk?"

She glanced around. "Give me a few minutes." She headed off into the crowd.

While she was gone, Owen looked at me and said, "Now what? What do you have planned?"

"I don't know. Maybe have them speak out? Even raising doubts may help keep this from being a big success for Sylvester."

Florence returned, dragging a few other elves with her. "This is the best I could do," she said.

"Okay, this is good," I said, rubbing my hands together as I thought of what I could do with this. "We control the sound system. Let's use that."

We hurried over to where the little gargoyle still sat on the stereo. I took the enchanted iPod out of my pocket and said, "First, a tiny bit of mind control might help. When they were under the spell, all they wanted to do was dance and have fun. That might distract them from Sylvester." I swapped out the players, then scrolled through the menu to find a song sure to get the elves' attention.

I went with something tried and true that I'd already seen them react to. After the first few words of the enchanted extended dance mix of "I Will Survive," most of the elves on the dance floor were singing along. When the tempo picked up, they started dancing, oblivious to anything going on around them.

Up on the balcony, Sylvester hadn't noticed that he'd entirely lost his audience. I saw it dawn on him. He tried shouting louder, but the little gargoyle adjusted the volume, making the music even louder. Florence and her friends fell into the dancing like everyone else, and Owen took my hand and spun me around.

"You're not under the spell, are you?" I asked him.

"No, I think it's elf-specific. But we might as well enjoy ourselves a little."

When the song ended, I swapped out players and put on "How Deep Is Your Love?" The elves might not have been under a literal spell, but they all swayed and sang along, creating harmonies that the Bee Gees only dreamed of. Even Sylvester seemed to get caught up in the moment.

During the song, I searched around the table and found a microphone connected to the stereo, then I figured out how to switch over to that input. I let the song fade out when it ended, turned on the microphone, and handed it to Florence. "Give it your best shot," I whispered to her.

"All of this is a lie!" she shouted, her voice echoing throughout the warehouse. "The only invasion here was to support the Elf Lord. He was the one to open the portal. He was the one who created the prison in the elven realms. I was a guard there, and he was the one who gave us our assignments. He was the one having people kidnapped and sent there if they had any inkling of the plan. He was the one who stranded his own people there so no word would leak out, and he was the one kidnapping elves from the other realm and bringing them here as an army."

She handed the microphone over to one of her colleagues, who backed up her story with an additional tale of Sylvester being present when a prisoner was sent through the portal. Soon, there was a line forming for the microphone, each elf with a story to tell.

We'd broken Sylvester's spell on the crowd. Enough elves were listening to the testimony that I didn't think his innocent victim act would survive. However, Sylvester wasn't about to roll over and play dead, even as angry elves headed up the stairs toward him.

He turned to run, right toward the staircase that led to the roof.

CHAPTER TWENTY-ONE

"He's getting away!" I shouted, then realized that didn't do any good because no one could hear me. I dialed Sam on my phone. "Stop Sylvester! He's headed to the roof!" I said when he answered.

"Got it, doll," he replied, and I saw him already flying toward the balcony.

"When did you get that?" Owen asked.

"A lot has happened since the last time you saw me," I said mysteriously as I slid the phone back into my pocket.

We moved through the crowd toward the stairs. "It has? How much time has gone by?" Owen asked as we ran.

He looked so alarmed that I didn't have the heart to keep teasing him. "Only a couple of hours. Merlin gave me the phone. I guess when we went missing they decided it would be a good thing for people to be able to reach me, and I'll admit it's come in handy tonight."

Sam could only hamper Sylvester's escape, since Sylvester fought back with magic. I got out my phone again and called Merlin. "Are you here yet?" I asked.

"Almost."

"The roof!" I shouted, forgetting the fact that I was giving orders to my boss. I didn't think he'd mind my tone under the circumstances.

Owen and I reached the balcony and rushed for the stairwell door where Sylvester had just disappeared. Earl and Brad were right behind us, and when they saw us running, Mac and McClusky joined the chase. Rod came after them. All those people running up the stairs sounded like a herd of stampeding elephants as our footsteps echoed around the stairwell.

We made it out onto the roof just as Merlin stepped nimbly off a flying carpet hovering a couple of feet off the ground. He then turned to help Granny down. When Sylvester saw Merlin, he stopped so abruptly that he skidded a few inches. The rest of us fanned out to surround him.

"Why, Sylvester, imagine seeing you here," Merlin said, sounding like he was paying a social call. "I was just at your office, looking for you."

Sylvester started to run for the stairs, but Owen and I blocked the way. The Elf Lord did a double take when he saw us. "You? But how did ..." His voice trailed off as his expression clouded.

"How did we get caught in your trap and taken prisoner in your freaky other world?" I finished his sentence for him. "Well, there was an unintended consequence to your last little scheme, so when we stumbled upon your portal, we got zapped."

"If that's the case, then out of my way!" he shouted, raising his arms to do a spell.

I stepped in front of Owen and felt the magic hit me, but it had no effect. "Sorry, I'm back to normal," I said with a shrug.

"And so am I," Owen said coolly. He raised his hands, as though preparing to do a spell, but then he froze. I followed his gaze to see that he was looking across the circle at the two Council men, who were staring at him. McClusky looked smug, like he'd been vindicated, and Mac's forehead was creased with concern. Owen lowered his hands.

Sylvester didn't get the opportunity to take advantage of that, though, because Merlin and Granny were on him. They worked surprisingly well as a team—disturbingly well, really. Sylvester whirled to face them, and it appeared that Granny was blocking his spells while Merlin focused on attack.

Merlin was able to hold Sylvester. The Elf Lord was still doing enough magic to keep the rest of us at bay, but he wasn't going anywhere. Brad moved in as close as he dared and said, "You thought you could silence us, but now your treachery will be even more widely known." He smiled and added, "But perhaps there's a nice place you could start over, a whole city where you can rule to your heart's content."

"You wouldn't!" Sylvester snarled.

"Why not? You did," Earl said.

"Quick, pick your favorite fantasy, and maybe they can give it to you," I said. "But I don't recommend the romantic comedy one."

"There is a bookstore that needs someone to run it," Owen put in. "Do you like books?"

"Oh, no, he's not getting away that easily," Mac said. "He has to answer for multiple counts of kidnapping."

"This isn't Council jurisdiction," Merlin said mildly. "This is an elf matter. We wizards are merely lending our support."

"The leaders of the elven lands should decide his fate," Brad said. "More elves were taken from their realm than wizards were taken from this world."

"I will accept the authority of the Council," Sylvester shouted. I wasn't so sure he was making the right choice, but I figured it was his funeral. Just so long as he couldn't interfere in my life again, I'd be happy.

Mac and his partner looked awfully pleased with themselves as they stepped forward to take Sylvester into custody. When they reached him, he suddenly grabbed their wrists, and their faces went strangely blank, as though they'd forgotten who they were. Then they went blanker than that, like they were losing consciousness. He wasn't just giving them the same identity-erasing whammy he'd given us. He was killing them, and they were too dazed to do anything about it. Owen shouted a warning. When they didn't respond, he jumped forward to break Sylvester's grasp on them. But when he touched Sylvester, the Elf Lord's touch had the same effect on him as it had on them, and he fell to his knees. Mac and McClusky staggered, still too stunned to help, so I ran over and brought the point of my elbow down hard on Sylvester's wrist, forcing him to release Owen.

As the others teamed up to stop the Elf Lord, I leaned over Owen. He was conscious and breathing, but he seemed a little unsteady. "Do I need to remind you who you are?" I asked him without taking my eyes off the Elf Lord.

"I'm good," he said, pushing himself back to his feet.

Mac and McClusky, now recovered, came over to Owen. "Thanks, man," McClusky said, extending his hand to Owen. Owen looked at it skeptically for a moment before shaking it. Mac clapped him on the shoulder and gave him an approving nod.

"So, you'll be giving a good report to the Council, right?" I prompted. "After all, he may have just saved your lives, at risk to himself."

"I think we can put in a good word," Mac said. He glanced at McClusky, who gave a reluctant nod.

By this time, more elves had come up the stairs and joined us on the roof. Brad went over to one of them, and they had a brief conversation, then Brad returned to Merlin. "They'll take him through the portal and lock him in the containment area," Brad reported. "That should keep him from being a problem here. A few of the elves want to stay, at least for a while, but the rest will return home, and they'll find and return any remaining prisoners there."

"That does appear to be the best solution," Merlin said. "Thank you for your assistance."

Brad shot me a smile. "Actually, it was Katie who saved us all. She was our resistance leader."

Merlin turned to me and raised an eyebrow. "You neglected to mention that in your report."

"I skipped the trivial details," I said with a shrug.

"Now that her immunity's back, maybe she should talk to Sam," Owen suggested. "He could probably use her in Security. She has a knack for covert operations."

"Is that something that interests you, Miss Chandler?" Merlin asked.

"Yeah, I think it does," I said. "Just as long as I don't have to make coffee anymore." Merlin looked completely blank, since that was another of the trivial details I'd omitted, but Owen and I laughed.

We returned downstairs, where the elves who wanted to return to their realm were already going through the portal. Two of them took Sylvester through between them, using something that looked like the elvish version of the wizards' silver chains as restraints. Every so often, a few people came through from the other side, blinking and looking a little confused.

When I went back to the stereo to retrieve Jake's iPod, I was surprised to find my purse and Owen's coat in a pile under the stereo table. It looked like they'd just tossed their captives' personal effects aside. That meant I still had my apartment keys, ID, and credit cards and he had his wallet and phone. We'd gone through all that and hadn't lost anything but a week.

But I wasn't quite ready to return to normal reality yet. I'd spent the entire time I was a prisoner wanting to get home, and now I found myself thinking a little longingly of the world I'd left. Well, mostly my apartment. I'd gotten used to having that lovely brownstone apartment all to myself. Going back to sharing a two-bedroom in an old tenement building with three other people was going to be a real adjustment.

While the others were still wrapping things up, I went back up the stairs to the roof for perhaps the last bit of peace and quiet I'd probably have for a long time. But when I reached the roof door, I found that it had started raining.

"What was that about dancing on a rooftop in the rain?" Owen's voice said from behind me.

"It's a romantic movie cliché," I replied.

"Still, don't you think we should give it a try? We hit all the other clichés. Why not that one? They're even playing our song."

"I didn't know we had a song. And where did they get the music? They aren't using the enchanted iPod, are they?"

"I think they're singing."

I listened for a moment before I realized that what I was hearing was a hundred elves singing a Bee Gees song. "Okay, in that case, we have to try dancing," I said, turning to face him. "This is a once-in-a-lifetime opportunity."

He took my hand and led me onto the roof. It was only a light rain, just enough to make my skin tingle where it touched, which felt a lot like magic surrounding me. Owen took me into his arms, making my skin tingle in a totally different way, and we moved to the unearthly sound of the elven chorus singing "How Deep Is Your Love."

"Well, that was interesting," I said after a while.

"Dancing on the rooftop in the rain?"

"No, though I am starting to see the appeal. But I meant everything that's just happened to us."

"Then 'interesting' is the understatement of the century."

"I don't even know what to make of it. It's almost like a dream. Now that we're back in the real New York, it doesn't seem like it was real, and yet it's more real to me right now than my real life."

"Do you know what I find most amazing about that whole experience?"

"What?"

"That even when they made us forget not only each other but who we really were, we still somehow found each other and knew we belonged together. It happened all over again when we weren't even ourselves, and I'm pretty sure that wasn't their plan."

"Florence did help nudge things along."

"But did she really make that much difference? She mostly planted doubts about the other guy."

"So I suppose that means we really do belong together," I said, feeling my heart fluttering a little as I rested my head on his shoulder.

"It does seem rather inevitable, doesn't it?"

"I don't mind," I said with a smile.

"I was hoping you felt that way." He loosened his hold on me, then with a casual wave of his hand, he started a small shower of sparks, like the ones we'd created in the bookstore. As useful as magic could be, that little trick was the one I thought I'd miss the most.

And then my heart leapt into my throat when he went down onto one knee. With another wave of his hand, a glowing circle of light appeared in his palm. "Since it seems like we'll end up together no matter where or who we are, that we love each other in any realm we visit, will you marry me and make it official?"

It wasn't the way I'd ever imagined being proposed to, but it was exactly what fit for Owen. It was private, magical, and meaningful. I couldn't seem to find the words to respond, so I nodded and held my hand out so he could slide the glowing circle onto my finger.

"This is just a placeholder," he said, his voice shaking a little. "We'll go shopping for a real ring."

I pulled him to his feet, then kissed him as showers of sparks continued to fall around us. It seemed that the romantic comedy the elves had forced us into had reached its happy ending.

The strains of "Too Much Heaven" floated up the stairwell as the elves began a new song. "I guess that's the closing credits," Owen whispered.

"Thank goodness I ended up with Mr. Right," I responded. "And we'll live happily ever after."

ABOUT THE AUTHOR

Shanna Swendson is the author of the Enchanted Inc. series of humorous contemporary fantasy novels, including *Enchanted, Inc.*, *Once Upon Stilettos*, *Damsel Under Stress*, *Don't Hex with Texas*, *Much Ado About Magic*, *No Quest For The Wicked*, and *Kiss and Spell*. She's also contributed essays to a number of books on pop culture topics, including *Everything I Needed to Know About Being a Girl, I Learned from Judy Blume*, *Serenity Found*, *Perfectly Plum* and *So Say We All*. When she's not writing, she's usually discussing books and television on the Internet, singing in or directing choirs, taking ballet classes or attempting to learn Italian cooking. She lives in Irving, Texas, with several hardy houseplants and a lot of books.

Visit her Website at http://shannaswendson.com.

CPSIA information can be obtained
at www.ICGtesting.com
Printed in the USA
LVOW13s1539150117
521008LV00013B/650/P

Kiss and Spell

SHANNA SWENDSON

ALSO BY SHANNA SWENDSON

Books in the Enchanted, Inc. Series:

Enchanted, Inc.
Once Upon Stilettos
Damsel Under Stress
Don't Hex With Texas
Much Ado About Magic
No Quest For The Wicked
Kiss and Spell